Praise for
The Shape of Mercy

"As raindrops become mighty rivers, Susan Meissner's words seem simple in the beginning, but one thought builds naturally upon another, phrases and sentences flow together with effortless fluidity, and before you know it, you are totally engrossed by the powerful undercurrents of her story. To read Ms. Meissner is to put yourself into the hands of that rarest kind of author: an artist working in the medium of words."

—ATHOL DICKSON, Christy Award–winning author
of *The Cure* and *Winter Haven*

"I loved *The Shape of Mercy* from beginning to end. Ms. Meissner's prose sings, and her characters captured my interest from the start. As the story unfolded, those same characters captured my heart. I won't soon forget Mercy, Lauren, or Abigail."

—ROBIN LEE HATCHER, award-winning author
of *Wagered Heart* and *When Love Blooms*

"*The Shape of Mercy* is vintage Susan Meissner: tender storytelling that keeps you hooked; living, breathing characters that capture your heart and madden you too; and a message of redemption that sticks with you. Meissner deftly weaves the stories of three women of vastly different generations, connecting them perfectly and crafting a winsome, interesting, powerful read."

—MARY E. DEMUTH, author of *Watching the Tree Limbs*
and *Daisy Chain*

"A compelling tale that will resonate long after you turn the last page. A haunting story, deftly woven, full of layers and textures that will quickly pull you out of the present and into the long forgotten past. Meissner recalls a tale that must not be forgotten, about the tragedies and senseless cruelties that happen when we abandon grace and turn our backs on mercy."

—SIRI MITCHELL, author of *A Constant Heart*

"*The Shape of Mercy* is a truly lovely story, one to savor again and again. In a fantastic blend of old and new, this modern-day novel has the scope and feel of a historical. The characters and their journeys will touch your heart."

—MINDY STARNS CLARK, author of *Whispers of the Bayou*

"A bit of mystery, fascinating history, and the biggest question of all: what would you do for love? I can't stop thinking about *The Shape of Mercy.*"

—ROXANNE HENKE, author of *After Anne* and *Learning to Fly*

"With a deft hand, Meissner blends an intriguing storyline, artful writing, and memorable characters for a truly delicious read. This one's a keeper!"

—DENISE HUNTER, author of *The Convenient Groom*

The Shape of Mercy

The Shape of Mercy

A Novel

SUSAN MEISSNER

WATERBROOK
PRESS

THE SHAPE OF MERCY
PUBLISHED BY WATERBROOK PRESS
12265 Oracle Boulevard, Suite 200
Colorado Springs, Colorado 80921
A division of Random House Inc.

Apart from well-known real people and real events associated with the Salem witch trials of 1692, the characters and events in this book are fictional and any resemblance to actual persons or events is coincidental.

ISBN 978-0-307-73155-5

Published in the United States by WaterBrook Multnomah, an imprint of the Crown Publishing Group, a division of Random House Inc., New York.

WATERBROOK and its deer colophon are registered trademarks of Random House Inc.

Library of Congress Cataloging-in-Publication Data
Meissner, Susan, 1961–
    The shape of mercy : a novel / Susan Meissner.
          p. cm.
    ISBN 978-1-4000-7456-3
 I. Title.
    PS3613.E435S53 2008
    813'.6—dc22

                                        2008017945

Printed in the United States of America
2012

10 9 8 7 6 5 4 3 2 1

In memory of Connie Dorough,
who loved without hesitation.

Fear is the enemy of love.

—St Augustine

One

I've heard the story countless times, how I grasped the delivering doctor's scrubs as he guided me into the Durough family universe of opportunity and duty. My father likes to say I came out of my mother's body insistent on being taken seriously, declaring to the doctor who held my slippery limbs that I was no helpless female unable to forge her way through the world of men.

I've seen the video. My father had the camcorder rolling when my mother pushed me into waiting hands. Dad's aim was discreet, thank goodness, because he'll sometimes show that video when he tells the story. He's even downloaded it onto his iPod. I've seen my open, squalling mouth, heard my mother's throaty cries and a nearby nurse's words: "It's a girl." My infant body is a glistening, angry shade of pink, and I am indeed grappling for the doctor's clothes as if prepared to wrestle him to the floor. My father loves that.

Whispered conversations over the years—which I wasn't meant to hear—have suggested my father enjoys retelling this story because he needs to reassure himself it's not the end of the world that God didn't bless him with a son. Neither was I supposed to hear that my clutching at the doctor's clothes could just as easily have been a cry of, "Help! I'm falling!" rather than, "Stand aside! I've arrived!"

I've long wondered if the whispering people are right. About both.

Imagine you are six, and you're hiding under the dining room table, hidden by the damask cloth that covers it, and all you can see are the shiny, pointed toes of women in stilettos, clicking their way from room to room. Their skirts swish. Their porcelain coffee cups make delicate scraping sounds as they lift and lower them onto saucers. They've just heard Bryant Durough tell the story of how his daughter, Lauren, was born.

His only daughter. His only child.

Born grappling for power.

One of them titters. "So like a man to see it that way."

"I heard Bryant and Julia have tried everything to have another child," another says.

"Really?"

"Oh, that's so sad. They're such wonderful parents."

"In vitro, too?"

"Yes. They tried in vitro three times. Three times it didn't take."

"Oh, dear."

"Think they'll adopt?"

"Goodness, no."

"No, I suppose not."

"I imagine it's hard for Bryant to be unable to pass along his side of the Durough name."

"There have always been sons born to Duroughs. He's the first not to have one."

"And to think his brother has four sons. Four!"

"Bryant puts up a good front, but I bet it drives him nuts."

"Well, at least they have Lauren."

"Mmm. But you know, for a man like Bryant Durough, it's not the same."

You hear this, and you haven't a clue what *in vitro* means, and you don't know who didn't take what they should have taken and why that is so oh-dear sad.

You do know who Bryant and Julia are.

And you know what the words "have another child" mean.

And the words "at least they have Lauren."

You crawl away unseen and ponder the idea of another child, another child, another child for hours.

You wonder if having another child means someone wants to buy a new one. You wonder what happens with the old one.

What do they do with the old one?

Throughout the day you consider this, but you don't say anything. You just let it tumble around in your six-year-old head. You stare at the picture in your bedroom of Jesus watching over a boy and a girl as they walk a dark forest path, and you wonder if the boy and girl are brother and sister and if Jesus loves them both the same.

When your mother tucks you in later that night and she leans down to kiss you and the scent of sweet apples is all around her, you look into her face and see nothing there but loveliness. The worry begins to fall away into the darkness, and you reach out your hand to touch her tummy, the place where babies grow. It is flat and smooth. She looks down at your hand and then back up. Her eyes are wide.

You pull your hand away.

She stays a moment longer, caressing you on the forehead where a damp curl rests, and whispers, "Sweet dreams."

She moves away from the canopied bed with its matching French provincial armoire and dresser. A seashell night-light glows at her ankles as she stands at your half-open door and blows you one last kiss.

It will be another six months before you hear again the story of how you were born.

It will be years before you find out what *in vitro* means.

And you will never be sure why you grabbed the doctor's clothes.

When I met Abigail Boyles, the woman who hired me to transcribe the diary of a girl who died too young, she said to me, "You're an only child, aren't you?"

I asked her how she knew.

She said, "I'm one too."

As if that were answer enough.

❧

I'm not the person my father thinks I am.

I am not the determined daughter out to prove she is all the unborn son would have been.

My recent acts of defiance—choosing a state school instead of Stanford and living in a dorm with a shared bathroom instead of a gated condo—are not evidence of my determined, lapel-grabbing nature. I'm not out to prove anything. I grew up believing I was supposed to be what all Duroughs have been: industrious, entrepreneurial, and shrewd—an amasser of wealth, not for the joy of spending it but for the prestige in having it. How could I be anything else?

This is what Dad is, what his father was, his grandfather before him, and his great-grandfather before him. It is what my Uncle Loring and his sons are.

But that's not what I am.

Being a woman isn't what makes me different from all the Durough heirs before me. There are plenty of women in the family who gracefully embraced a life of privilege. My mother, for one, didn't have to stretch out her arms very far; she married into a life she already knew. My grandmother—another Durough by marriage—was tutored in the ways of wealth by her mother-in-law, a woman whose own wealth significantly outmatched the Durough fortune. You don't have to be a man to appreciate the muscle of affluence.

You don't have to be a man to inherit a destiny.

The thing is, I don't want my destiny handed to me. I want to choose it.

This is the treasure the impoverished forget they have: the ability to choose a new road. They may struggle all their lives to stay on it, but at least they chose it for themselves.

This is why I went looking for a job to earn a paycheck I didn't need. Not because I wanted to prove I could earn my own money, but because no one expected me to do it. When you only do what is expected of you, you never learn what you would've done had you chosen for yourself.

Think of it this way. Suppose you have before you two choices: wealth or poverty. Suppose there is no middle ground. Which do you choose?

I'm young, but I have spent my two decades as an only child in the cloistered huddle of affluent adults. I've watched them, learned their language, and observed them scrutinizing the world around them, noting the disparity in the masses. And I have found that the rich and the poor have a hugely significant characteristic in common. As do the accuser and the condemned, the loved and the unloved, the free and the bound. We each think we understand the other.

We don't.

I see the truth of this in Abigail Boyles's wasted life and in a young woman's needless death.

And I see it in me, every time I look in the mirror and see the rich girl who stares back.

We understand what we want to understand. That's how it is. How it's always been.

Two

Sometimes I think I didn't find Abigail Boyles at all; she found me. I have this crazy idea that if I asked her how long she'd been searching for a writer to breathe new life into the story of a young colonial woman wrongfully accused of witchcraft and sentenced to die, her answer would be, "All my life."

Abigail had been waiting for me, for someone to tell Mercy Hayworth's story. It was a story meant to be told.

I met Abigail after I returned to UC Santa Barbara from a long summer at my parents' home in Pacific Palisades, fresh from the lap of luxury and itching to be like the other sophomores in my dorm. Abigail's job posting, skewered to the English department bulletin board along with half a dozen other openings, was the only handwritten notice. The fontlike precision of her script caught my eye. The personal touch drew me.

I had just decided that day to end my dependence on Dad's monthly stipend for my living expenses, though it was something that had gnawed at me all through my freshman year. I had a vat of money I could dip my hand into any time I wanted. I'd always had it. My roommate Clarissa worked in the college bookstore and at a coffee shop, sneaking in study time whenever she could. I hardly ever saw her. I don't know that she resented my unlimited debit card, as she never said anything about it. Maybe that's what bugged me the most. That she never said anything.

Abigail had written her notice on lavender stationery using a black, felt-tipped pen. The *W* in her *Wanted—Literary Assistant* was perfectly formed, just the right amount of arc and sweep. Abigail's posting had a slightly faded patina, and it wasn't dated—that should have been a clue. It was surrounded by job postings printed on ink jet printers and bearing informational tabs torn off here and there by hurried hands.

Hers was the only notice that bore the unseen fingerprints of human touch: lavender paper meant for a personal note and words penned with a steady hand. There was no mention of Mercy's diary, just these lines and a phone number: *Wanted—Literary Assistant for transcription project. Ten hours a week for four months. Eleven dollars per hour. Prefer someone with knowledge of seventeenth-century literature.*

It was the word *literature* that made me write down Abigail's phone number. The other postings were for research assistants, copyeditors, proofers, and writing mentors. That, and the humanity of the posting itself: the artistic *W* and the unspoken knowledge that this technologically bereft employer had a project different from everyone else's.

A classmate, Lira, walked by as I was writing down Abigail's phone number on a Starbucks receipt I'd found in my backpack.

"You looking for a job?"

There was nothing unkind in the way she said it, but I felt my cheeks grow warm nonetheless. I'd had enough short conversations with Lira to know she was paying her own way through college. And she knew what most of my college acquaintances had been able to pick up, though I had made no conscious effort to convey it: my parents were wealthy.

"Um. Yeah."

Lira, a journalism major, leaned in to look at Abigail's lavender paper. My guess is she wanted to see what kind of job appealed to someone who didn't need one.

"Hmm," she said. "What do you suppose that's about?" It was clear

Lira had no interest at all in a posting like Abigail's. If anything, she distrusted it.

I feigned casual curiosity. "Could be interesting." I shrugged and clicked my pen closed.

"This one looks good." Lira pointed to a mauve-and-taupe-colored flier for a copywriting internship at an ad agency. Half its phone tabs had been yanked off.

I could tell Lira meant well. I know now that it was a joke among the students in the English department how long the handwritten ad had been posted, and that many English majors had in desperation called Abigail and either declined her strange job offer or failed to impress her.

But I didn't know this yet.

"I'm going to give this one a try." I nodded toward Abigail's posting. "Can't hurt."

Lira readjusted her book bag on her shoulder and smiled. "Well, I hope it works out." Her eyes, kind but discerning, told me that if someone needed a job for income and résumé-building, they would've torn off one of the ad agency's tabs. But if a rich girl just wanted a little diversion for a few hours a week and the money itself didn't matter, well, here was the perfect match.

We said good-bye and she walked away.

I wondered all that afternoon if she was right: that I wasn't looking for a job because I needed the satisfaction of earning my own money. I needed something else.

Back in my dorm room, I called the number. A woman with a gentle Spanish accent answered the phone and told me she needed to ask me a few questions before setting up an interview with Miss Boyles. In the background I heard her fiddling with papers.

"What is your major?" she asked.

"English with a concentration in Literature and Cultures of Information."

I had to repeat that.

"And your year in college?"

I figured this was a sly way to guess my age. I answered anyway. "Sophomore."

"And where did you earn your high school diploma?"

This, I learned later, was to see where I was from, where I grew up, where I had learned how unfair the world can be.

"Palisades Point Academy." I had to repeat that, too.

"Can you wait a moment?" the woman asked. She put me on hold before I could answer but was back within a minute.

"Miss Boyles would like to know if you can come for an interview on Thursday. Five o'clock?"

"Uh. Well, yes."

"Okay. You have a pen? I give you the address."

I didn't recognize the street. It sounded like the address of a residence rather than an office. Abigail's home.

"Just ring the bell at the gate. I will let you in."

A gated home. Like my parents'.

"Okay?"

"Wait," I said. "Can I ask what I would be transcribing?"

The woman hesitated. I heard her cover the phone with her hand. She was consulting someone. "A diary. It's three hundred years old. It belonged to an ancestor of Miss Boyles who lived during the Salem witch trials."

The connection to Mercy Hayworth was immediate, and I hadn't even heard her name yet. My interest instantly soared. A diary. Literature of the most intimate kind, amazingly personal and revealing. Penned during the Salem witch trials and kept for three centuries. Somehow I knew it was the diary of a woman, not a man. A woman with secrets. This resonated within me more than anything else: a diary was where secrets were recorded.

I wanted this job. I had secrets of my own.

"Okay?" the woman asked.

"Yes," I said. *Yes, yes, yes.*

"Okay." She hung up.

I stared at the address in my hand for a moment, then went to my computer and googled it. I studied the map and realized Abigail lived in an older, stately neighborhood where the moneyed families of early Santa Barbara built their mansions.

I wasn't sure how Dad would react to my taking on a part-time job that had nothing to do with Durough enterprises, but I knew he would approve of this: my prospective employer lived the kind of life he was familiar with and trusted.

I waited until after I knew my parents had eaten dinner to call my dad and tell him he no longer needed to deposit the spending allowance in my checking account. I practiced saying it a couple times before I called so I would sound calm and confident, like it was the most natural thing in the world to earn my own money.

He took the news better than he had taken my other decisions that made no sense to him, like choosing Santa Barbara instead of Stanford and majoring in something other than economics. Dad was slightly amused, a bit perturbed, but subtly proud of me for doing—albeit without grace—what all Duroughs of the past had done: made things happen instead of let things happen.

I wanted to earn my own money. I was making a business decision. He liked it.

My father does not control by domination; he controls by persuasion. There is a huge difference. I have never felt ignorant or inferior around him, only the pull to conform. It's a very strong pull. My father possesses a keen ability to make people do what he wants them to do. Couple that with his good looks, calm demeanor, and disarming confidence, and it's no wonder I tremble at the thought of disagreeing with him. I'd won the battle of where to get my undergraduate degree, but I doubted he would concede anything else.

When I told him about the job, I could almost hear him thinking, *This will be good for Lauren. She'll come to see success lies on just one road. The Durough road.*

He wanted to know the details.

"So it's hourly?"

"Yes."

"How much?" he asked, even though we both knew it didn't matter.

"Eleven," I said as confidently as I could. I knew his gardener's assistant made more plucking snails out of the Durough flower beds.

"And you'll be doing what, exactly?"

"Transcribing a diary."

"Well, that's different. What kind of diary? Whose is it?"

"It belonged to someone who lived three hundred years ago. I think it'll be very interesting."

He paused for a moment. "You know you could do consulting work for me online for a few hours a week, Lauren. I told you that a long time ago."

Yes, I knew. "I just want to try doing something on my own."

"Well, if you really want to do this, I won't tell you not to."

I refrained from telling him I was not asking for his permission.

"And if you're set on earning your own spending money, I can appreciate that. I can even get behind that," he continued.

I cringed. The words "spending money" put my experiment instantly and squarely into perspective. It was clear to us both that I was still wholly dependent on his wealth for everything else. He didn't mean to sound condescending. He meant to remind me of the big world that awaited me—his world. My little project was just that: little.

"Thanks, Dad."

"Good luck with your interview."

My cheeks felt hot. "Yep."

"Mom wants to say hello."

"Okay."

"Let us know how this works out, okay? I'd like to hear more about it sometime."

"Sure. Bye."

I heard the phone being passed from one hand to another. I raised my free hand to my face to rub away the warm hues of humiliation.

"Lauren! You're getting a job?" My mother didn't sound alarmed or annoyed. Just surprised.

"Just a few hours a week, Mom. And I may not even get the job. The interview's tomorrow."

"Well, I'm sure if you're being interviewed, you'll get it," she said, as only a mother can. Then, as if to prove she had no doubt I would get the job if I wanted it, she moved on. She reminded me that my Uncle Loring's fiftieth birthday party had been moved up a week. She'd told me several days earlier that the two-day affair was now being held in two weeks instead of three because Uncle Loring had to go to Singapore. I told her I'd be there.

I don't think Mom thought I had forgotten. She just wanted to remind me where I belonged.

Three

My first impression of Abigail Boyles was that she was unbreakable. Despite her delicate, eighty-three-year-old body with its transparent skin and her glistening, over-watered eyes, she stood straight and stiff-necked when we met on her threshold, with not a hint of frailty to her. A map of wrinkles hardened her face rather than softened it, as if the creases had been massaged into place by sleepless nights, hours of regret, and steady frowning. I knew in a moment she was a woman who had always been alone, yet this did not mean she hadn't loved or been loved. There was an underlying sadness about her, though she smiled genuinely. A sadness that made her unyielding rather than vulnerable.

I was let into Abigail's massive Tudor-style home by Esperanza, the woman who had answered my phone call two days before. She introduced herself as Miss Boyles's housekeeper. Abigail stood behind her, wearing lavender pants the same color as the stationery she had used for her ad. She stood so close she could've easily answered the door herself, and I wondered why she had shadowed her housekeeper to the door. I found out later she wanted to look past me to her circular driveway and see what kind of car I drove.

I drive a BMW.

When she spoke, Abigail's voice was low, controlled, and carefully measured out. It seemed the voice of a younger woman. She extended her hand.

"Abigail Boyles," she said.

"Lauren Durough." I took her hand. It was cool and watery-soft, like she had just lifted it from a jar of formaldehyde. I let go as soon as it was polite to do so.

"Esperanza, Miss Durough and I will meet in the library." Abigail looked straight at me as she spoke.

"Right this way." Esperanza closed the front door behind me and motioned to a set of closed double doors on one side of the tiled entryway. I saw matching double doors on the other side, open to reveal a sitting room in maroon and cream. From the doorway I could see it was beautifully but sparsely decorated and looked as if it were never used. Ahead of me, an L-shaped staircase with paisley-carpeted steps led to the upper floor, and more doors lay beyond the staircase at the end of the long hallway. One door was fully open, revealing large black-and-white floor tiles, flashes of chrome hanging from the ceiling, and countertops free of clutter. Afternoon sunlight fell on a bowl of strawberries sitting near the edge of an island topped with polished granite.

Esperanza opened the double doors across from the sitting room, exposing a room that did not fit with the little I'd seen of the house. Abigail's library was overly furnished, exploding with paintings, tiered candles, vases of flowers, pillows and cushions—and bursting with books. While the sitting room appeared purely decorative, the library looked as though Abigail spent every waking moment in it, surrounded on all sides by piles and stacks and cases of books.

It was the first time in my life I'd been surrounded by books and felt uneasy. Only half of them were housed on shelves. The rest were loose, unfettered, poised as if to attack.

"Please have a seat." Abigail pointed to an armchair that sat among towers of pages stacked around it like scaffolding.

I walked to the chair, sat down, and minded my ankles as if the books closest to me might nip at my feet. Abigail sat across from me in a similar chair, surrounded by Shakespeare, Milton, Chaucer, and Socrates.

Esperanza closed the door and I immediately felt claustrophobic. Abigail smiled as if she knew and wanted to assure me I was safe.

"So, what intrigues you about this job, Miss Durough?"

I'd practiced the answer to a question like this after searching the Internet the night before, educating myself at midnight on how to nail a job interview. I was prepared to say the job called for an interesting blend of skills and abilities I happened to have, but what came out of my mouth were two unrehearsed words:

"The diary."

Abigail's smile deepened; she liked my answer. I mentally formed answers to the question Abigail would surely ask next. *Why is that?*

But that's not what she said.

"You like secrets."

I colored. "I like autobiographies. I like seventeenth-century literature."

"Mmm." She waited for more.

"And I'm drawn to what a woman who lived three hundred years ago would write if she thought no one would ever see it."

Abigail nodded once. I satisfied her on this point and on another: I correctly guessed the diary belonged to a woman.

"Tell me about yourself," she said.

The nail-the-interview sites told me, when asked this question, to stick to details that matched the job's requirements.

"I'm an English major, an honors student, and I like to write fiction in my spare time. I love to read. I like Jane Austen, the Brontë sisters, George MacDonald, some Hemingway, some Steinbeck. I've studied a wide variety of writers: Shakespeare, Dickens, Dostoevsky, Tolkien."

"A true fan of literature," Abigail said like she was announcing it to the audience of books all around us, convincing them I could be trusted. Another point for me. "I think literature reveals more about us than history does." Abigail settled back in her chair. I hadn't realized she'd been sitting forward.

She was right. I told her so.

"You've chosen a very interesting focus for your major," she said next.

I didn't know if that was a compliment. I said nothing.

"I think Santa Barbara might be the only UC school to have an English concentration in Literature and Cultural Information," she continued. "It's a very interesting blend."

"UC Merced has something like it, I think."

"But you chose to come here."

"I liked the campus. And I would've missed the ocean."

"And I suppose Merced would have been a little far from home." She cocked her head, as if gauging my response to her snooping. She had obviously looked up Palisades Point Academy and knew where it was, a stone's throw from Malibu, situated in a gated haven where the wealthy laid their heads at night.

I wondered for only a second if she'd figured out who my father was. Of course she had. My Duroughness kicked in.

"Do you have any questions about where I grew up, Miss Boyles?" I kept my tone light, like hers.

Her grin was wide and appreciative. "No, I don't think I have any questions about that."

I waited.

"How about if I tell you a little about me," she said. "I'm eighty-three years old and I'm a retired librarian. My family is originally from Boston, but I've lived in this house since I was five. I've just one living relative in Maine, who surely expects to inherit my estate but is in for a surprise." She looked at the wall of tomes on her left. "I've a mind to will him just the books, since I know he cannot wait to get this house and toss them all out."

I didn't know what to say.

"I've had the diary since I was thirteen," she continued, turning back to face to me. "It's been passed down through eight generations of my family, and it belonged to an ancestor of mine. Her name was Mercy Hayworth and she was my cousin, eight times removed. She lived in Salem in the late 1600s."

Abigail waited, letting the date and the town's name coalesce in my mind with what I surely knew of colonial American history.

"I would like for you to transcribe the diary for me," she continued, "and edit it for clarity. I want the language to be readable for today's audience, and I want it typed onto a computer disk. I'll need help finding a way to have it bound, too. Do you prefer PC or a Mac?"

"What?" I had the distinct feeling the interview was coming to a close.

"PC or Mac. Do you have a preference?"

In a half stutter I told her I had my own laptop.

Abigail shook her head. "No. I'll provide the computer. Do you have a preference? I will buy whichever one you prefer."

"Um, a Mac, I guess."

She nodded. "Do you think you can do this job for me, Miss Durough?"

I couldn't believe we were finished. Abigail had barely asked me about my qualifications. She had barely asked about anything. I didn't even know why she wanted the diary transcribed. She didn't appear to want it published.

The words, "Just like that?" filled my mind, and as I thought them, they climbed out of my head and into my mouth.

"I don't see any reason not to hire you, Miss Durough. Do you?" Abigail grinned.

"Yes. No. I mean, no, I don't and yes, I'd like the job."

"Good. Which days can you come? I was hoping to have you three times a week for several hours at a time."

"I get out of class on Mondays, Tuesdays, and Thursdays at three thirty. I could come then."

"Excellent. You can have your dinner here with me on those days and work into the early evening hours, until seven or so. Will that work?"

"Uh, yes. That's fine."

She stood. "I'll see you on Monday, then. Esperanza will give you the code for the gate so you don't have to use the buzzer each time."

I stood as well. Abigail made no move to see me to the door. An awkward moment followed where we just stood and stared at each other.

"Good-bye," she said. Her voice was strangely kind.

"Good-bye, Miss Boyles."

I took a step toward the library door and she called out to me.

"Miss Durough, would you consider letting me call you Lauren? And you could call me Abigail. The formality of using our last names will drive me batty."

I smiled. "Sure. That would be fine."

"See you on Monday, then, Lauren."

"See you then."

I didn't call her Abigail that day.

I walked to the library doors and opened one of them. I looked back as I stepped through, not knowing if I should close the door or not. Abigail stood in her ocean of books, perfectly relaxed, watching me leave her.

I closed the door behind me.

When I got into my car, I called home. I knew Dad would be on the golf course at five thirty on a Thursday and that I would get his voice mail.

It took only seconds to leave a message telling him I got the job.

Four

Before I met Mercy on the pages of her diary, I dreamed of her. The night before my first day at Abigail's, I dreamed of a woman wearing a dress like the one I wore in the Thanksgiving play in fourth grade. Dull wool skirt, muslin apron, and a white cap with puckered edges. She sat at a table, a candle burning beside her, writing. I knew she was Mercy, and I knew she was writing in her diary. She bent over a page, her hand flowing across the paper in swirls and slow flourishes as she spun the words with a feather quill. Her features were soft and unfocused in the dim candlelight, and she seemed deep in thought. I moved toward her and she heard me. Her head lifted and her eyes met mine. With the quill poised over the diary, she stared at me, her eyes kind but sad.

She didn't ask me who I was or what I was doing there. I wanted her to, but she didn't.

Instead, she looked past me. I turned my head and saw a woman in a chair in another part of the darkened room, sitting amid a pile of books, the titles of which I couldn't read in the darkness. The woman was asleep.

Abigail.

I looked back at Mercy.

She was gone. The diary was there and the burning candle, but the chair where she had been sitting was empty. The quill lay on the pages with the feather pointed toward me.

Like an invitation to pick it up.

The candle went out and I awoke.

I felt alone, though Clarissa murmured in her sleep in the bed next to me. It took a while before I fell back asleep, and when I did, I dreamed of nothing.

Abigail's first question when I returned to her sad house surprised me. We settled at a sturdy wooden table in her suffocating library, and instead of asking if I wanted a cup of tea—I could see she had one—she asked if I talked to God.

"You mean, do I pray?" I said. I might have stuttered.

"What is prayer but talking to God?" She lifted a withered hand and flicked her wrist, as if to wave away a cartload of my naiveté.

This wrinkled dismissal annoyed me. I may not have the Durough drive, but I don't lack the household dignity. We've always been quick to defend our intellect. A second or two ticked by as I debated how to answer her. How does the brand-new employee answer the employer's arguably inappropriate question? I'd never been an employee before. I *do* talk to God, but I didn't see how or why that should matter to her.

And what did that have to do with transcribing a three-hundred-year-old diary? Mild irritation gave way to momentary boldness. I looked her straight in the eye.

"Yes. I talk to God." I said it with such self-assurance. There is a jolt of satisfaction people my age get from answering an elderly know-it-all with confidence.

The corners of Abigail's mouth rose in slow symmetry. My answer amused her.

Irritation swelled within me. "I don't see how—"

"And do you believe God talks back to you?" she interrupted.

"What?"

"Do you know what happened to Joan of Arc?" Abigail posed the question as easily as if I had just said, *Sure, I believe God talks to me.*

"Joan of Arc?"

"Yes."

"She was executed. Burned at the stake, I think." That was all I could remember from high school social studies. I was only a month into my college Western Civ class. We were a ways off from Joan of Arc.

"Yes, she was. Do you know why she was executed?"

I scratched my neck. It didn't itch. "Well, if I remember right, France was at war with England and she led the French troops. English troops captured her. The charge against her was treason?"

Abigail inclined her head, entertained by my recap, I think. "You don't remember right."

"She led troops. She was captured. I'm sure that part is right," I said, mentally massaging my wounded ego.

"Yes, all that's true. But she wasn't executed under a charge of treason."

I was about to ask what the charge had been when I suddenly remembered why Joan of Arc was executed. "She believed God talked to her."

Abigail's eyes seemed to brighten. I had surprised her.

"She was about your age when she died, did you know that? You are nineteen?"

"Twenty."

"They called her a heretic. A witch. They lit her on fire."

I shifted in my seat.

"But she wasn't a witch, of course," Abigail continued. "Everyone knows that now. She's a saint. St. Joan."

"Yes, I remember that," I muttered.

"Of course, that doesn't change how she died, how the flames ate her body while she stood tied to a pole."

"No, it doesn't," I said.

Abigail said nothing for a moment, just looked at me. Then she leaned forward. "Do you see all these books?" she asked in a low voice, as if passing on a secret I should keep close to me. Abigail's books were everywhere, stuffed into shelves, lying in piles, peeking out from under tables. I'd have to have been blind not to see them. I was in awe and afraid for the same reason—there were so many.

And I didn't care that she had again made a hairpin turn in the conversation. We were leaving behind the burning body of an innocent woman.

"Yes," I said, looking about me.

"You love books the way I do. You love to write. I know this. That's one of the reasons I hired you."

I nodded and waited.

"Mercy Hayworth loved to write too," Abigail said, tipping her head. "Stories. The once-upon-a-time kind. The men who demanded her execution said she wrote the devil's words, that her stories were tales from hell, that she was the devil's scribe. Her writings were proof she was a witch. They were just stories, Lauren. The kind of stories you and I like to read. The kind you like to write."

She sat back in her chair. "This is why I want you to tell Mercy's story," she said. "Mercy was a beautiful young girl who loved many good things. She was wrongfully accused, convicted, and hanged, and no one remembers her."

"I see." I swallowed, keenly aware of the muscles in my neck.

"I wanted you to know why you're doing this."

"Okay," I said.

Across from me, Abigail inhaled and exhaled heavily. A cleansing breath. She was ready to move on.

I barely felt my lungs moving, the ghosts of Joan of Arc and Mercy Hayworth hovering at my shoulders, lamenting their ruin.

"Now, then," Abigail said. "Perhaps you'd care for a cup of tea before we get started?"

Five

The diary's pages were the color of toast in some places and in others, the color of wet ashes. The ink, made long ago from ground walnut shells mixed with vinegar and salt, was so faint it looked as if I could blow it away if I leaned over it and merely exhaled. The frail letters on the first page were barely legible; they looked like whispers, if whispers had form. I'd never seen a book that old that wasn't in a museum. I could tell without touching it that Mercy's diary was too fragile to be held in my hands, too delicate to bear the weight of my fingers. The thought made me sad.

As I stared at the diary's pages, I felt I was just inches from this woman, a breath away. Three hundred years of time and space seemed to vanish. This was Mercy's very touch, the last vestige of her existence.

Abigail told me Mercy had penned her stories in a separate volume, a business ledger her father bought at Ingersoll's Ordinary—the colonists' version of a public house—which she kept a secret as her father had asked. But Mercy's accusers found her hiding place when they turned her cottage upside down looking for proof of her alliance with the devil. They found the ledger of stories, and after her trial, they burned it.

They didn't find the diary.

The only words of Mercy left on this earth lay on paper too fragile to be touched. And I so wanted to touch it.

Abigail showed it to me that first afternoon, after she had finally handed me a cup of tea. She brought it from another room, inside a box that made a snorting sound when she opened it. An airlock.

"I don't get it out very often," she said, as she slipped a pair of thin white gloves on her hands and gingerly lifted the wrapped book out of a foam-covered slot. "I'm afraid it will disintegrate in my hands."

"I'm surprised you keep it here," I said. "If there was a fire..." I stopped. It wasn't any of my business.

"I keep it in a fireproof safe," Abigail said, apparently unruffled by my comment. She laid the book down in front of me and gently removed its plastic covering. The leather cover looked like a layer of thin chocolate. A musky odor met my nostrils.

"The cover is in remarkable shape," Abigail said, as she nimbly opened the diary. "The pages, though, are as fragile as a house of cards."

The first page lay open before me, dated the fourth of January, 1692.

I could see the first few lines. The script was both foreign and familiar. Mercy's letters bore strokes I didn't recognize easily. Reading her words would be like deciphering a code, like uncovering buried treasure or peeling back a veil. They beckoned.

I am hiding high up in my elm tree as I write in this little book.
'Tis true I have been told not to climb any more trees. Papa
said if the Village leaders see me they will think me mad. What
Gospel woman in her right mind climbs a tree? An elm tree?
A tree that bears no fruit to be plucked? But I cannot stay on
the ground. I yearn to be up. I yearn for...

The ink grew faint. I couldn't read the rest of the first page. "Are all the pages like this?" I lifted my head to look at Abigail.

"Many are that way. But not all. Some are better. Some are worse."

I sat with the diary inches from me, surrounded on all sides by Abigail's horde of books. I couldn't help but ask the obvious. "You're a lover of stories. Why don't you just transcribe this yourself?"

Abigail didn't look at me. "I cannot write what needs to be written. One can appreciate art and yet not have the talent to paint a picture. Besides, I am too old."

She wasn't being truthful. I was sure of it. A retired librarian obsessed with books surely had the talent to transcribe a diary. And Abigail's age didn't appear to limit her in any other way. She was keeping something from me.

She reached into her pocket and silently handed me a pair of white gloves just like the ones she wore.

I slipped the gloves on my hands and placed my thumb and fore-finger on the edge of the first page. My pulse quickened as nervousness swept over me. I had an immediate vision of the page crumbling to dust at my touch. I eased my finger under the page's lower corner and slowly moved my hand upward, holding my breath as the page rose vertical. The binding made a yawning sound; I had awakened it. I clamped my mouth shut and pursed my lips together—as if this would keep the trea-sure in one piece—and let gravity ease the page down on the other side. The page creaked to its resting place and lay still. I exhaled.

Page two of Mercy's diary was legible almost in its entirety. I leaned over the ancient words and a strange love affair began. There is no other way to describe it. I devoured those first few words like I was ravenous.

I am so pleased Papa gave me this little book to record my thoughts. On occasion my thoughts find their way into the stories in mine other little book. But these pages will be filled with all that stirs me, all that I wonder about. And it won't be a story. Unless I call it my story.

Papa is feeling better today, though he still looks pale to me. Oh, that the sun would come out blazing and warm him.

But there is not much sun today. The little of it we saw shone through the window of the Meeting House this morning when the Reverend brought us the lesson. I tried with all my strength to listen to him speak from the Book of Isaiah, but mine eyes kept traveling to the shaft of light falling on the floor. Dust motes were at play in the beam, and I could nigh hear the music they danced to. Goody Collier's son, John Peter, witnessed me smiling at the sun's little ballet. He was looking at me from the men's side. I feared he might be of a mind to tell my father, but he smiled as if pleased I had seen the dance within the sunbeam because he had seen it too.

It near transfixed me, his gaze. I had to look away.

It is nigh unto nightfall. I hear Lily, our milk cow, teasing me to go to her. On the morrow I shall write a story of a fairy maiden who dances for the queen of the sky and of the fairy prince who secretly loves her. He will...

The ink faded away with the fairy prince on the cusp of discovery. I wanted to read more but I didn't know if I could handle the stress of turning another page. Abigail spoke, and the sound of her voice startled me.

"I don't want you merely to copy the diary, Lauren. I want Mercy's life to be remembered in language that is understandable. I want it to be a story. There's more to Mercy than this diary."

"More?"

"Of course there's more." Abigail frowned, as if wondering how I could not know a woman is more than what she says about herself. "There's everything I know in my head about her; what has been told about her down through the decades, what has been passed from generation to generation—all of which I will tell you, Lauren, because I have no daughter."

At that moment, I understood Abigail had arrived at a place of decision and the lore that surrounded her beloved cousin was with her at that meeting place. Abigail stood at a crossroads, burdened by her status as sole heir, to decide if Mercy Hayworth would slip away into anonymity when Abigail died, or if she would unseal the vault that kept Mercy's memory alive and command us to weep for her.

She wanted what Joan of Arc finally got five hundred years too late—a crown of sainthood on a tragically bowed head.

I should have realized then that this wasn't about Mercy alone.

Six

5 January 1692

A bird the color of sky flew into our barn today. It has an injured wing. He must have been hurt before the autumn snows and so could not fly south with his brothers. Papa thinks he must be roaming from barn to barn in the settlement, looking for a warm place to spend the winter. Poor thing. He'll not find a warm place this winter, I dare say. I cannot remember a January as cold as this one. Clouds are collecting, and I fear we are in for a terrible blizzard. I can hear it in the wind. Lily senses it too. When I milked her she kept her nose in the air, sniffing like a dog.

Goody Dawes made a strange face at the Ordinary today when I told her the wind whispers of heavy snow for tonight. I don't think she cares to listen to anything save gossip. Gossip is seldom about the weather.

I heard her tell Goody Wyndham that 'tis a disgrace John Peter Collier isn't in the militia with the other young men of the Village. They meant with their own sons, of course. I was of a mind to remind them that since the passing of John Collier Senior, John Peter's mother has relied solely on him to tend to the mill. If he left, there would be none but his young sisters to help. There's not a one of John Peter's sisters who could manage the grindstone.

But I minded my tongue. Not because I wanted to, but because Papa would have wanted me to.

Ah, I see the first flakes of snow as I write. A wall of whiteness descending.

I do hope the little bird stays in the barn tonight.

'Twill not be safe to be out and about.

7 January 1692

Snow covers all. I shoveled a path to the barn, and the traces of my steps disappeared even as I stepped away. Lily was fretting to go out. She does not care for being wedged in the barn all day long. She gave me little milk for wanting to be out in the sun. I told her there was no sun today. She tossed her head at me as if to say, if there is daylight, there is sun. I told her the light she senses is but the wide whiteness of last night's blizzard. Snow has a light of its own when it is angry. A cold light. Menacing.

The little bird sat watching me as I milked Lily. He chirped. I threw him some crusts of bread that I carried in my apron.

I have named him Wanderer.

John Peter likes the name.

Mama would have liked it too.

The first afternoon I spent with Mercy began with these two January days, one promising a storm that would leave its cold mark on everything in its path and the other promising that there would be no escaping it, not even for the smallest and delicate of creatures.

When I finished transcribing Mercy's first entries, I felt as though I had been sucked into a portal of shifting moments and then spit out. I sat back in my chair and rubbed my right shoulder. Handling the pages of Mercy's diary kept the muscles in my neck and arms tense with worry. It had taken me an hour to transcribe the first entry into language that made sense and yet didn't alter what Mercy had written. Then another hour for the second.

I wanted it to be perfect.

I wanted to let my mind conjure the scene as Mercy wrote. The cold whiteness of winter. The fluttering of tiny wings. Bittersweet memories of a deceased mother. The hard life of a young woman in colonial times who had already lost much. And over all these images was my knowledge that something was about to descend upon Mercy, far worse than a snowstorm. I wanted to shout across the centuries and warn her even though I knew full well, as Abigail had told me, that Mercy's destiny was sealed.

I had read Arthur Miller's *The Crucible* in high school. I remembered enough of the play to know that the coming days in Mercy's snowy white world would usher in a nightmare, a truly dark moment in our nation's history. As I rubbed an ache in my neck, I had a sudden desire to research the Salem witch trials, to read up on what I would soon see through Mercy Hayworth's eyes. Surely in a library as overweight as Abigail's there would be books on the Salem trials, especially since Abigail's long-ago cousin had been a victim of them.

I looked up from my work to face Abigail, who sat behind me as I read and typed. Abigail didn't stand over me as I plucked away at the laptop. In fact, she never seemed to let her eyes glance over the text of Mercy's diary. When she was in the room with me, helping to fill gaps where pages were missing or not legible, or where Mercy's ancient words needed clarification, she always stood off to the side. She never looked over my shoulder at the faded pages.

She sensed me looking at her and raised her head. "Do you need something, Lauren?"

"I was just wondering if you had books on the Salem witch trials I could take home and read on my own time."

She blinked at me. "What for?"

"I'd like do some research. I think it would help me understand the times Mercy was living in and what she went through."

Abigail licked her bottom lip. "Honestly, Lauren, the diary is all you need to understand Mercy and what she went through." She looked down for a moment, as if concentrating on choosing just the right words. "In fact, that kind of research would interfere with the work you're doing. Many have hypothesized on how the hysteria began and why. No one is really sure. It can get a little muddy, even political."

Abigail paused for a second, then continued. "I am asking you, Lauren, to read nothing written about the trials. Nothing. Not until you are done with the diary. When you're done, you may borrow any book I have on the subject. And I have many. But I ask that you wait until you're finished. And don't meddle with those Web sites on the Internet. Not yet. Just concentrate on the diary."

Abigail locked her eyes on mine, pleading with me. A strange sensation fell over me as I realized I was in a position of power over her. There were not to be many moments like that one.

"May we agree on that? Just until you are finished with the diary?" she asked.

It occurred to me then that the diary might be a forgery. It didn't look like one, but her anxiety made me question it.

"Is this diary genuine?" I asked.

"I assure you it is genuine. God is my witness."

We looked at each other for a moment.

"So may we agree on this? It is essential that we agree." Her eyes were hard on mine.

I could sense that my job hung in the balance. She was ready to pull the diary out of my hands and send me away if I refused. It mattered that much to her.

But that's not what bothered me most, that it mattered. I was thinking about what my father would say if I got fired from a job he thought was silly to begin with. I had no desire to find out.

"If you think it's necessary," I said.

"It is. Not for the diary, but for you."

She looked back down at her book, the conversation over.

I had no idea what she meant.

Seven

I kind of broke my promise to Abigail the moment I got back to my dorm room. "Kind of," because I didn't promise I wouldn't look at any *plays* about the Salem witch trials. I promised not to read historical accounts or Web sites.

I couldn't go back to my empty room—Clarissa would be working or studying somewhere else—with *The Crucible* sitting on my bookshelf and not look at it.

I had no trouble rationalizing it. I'd already read the play, and it wasn't a historical account. It was based on fact, but that was all.

I'd brought quite a few books with me to Santa Barbara my freshman year. Far more than I needed, more than the average dorm room could hold. Half of the boxes of books I brought went back with my parents that same night. As my father replaced the extra books in his company car, he reminded me that if I had gotten the condo like he suggested, I could've brought as many books as I wanted.

He hadn't thought much of my idea to live in a dorm. Not enough security (he still worries I will be abducted and held for ransom), too much partying (even though I am not much of a party girl and he knows it), and not enough attention paid to studies. He had yet to meet Clarissa, the woman who could do it all—stay safe, work, party, and study, all at the same time.

I'm sure he also felt that if I had at my disposal the means to live on my own, in the manner to which I am accustomed, why settle for anything less?

Historically, Duroughs don't settle.

Clarissa was gone, and the room was quiet except for heavy bass booming from a stereo next door. I was caught up with assignments for my classes the next day, so I made a cup of green tea and eased *The Crucible* out from its thin space on my bookshelf.

I opened it and fanned through the pages, noting my high school scribbling from my junior English class. I'd highlighted snatches of dialogue, penciled in a few insights from my seventeen-year-old mind, and drawn little daisies in the margins.

The moment I held the pages still and my eyes swept the script, the details of the story came back to me. The names, the places, the remembered fear that someone can say something untrue about you and as long as there is someone else to believe it, you are whatever they say you are.

The remembered names filled my head: John Proctor. Betty Parris. Abigail Williams. Martha Corey. Tituba. Rebecca Nurse.

And I was suddenly aware that these people weren't merely characters in a play. They had been real. Arthur Miller had fiddled with the details—like creating an affair between John Proctor the accused and Abigail Williams the afflicted, which would have been unlikely, as the real Abigail Williams was only eleven years old—but the people had actually existed. Mercy probably had known them all by name.

And they knew her.

Inside the book, just before the first scene, I found a folded piece of paper. Study notes from my American lit teacher. I read them and remembered.

In 1692, several young girls in Salem, Massachusetts, began having hallucinations and seizures. Unable to account for their afflictions, and believing as most Puritans did that anything unexplainable and terrible was of the devil, the local physician declared that they were bewitched. Fear quickly took hold, and the girls were pressed to name their tormentors. They began to name names, perhaps arbitrarily and perhaps at the coaching of their parents. First to be accused were those considered socially deviant, but soon anyone who challenged the girls or the ruling authorities, or who defended the accused, became accused themselves. Seemingly devout people were suddenly charged with witchcraft, and as panic spread throughout the colony, others began to claim they were also bewitched. Old grievances were aired, grudges were unearthed, and ordinary people were charged, arrested, and many convicted based on little more than the claims of young girls writhing on courtroom floors. In all, more than one hundred forty people were accused of witchcraft, though not all were imprisoned or tried. Nineteen people were hanged in Salem alone.

Your first discussion question is due Friday. Be prepared to discuss one of the following:

- How does hysteria defy logic?
- What are the ramifications of moral law equaling state law?
- How were the afflicted girls empowered, and what was the direct result of that empowerment?
- What is the basis for social intolerance?
- What is the opposite of deviance?

My cell phone trilled, and I jumped in my chair as if Abigail had walked in the room and found me cheating. I grabbed my phone and saw the word *Dad* on the screen. I knew why he'd called before he even asked.

"Hi, Dad."

"Lauren. So. How goes the job?"

Dad's not much for small talk. Big talk gets more done.

"Um. I like it. It's really interesting." Interesting probably wasn't the most accurate word, but it fell off my lips first.

"Tell me."

Those are Dad's favorite two words as a parent. Maybe they're his favorite two words as a CEO too. They sound like an invitation to be heard, and they are. But they are also the means to enlighten. Dad has a fondness for information. He wants to know all that can be known. "Tell me" is the same as saying, "Increase my knowledge," which is the same as "Empower me." Dad has always understood that knowledge is power.

"Well," I began, "the diary is in really good shape. Abigail has a special box she keeps it in that has an airlock. I wear gloves when I handle it. Some of the pages are missing or torn, and sometimes the writing is hard to decipher. And of course, the language is a bit of a challenge. Abigail wants the transcription to be easy to read, so I'm rearranging some of the sentences and replacing the 'thees' and 'thous' with 'yous' and 'yours.'"

Dad was quiet for a moment. Processing.

"Why does this Abigail want to change the language? It seems to me a transcription should be an exact representation of the original."

"Well, she'd like it to be readable for today."

"Readable for who?"

My eyes widened as I held the phone to my ear. I hadn't a clue who'd be reading it when I was done. Abigail had said nothing about what she planned to do with the transcription. She'd only said she didn't want Mercy to be forgotten.

"Readable for who, Lauren?"

"Um, well, anyone, I guess."

"But who's going to read it?"

Dad was not being belligerent or excessively nosey or even accusatory. He was gathering information. Increasing his understanding.

I quickly decided it didn't matter to me what Abigail planned to do. I was hired simply to transcribe.

So instead of saying, "I don't know," I said, "Well, it makes no difference to me."

Even though, right then, I knew it did.

"She must have a plan of some sort, " Dad said. "I mean, by the time you're finished with this project, she'll have spent several hundred dollars. And for what? If she's planning on publishing, you should get it in writing that you're the coeditor. Editor, actually. You might want to ask what her plans are."

"I don't think she has any plans."

"It's not too late to tell her you want credit on the byline."

"Well, it's really Mercy's story, not mine."

"Is it worth publishing?" Dad the entrepreneur, always thinking big.

"Possibly. Probably. Mercy was hanged as a witch in Salem. But she was innocent, like most of the people executed for witchcraft back then were."

"Hanged? As a witch?" He sounded appalled.

"She was innocent, Dad. That's the point. She was innocent."

"Not very pleasant subject matter."

"No. Not pleasant. But historical. It really happened."

"Kind of a sad way to spend your afternoons." He said this in a fatherly way. I don't know how else to describe it.

"Sometimes history is sad."

"Hmm."

We were silent for a moment.

"Do you know much about the Salem witch trials, Dad?"

"No more than the average person, I guess."

"A bunch of teenage girls started acting strange and accusing people of bewitching them. And everyone believed them even though there was no proof. How does a person convince people to believe things they can't prove?"

My father was quick to answer. "That's easy. People always believe what they want to believe. Hitler didn't force anybody to jump on his bandwagon. All those men who jumped on it used their own legs to do it."

"But *how* did he convince them to jump?"

"How does anybody convince anybody else of anything? You catch them at a weak moment, when they're feeling alone or afraid, and you offer them the security of solidarity. Advertising execs use this tactic all the time: Buy this and be like everyone else. Don't buy it and be the loser no one respects."

"So I guess the key is to never let yourself feel alone or afraid."

"No," he responded. "The key is to never let someone else tell you what to think."

Eight

8 January 1692

Spent the day in the cottage. Papa coughed most of the morning. I made him a hot drink of dried herbs to settle his lungs. He told me it tasted like summer.

I spun thread all afternoon and my fingers are sore. This is one chore I would gladly give up. I would wear fig leaves like Eve rather than spin thread. Papa reminded me that fig trees do not grow in the colony and even fig leaves must be sewn together.

It seems the world will not function without thread. And even though my fingers are red and angry, supper must be made.

Papa wants rabbit stew. I do not, but I will make it because I know he will eat it.

And because I must go to John Peter's house to get the rabbit. I will trade thread for it.

'Tis not a long walk.

Evening

The rabbit tasted a bit different tonight.

John Peter insisted on bringing me home on his horse after I went for it. So I sat on a horse with a

*dead rabbit in my lap and my arms around John
Peter's waist.*

I may yet develop an appetite for rabbit.

11 January 1692

*Tonight I miss Mama. 'Tis her birthday today. Papa
said this would be her thirty-seventh winter if she had
lived. 'Tis strange to think that when she was my age,
she was already a mother.*

*I am eighteen. Most of my friends are wedded
already. Papa worries that his illness prevents him from
finding a suitable man for me to marry. He does not get
out very often.*

*I want to be married, but I do not want to marry
just any man.*

And I am fearful of what happened two years ago.

I have been betrothed before.

*When I was sixteen, I was to marry a man from
Marblehead named James Luddy. He was two years
older than I, and his father owned a ship like Uncle's.
That is how my father knew him. James was tall and
red-headed, and he scarce spoke a word to me the day I
met him. His eyes were as gray as a stormy night and
very large. They looked like they wished to pop from his
head altogether. I think he was as afraid of me as I was
of him.*

*When James and his father left our cottage, I told
Papa I did not think I should marry James Luddy. He
said, "Why ever not?" And I said because within me
there was not a hint of affection, or even its opposite.*

I felt nothing. Papa said marriage is not kept by affection but by a pledge. Affection does not beget the pledge; the pledge begets affection. When you share a life and a home and a bed with someone, you become soul mates as surely as cream and effort produce butter. Papa told me James Luddy was a good man, a Gospel man, who would be a good husband.

And so I began to imagine my life with James Luddy. I imagined being butter.

But before I finished sewing even one tablecloth for my future table, James Luddy came down with brain fever and died.

I did not know how to weep for him.

Papa has not tried to find me another match. I believe James's death affected him greatly. Or perhaps he has tried, but no man wants to take James's place and wind up where he is: in Abraham's bosom.

I wonder if I should tell Papa that I fancy John Peter. Can it not be that for some, affection begets a pledge?

Abigail hadn't mentioned that Mercy had been in love. And I knew the moment I finished reading the January 11 entry that she had been. The shape of the words on the paper, the underlying tone, the lift in the script.

Mercy had been in love.

The story was taking a painful turn already, and it was only my fifth afternoon with the diary. Here was a woman in love about to be hanged. An innocent woman.

I turned to look at Abigail who, as usual, sat behind me, her nose in a book. It was a few minutes before six o'clock. Esperanza hadn't called us to dinner yet.

"She's in love with John Peter," I said.

"You can tell that from four pages in, can you?" Abigail kept her eyes on the book she held in her lap. I didn't know what she was reading.

I turned to face Mercy's pages. "It just surprises me."

Abigail raised her head. "Why is that?"

"Because," I began, but I had no good reasons for thinking a woman my age in colonial New England wasn't capable of falling in love.

"I am sure you've been attracted to someone before, haven't you?" Fatigue edged Abigail's voice. She waited for me to answer.

Of course I'd been attracted to people. Tyler Prindell in sixth grade. Adam Bosch in tenth. Steve Lynde had escorted me to a debutante ball when I was seventeen. I liked him. We had a lot of the same friends, and we played tennis a couple times. He was attractive. He kissed me once, but I hadn't been in love with him.

I wouldn't have walked to his house through the snow to trade thread for a dead rabbit.

Attraction was one thing. Love was another.

"Yes, I have. I just…"

"Makes it harder, doesn't it?" Again I caught the weight of weariness in her voice. She meant that knowing Mercy had been in love would make the transcription work more emotionally difficult simply because I knew Mercy was doomed. But there was something else there, lurking just under the surface of her words: being in love complicates things.

I thought back to that moment two weeks earlier when I saw Abigail for the first time, when I visually took in her physical resilience. I had known somehow that she was alone. That she had always been alone.

But that she knew what it was like to be in love.

"Have you ever been attracted to someone?" I was only asking her the same question she asked me, but it was more than that and we both knew it. I was asking her if she had ever been in love.

She looked at the book in her lap. "Yes. Once."

"Who was he?" I asked softly, hoping she liked mentioning his name from time to time. If he was dead, she might. If he'd left her for another, then maybe not.

She ran her finger absently down the length of a bookmark resting on her open book. I expected her to say, "Oh, he was just someone I met in college," or "He was a librarian in the next county over," or "He never even knew I liked him."

But as her finger slid down the bookmark, she said, "He was the man I should have married."

Then she closed the book.

"Time for dinner," she said, looking up.

Esperanza had not called us.

Mealtimes with Abigail were never predictable. Sometimes she was silent the whole time we ate. If I asked a question or attempted to begin a conversation on one of those evenings, her response was a short one-word answer that clearly meant, "I don't want to talk." Other times we discussed books the entire meal. She especially liked to talk about books we'd both read. Her eyes lit up if she looked up from her plate and asked, "Have you read this?" and I responded that yes, I had.

In the beginning, I chalked up her talkative moods to being a retired librarian who missed being around people who loved books. I suppose that was a small part of it. But there were other reasons Abigail pounced on any opportunity to discuss a book we had both read. Dissecting a book was the same as making sense of life. You have to find a way to interpret life, or you'll go nuts. That's her way. It is also mine.

As we walked to the dining room that evening, I could almost hear the heavy fabric of Abigail's lifelong disappointment swishing. This was to be a silent meal. I dreaded it already.

Esperanza, a truly wonderful cook, had made a dish she called *bifana*—a pork roast she slow-cooked with ginger, cloves, and garlic, and which she served with rhubarb chutney. The sweet and spicy aroma met us halfway down the hall. I said something about how wonderful it smelled, and Abigail said nothing.

The dining room was at the far end of the long entryway, just off the kitchen. It was paneled in dark wood, and the table that ran the length of the room was dark also. Cherry, probably. The curtains and valances were a deep crimson with gold brocade. A few family portraits and one seascape hung on the walls. The Persian rug under the table, the same bottomless shade of red as the curtains, was fringed in light beige. Those threads were the only hue in the room that hinted there were other colors in the spectrum besides heavy ones.

Abigail sat at the head of the long table, and I took a chair to her right. She prayed for our meal, a rote prayer, but one I sensed she genuinely meant. And we began to eat.

I didn't even bother making a stab at conversation. There didn't seem to be much point, since Abigail had clearly slid into silent mode. I would just eat my dinner, spend another hour or two afterward with the diary, and then go back to the dorm. Clarissa needed help with a research paper, and I had promised to give it.

But after two bites of Esperanza's bifana, Abigail lifted her head to look at me.

"Have you read *Great Expectations*?" she asked.

My fork was poised at my mouth. I'd been musing on what could have happened between Abigail and her lost love, and she brought up *Great Expectations.*

Not exactly a love story, but certainly a story about regrets.

"Yes." I slipped the fork in my mouth, chewed, and waited.

"Do you have a favorite line?"

I licked a drop of rhubarb chutney off my lower lip. I don't tend to memorize whole lines verbatim from any book. The only ones I know are the ones everybody knows. *Call me Ishmael. It was the best of times, it was the worst of times. Et tu, Brute?* And I certainly didn't have a collection of quotes from *Great Expectations* swimming around in my head.

"No, sorry. I don't."

I expected a look of subtle dismay, but Abigail looked past me to the sea of empty chairs around the table, smiling as if I had rattled off a great quote from chapter eight.

"Mine's fairly near the beginning," she said, "before Pip becomes someone who judges people by outward appearance. 'In the little world in which children have their existence…there is nothing so finely perceived and finely felt as injustice. It may be only a small injustice that the child can be exposed to, but the child is small, and its world is small.' " She turned to me. "I like that line. It suggests what I've always known to be true. We are born knowing how to be just. And we die knowing we spent a lifetime pretending we didn't."

I stopped chewing. At twenty years old, I certainly wasn't going to argue with her. Perhaps she knew I wouldn't and that's why she went on.

"Why do you suppose Pip loved Estella and not Biddy?"

I shrugged. "Estella was beautiful. Wealthy. Desirable."

"But she was cruel to him."

Again I felt Abigail was revealing something about herself to me. Had she been cruel to the man she wished she had married?

"Well, then I guess he loved what she represented," I said.

Abigail cocked her head, studying me. "Which is why he didn't love poor, plain Biddy, isn't it? Even though she was kind to him. Because of what *she* represented."

"Yes, I think so." It didn't seem like a terribly shrewd observation on my part. I thought it was rather obvious. But Abigail still looked at me like I had said something insightful.

"Did you know, Lauren, that in the original ending, Charles Dickens didn't have the garden scene at the end where Pip and Estella leave hand in hand? Did you know that?"

"No."

"Instead, Pip one day hears that Estella has remarried. They meet only briefly and shake hands. They just shake hands. And then they part."

"I didn't know that."

Abigail nodded. "Not many people do."

She began to cut the rest of her meat.

I waited for her to say something more.

We ate the rest of the meal in silence.

Nine

15 January 1692

Papa was outside for a little while today, watching the icicles melt into muddy puddles. He wanted to muck out the barn but I told him I had already done it.

God forgive me, I lied.

I did it later while he slept.

This afternoon Papa wanted to write a letter to his friend Rev. George Burroughs, who was a minister here in the Village some years ago, but he was too weak to form the letters. I wrote it for him. Rev. Burroughs is not at all like our Rev. Parris. I do not think he is like most ministers of the Gospel. He is loud and immense and I think he could break my arm just by looking at it if he wanted to. I do not think he should ever want to, but he could if he did. Papa likes to talk theology with him. Not because they agree on spiritual matters but because Papa likes to converse with people who are not afraid to say what they think. Papa told me once that George Burroughs left Salem under difficult circumstances. He owed someone money, or maybe someone owed him. I was too young at the time to know or care which and Papa does not discuss it. His letter to George Burroughs was brief today. Papa talked of the frustration of illness, the depth

*of winter and the oddity of Lot's wife becoming a pillar
of salt. I shall see that the letter is posted tomorrow
when I go to the Village to sell my cider.*

*Of all the things I am glad of, I am most glad Papa
taught me how to write.*

*What would I do with all the stories in my head if
I could not form letters? Papa has told me not to make
bold of my ability to read and write. The Village elders
do not think it wise that I know my letters. Only a few
of my childhood friends know how to write their names.
I showed my friend Mary Graham how to write her
name when we were younger. I taught her other words
too. But she was wedded two years ago and lives in
Gloucester now. I never see her anymore. Prudence Dawes
pretends she has no desire to know more than she does. She
pretends knowing how to write is akin to knowing how to
spit tobacco or shoe a horse. And Esther Harding just
thinks whatever Prudence tells her to think.*

*But I think I would go mad if I could not write.
Papa says there is never any vinegar in the house because
I use it all to make ink!*

*Today I wrote a story about a girl who finds her-
self betrothed to a man who cannot speak. He must tell
her everything in pictures he draws on the ground with
a stick. After they are married, and after the pledge
begets affection, she becomes enamored with his drawings. And so the clearing in front of their house is covered with etchings in the dirt that she refuses to sweep
away.*

*Wanderer, my little bird, has been here ten days.
I think he likes it here. I think he will stay.*

17 January 1692

Today there was news from Papa's sister in Maine.
My cousin Samuel is to be married in the autumn. He
is bringing his bride from England this summer. I have
visited my aunt's home in Maine. Papa's friend George
Burroughs lives there, and he and Papa like to talk about
the things of God when they drink ale together. The last
time we visited Wells, Papa and Rev. Burroughs debated
yet again why our all-seeing God made the serpent that
tempted Eve. They have never happened upon an answer
upon which they agree. Many pints of ale and many
years later, they are still at it.

I hope Samuel's bride likes it here. I should imagine
the colony will seem very primitive. I hope she likes birds
and trees and wide spaces. And that she does not mind
linsey-woolsey in place of silk.

I am running out of ink again.

Mercy's mid-January entries were hard to transcribe. The ink was especially faint.

It became a puzzle to me, Mercy's long January 15 entry. I brought in different magnifying glasses, including a jeweler's loupe Abigail insisted on paying for, and a special light I borrowed from an art student. I studied other samples of writing from the same time period at the library. I was fairly confident when I finished that I had eked Mercy's original thoughts out of the faded words. I read the transcription to Abigail when I was done. She asked me to read the paragraph twice about the girl who marries a man who cannot speak. I could see her picturing the lines in the dirt as I read it to her.

She'd never heard this snippet of story before. It had been too difficult to read. I looked up at Abigail when I was done reading it for the second time, and she nodded, apparently satisfied.

"So you're going home this weekend," she said.

I'd expected her to say, "That was excellent transcription work." It took me a second to tell her yes, I was going home. My uncle Loring's fiftieth birthday extravaganza was set for that Saturday.

"So how do the Duroughs celebrate fiftieth birthdays?" A mix of cynicism and longing laced Abigail's voice, like she already knew how my wealthy family honored a milestone birthday: with excess.

After I saved the transcription, I decided to do what I'd always done in the company of adults who thought themselves shrewd, which in my childhood and adolescence was often. I answered her soft sarcasm with soft sarcasm.

"Pin the tail on the donkey and a water-balloon toss." I closed the laptop and heard Abigail chuckle behind me.

"Touché, my dear," she said.

I smiled back at her.

"Oh, I do miss the parties." The cynicism in her voice was gone; the longing was not.

I carefully closed the diary and placed it back inside its plastic sheath. I tried to imagine Abigail as a young woman dressed in chiffon or organza, milling about a rose garden filled with young party-goers, a cup of punch in her gloved hand. I couldn't do it. It was strangely easier to picture Mercy that way.

"Do you?" I said, as I laid the book in its foam-lined box.

"Don't believe me?"

I turned to face her. She sat in her usual place, in a lime green armchair with a tea service at her side, a hardback book open spine-down on her lap. She was stroking the delicate handle of a Royal Doulton teacup that boasted an explosion of roses on its porcelain sides.

"I didn't mean to sound like I doubted you," I ventured. "You just don't talk much about your past. It's hard for me to picture what you were like when you were young."

She looked at her withered hand holding the teacup. "It must seem to you that I've always been old and odd."

"I never said you were odd."

"Good heavens, Lauren, how many people say to other people, 'You're rather odd'?" She laughed. "You wouldn't have *said* it."

"So what were your parties like?" I asked, wanting to move on.

Abigail lifted her chin as if to peer into her past on tiptoe. The humor from before was replaced by sweet contemplation. "My parents held parties in our garden nearly every weekend in the summer. Just outside those french doors." She inclined her head toward curtained doors in the far corner of the room that I hadn't noticed before. Stacks of books lay against them. "My cousin Dorothea and I would be allowed to stay up late if the guests lingered into the evening. Dorothea spent every summer with us while her parents traveled for their business. She was my age and had the most beautiful auburn hair. We wore beautiful dresses and did each other's hair, and sometimes we snuck into my mother's bedroom and used her perfume and talcum powder. When the sun went down, Dorothea and I slipped our shoes off and danced about the patio in our bare feet. Sometimes there'd be a string quartet or a guitarist there. Dorothea was a wonderful dancer. My father let her dance for the guests sometimes. She took ballet. I wanted lessons, but my father wouldn't let me have them."

She paused for a moment. I asked why her father wouldn't let her take ballet lessons, but she didn't seem to hear me. Her gaze lingered on the curtained doors, but also on a far-off moment invisible to me.

"I couldn't dance like she could, but I could recite poetry," she continued after a moment. "I could recite bits and pieces of *The Song of*

Hiawatha. There was a man my father worked with who liked to hear me recite. He always asked me to tell him more about the Indian princess when he and his wife came to my parents' parties. I'd stand in the middle of his friends, they with their tumblers of expensive bourbon and me in my bare feet, and I'd recite whatever part of the poem I had memorized that week. After a few minutes my father would say, 'That's enough.' He said it to Dorothea, too, when his friends asked her to dance. He'd watch her with his lips pursed in a pained smile and after a little while he'd say, 'That's enough.' "

Her voice fell away. I hesitated to say anything. I didn't want to break the spell. This was the first moment of vulnerability I'd seen in Abigail. It intrigued me.

"Appearance was everything, and Papa didn't like show-offs," she continued, but not to me. "People are always watching you, so you can't give them something to talk about. If you reveal a weakness, they will use it against you. You must always guard your appearance."

Something clattered to the floor outside the library doors. Esperanza must have dropped something in the hallway.

The transparent moment skittered away.

Abigail flinched in her chair and blinked. The vulnerability disappeared, and in its place came the familiar resilience.

"I wonder if you'll miss the parties," she said, her eyes back on mine, and I wondered if she saw my future stretching out like hers, empty and solitary.

"Who says they have to end?" I reached down and grabbed my book bag.

"Oh, believe me, they end." She stood but made no move to see me to the front door. She never did.

"Have a nice weekend, Abigail." I meant it. I didn't think she would, but I meant it.

"Drive carefully."

I turned and walked toward the library doors. Her voice called out to me as I placed my fingers over one of the handles.

"Lauren."

I turned.

"Nice transcription work today."

Ten

My dad and his brother are perfect Durough specimens. They are inventive, perceptive, methodical, and sharp. They aren't afraid to take risks, but they don't gamble. They are generous but not extravagant. They thrive on the beauty of economics, the fact that it is both art and science. My father and Uncle Loring are smitten with it. I cannot count the number of conversations around the Durough dinner table that began with Ludwig Von Mises's ideas on free economics and ended with the Durough ideal that wealth isn't delivered—it is made. People who are free to choose will choose the best use for whatever it is they possess. Wealth and prosperity begin with the freedom to choose.

I'm not sure if this is beautiful. Or completely true.

Duroughs accumulate wealth, in my opinion, because that is what the concept of wealth is. It is the concept of having because it is there to be had. It is the concept of pride in ownership. To possess is to be successful.

My father once debated a man in our church parking lot about this concept. My father made the point that you can't be wealthy and possess nothing. The other man, an ordinary guy with an ordinary bank account, told my dad you certainly can be wealthy and yet possess nothing. My father said that was impossible. The very essence of the word *wealth* implies ownership of something. The other man said plenty of poor people are content with nothing more than their good health and the love of their families. And Dad said, "So you're saying good health and the love of your family is nothing? Means nothing? Has no value?" And the man said, "That's not what I said." My dad smiled cleverly and paused before replying, "My mistake. Have a nice one, Felix."

And we got into our Bentley and drove to the country club to eat Belgian waffles on a terrace awash in linen and sterling silver. I was probably eleven. I remember licking strawberry syrup off my finger and telling my dad I thought Mr. Turney—Felix—was probably jealous that we had lots of money and he didn't. Dad told me Mr. Turney's problem was that he wasn't content with what he had, so he pretended it didn't matter what he had.

At that point Mom told Dad to please pass the marmalade and for heaven's sake could we talk about something else. Other diners were stopping to listen.

The interesting thing is, Dad has never been where Felix Turney is. Money has always flowed in the family gene pool. He can guess what it might be like to want more than you can afford to have, but how can he know?

My great-great-great-grandfather Abel Durough might have known. He was the son of an East Coast aristocrat and a commoner mistress. The story goes that Abel left home at age sixteen when he was unable to win his father's affections, jumped a train bound for the West, and eventually landed in northern California during the height of the gold rush. He hooked up with a miner named Sam Cabot, who knew a lot more than Abel did about finding the mother lode, and who needed a pair of strong arms and a healthier set of lungs. Just days before Abel found a giant ribbon of gold, Sam Cabot suffered a heart attack and died. The claim went to Abel and so did the money. Lots of it.

Abel was only eighteen.

He bought land, a shipping company, and shares in a railroad. By the time he was thirty, he was one of the richest men in San Francisco, far wealthier than the man in Boston who fathered him but refused him his last name. Durough was the last name of the Boston washerwoman who did the rich man's laundry and gave birth to Abel out of wedlock. The rich man's name was Fellowes.

Abel had long since moved his mother out to California when Fellowes fell upon hard times and came crawling on his knees to San Francisco, begging his illegitimate son to have pity on him. Abel, so the story goes, gave Fellowes what Fellowes had given him when he told Abel he would never amount to anything—five dollars and a tin of cheap tobacco—and sent him on his way.

Fellowes walked back to the train station, opened the tin of tobacco, and found inside a nugget of gold the size of a walnut and a note from his son that read, *Make something of yourself.*

I've always thought that we Duroughs, who like to point to Abel Durough as a model of ingenuity and verve, forget his life made its monumental turn not by anything he did, but by being in the right place at the right time. All of Abel's successes thereafter were made with money in his pocket. Money gave him the confidence to do what he did.

Confidence tends to minimize the magnitude of the choice.

When I asked my father about this the summer I turned fourteen, he told me there is nothing wrong with being in the right place at the right time, and that getting to that place involves the freedom to choose. And the responsibility to choose.

As I drove home to attend Uncle Loring's party, Mercy hovering over me, I knew the freedom of choice was as dangerous as it was beautiful. I knew Mercy would soon be given the awful freedom of choosing her destiny. Confess or perish.

It's a lucky break—a providential one, rather—to be in the right place at the right time, like Abel Durough was.

But what about when you're in the wrong place at the wrong time?

How do you make something of yourself then? How do you show

that you are what you do, not what is done to you? What choices do you have then?

Two rooms in my parents' home are largely ignored by the rest of the household. One is the little library.

It's called a library because it contains books—mostly out-of-print first editions valuable because of their age, not the wisdom contained in them—and it is little because it's smaller than the main library on the first floor, which is also my father's home office. Mom and Dad both keep back issues of their favorite magazines in the little library, as well as banker's boxes of files and papers and records. Otherwise, to them, it is a forgotten room.

For me, it was a kind of prayer room, although I never actually prayed in it. It's where I went when I was especially mad or afraid or sad. It was hard to pray actual thoughts during those times. I don't know very many people who can piece together eloquent prayers when their souls are wounded. Words don't come at those times, but tears do. I have always thought of my tears as prayers. When Abigail asked me if I talked to God, I thought of the little library first, even though I never said much there. Bedtime prayers, offered with Mom at my side until I was twelve and now alone as I drift off to sleep, are far wordier, but those are not what popped into my head first on that afternoon in Abigail's house. I thought of my tears first.

The little library is on the third floor, along with two seldom-used guest rooms and a large storage closet that houses my mother's holiday decorations. Mom is big into holiday decorating. The closet is bigger than my dorm room and jam-packed. The library is next to it, and so is the Writing Room.

I named the Writing Room. It's a former sitting room, used by long-ago guests in the 1930s, when the house was new and it wasn't customary to chat with another guest in your bedroom. Mom let me keep my journals, books, and half-finished stories in the Writing Room and decorate it however I wished. My bedroom on the second floor was another matter. It was professionally decorated, along with the rest of the house, and kept photo-shoot clean every moment I wasn't in it. I painted the Writing Room a sunny yellow and brought in white wicker furniture from the main patio that had outlasted its usefulness. I started with pictures of cats on all the walls (I wasn't allowed a cat), switched to dolphins during my "I want to train dolphins" stage, and then to black-and-white prints of the streets of Paris, the place my parents took me for my sixteenth birthday. Those pictures are still there.

When I came home from college, I usually greeted my parents, hugged Eleanor, the housekeeper, and headed up to the third floor to the little library and the Writing Room. I didn't cry in the former anymore, nor write in the latter, but there was something comforting about visiting these rooms where I had done both.

It was a strange experience letting my eyes rove about the Writing Room, Mercy practically at my elbow, the day I arrived home for Uncle Loring's party. I could almost see her sitting in my white wicker chair by the dormer window, sunlight falling across her face, penning the story about the girl who loved the man who could not speak. Mercy would've liked that room.

When I came downstairs later, my cousins—Uncle Loring's sons— had arrived and were outside kicking a soccer ball on the immense patio while my mom and Aunt Denise scurried about, giving orders to the Spanish-speaking caterers. Tyler, twenty-five, who got his MBA at Stanford like a good boy, had brought a date named Bria, who sat with her cell phone to her ear while she watched the boys play. It was an hour before I actually talked to her. Cole, twenty-two, nodded a wordless greeting, and Blaine, my age and languishing at Stanford with Cole, greeted me with a playful punch and a reminder that he was going to fail his lit class because I wasn't there to help him. Kip, seventeen and preparing to take the ACT the following week, told me as he ran by that he was going to beat my score by at least two points. I had managed a 27. I watched him dash away and wished him luck.

There they were: the future of Uncle Loring's vast transportation and logistics company. Four young men in various stages of Empire Building 101. Confident, brash, single-minded, and with the blood of Abel Durough coursing through their veins. And there I was with the same blood, the lone heir to Durough Design & Development Inc.—a monstrously large development firm that turned ordinary land into resorts, skyscrapers, and whole cities—watching my cousins frolic while white-shirted caterers bowed to the half-understood wishes of my mother.

I lingered a few minutes and then went back inside the house. As I stepped into the tiled entry, my sandaled foot hit something wet, and I started to slip. A Hispanic man wearing an untucked white oxford shirt and black pants was about to glide past me, and he reached out to steady me.

"That was a close one," he said, smiling. "You okay?" His accent was pronounced but lilting. The other caterers did not have the command of the language he did. *Mom should be speaking to him,* I thought.

"I'm all right. Thanks." I bent down to rub my ankle. I had twisted it slightly when I began to fall.

"No problem." He started to walk past me, his concern already dissipating.

I called after him. "Hey. Maybe you could tell the kitchen staff to take care of that so no one else slips on it?"

He looked at the spill and then at me. He looked past me, as if he thought I'd been addressing someone else. Then he faced me again and slowly lifted the corners of his mouth in a relaxed smile.

"Sure." He turned and went back toward the kitchen. I'd begun to walk gingerly toward my father's library when he returned with a wad of paper towels.

"Everyone is busy doing other things," he said when I looked at him. "I can take care of it."

"Thanks."

Behind us, the patio doors opened and Cole stepped inside.

"Raul, what're you doing?" Cole gazed down at him.

"Just mopping up a little spill. We wouldn't want anyone to slip." The man named Raul turned to me and winked.

I felt my face drain of color and poise.

"We got a million people to do that, man," Cole said. "Do you even know how to clean up a spill? If you do, you've been holding out on me."

"I think I can figure it out," Raul said, smiling and rubbing the floor with the paper towel.

Cole looked at me. "Hey, Lars. Did you meet my roommate?"

I steadied myself on the wall behind me. His roommate.

"We didn't actually meet," Raul said as he stood and took a step toward me. "Hello. I'm Raul." He looked down at his right hand, which held a damp paper towel. He raised his head and shrugged. "I don't think you want to shake my hand."

I could say nothing.

"This is my cousin, Lars. I mean, Lauren," Cole said. "We call her Lars. Had to make her one of the guys."

"Nice to meet you, Lauren." Still the wide smile; still the calm composure. I noticed at that moment his oxford shirt was almost certainly custom-made. It probably cost him $200.

"Nice to meet you too," I whispered.

Cole stared at me. "Lars, you look like crap. You sick or something?"

"I'm fine."

"You don't look fine." Cole took the paper towel wad from Raul and started for the kitchen. "Bathroom's just down the hall to the right, Raul, if you want to wash your hands."

Raul lingered a moment.

I swallowed hard. He had made a fool of me, but I was the only one who knew it. "I owe you an apology," I said.

"Don't worry about it." He cocked his head, flashed a half smile, and turned to follow Cole down the hall, disappearing behind the bathroom door.

I just stood there, mindlessly rubbing my ankle.

A hired maid appeared from within the dining room, carrying a tray with empty glasses. She stopped when she saw me.

"Can I get you something, miss?"

I told her I was fine.

Eleven

23 January 1692

Papa went out for a little while today. After three weeks abed, he was near frantic for want of news and activity. He came home from the tavern with news that his brother's ship is expected in harbor next week. But he also brought with him strange tidings. He told me two young girls in the Village have been afflicted with a terrible sickness which sends them into awful fits. Betty Parris is the daughter of the minister. I know her. She is but nine. The other girl, Abigail Williams, is her cousin. She is eleven. Papa said the talk is that some terrible disease has fallen upon them. They are quite ill. He told me to stay away from the Village. Except for worship at the meetinghouse, he wants me to stay at the cottage.

I am afraid for the girls. James Luddy's sickness began with awful fits.

Wanderer flew away today. The sun was shining. He thinks winter is over.

24 January 1692

I did not think much of the sermon today. Rev. Parris is much interested in warnings of doom and the prospect of

*the fires of hell. He speaks of Satan as though the Devil
is God's equal instead of a mere created being. God could
whisper Satan out of existence with a word. Surely Rev.
Parris knows this.*

*And it was so cold in the meetinghouse. Too cold to
imagine the fires of hell consuming our sinful souls.*

*The tithing man saw me looking at John Peter. But
John Peter was looking at me, as well. And since he was
closer to John Peter than to me, it was John Peter he
poked with his long stick. I had to look away so as not
to laugh.*

28 January 1692

*Papa went into the Village again today to make ready for
the arrival of the ship at Marblehead. He came home
with news that the King has appointed for us a new governor. Papa said all the talk in the tavern was if the new
governor would stand in the way of the colony's having
its charter restored. I listened to Papa because he wanted
me to, but I am not of a mind to worry about a charter.
Which of us can truly say we do not need another soul
to help us tend to our affairs?*

*Betty Parris and Abigail Williams are still
afflicted. The younger Ann Putnam has become ill as
well. There is word that the girls are afflicted with the
same condition as the Goodwin children five years past.
Papa said he read the account of the Goodwin children.
A minister from Boston, Cotton Mather, wrote of it.
Papa said it was believed the children were bewitched. I
do not like that word, bewitched. I did not care to hear*

more, but Papa bade me pour him some cider and he
told me what Cotton Mather had written. The older
Goodwin girl was afflicted first and then her siblings.
Rev. Mather wrote that their jaws were out of joint
and they barked like dogs, that their necks would be
as dissolved one minute, then stiff the next, that they
screamed that they were being roasted on spits, and that
one of the Goodwin children flew from one end of the
room to the other. A washerwoman named Mary Glover
was accused of bewitching the Goodwin children. She
was tried, found guilty, and hanged.

I told Papa I didn't want to hear any more.

I went outside to my tree to finish my story about
the wind and the rain becoming good friends, but my
mind kept providing me pictures of children barking like
dogs and flying across rooms like bats, and I could not
think of any words.

When I came back into the cottage Papa was cough-
ing again. I fear the sickness in his chest was only sleeping.

I spent most of that weekend at my parents' house trying to avoid
Raul, which was nearly impossible.

I grew up hanging out with my cousins at the Sorries, as we called
them, kidspeak for the family soirees. We thought our parents' parties
were boring, so we played tabletop bowling with the hors d'oeuvres,
stole sips of champagne, played hide-and-seek when we were little, and
when we were older, *Super Mario Brothers* and Texas hold 'em. My
cousins were used to my being around. Actually, they insisted on it. If
left alone, I disappeared to the third floor or got sucked into conversation with my parents' friends. Mom and Dad's friends all seemed to

think I acted mature for my age. My cousins didn't approve of escapes to the third floor or Sorry guests who enjoyed my company.

So at Uncle Loring's two-day party, Cole expected me to be available for a quick pickup game of just about anything, and since we didn't see much of Tyler—he, Bria, and Bria's cell phone kept to themselves—and Kip needed to study for the ACT, I was enlisted to play any game that required teams of two. Blaine and me against Cole and Raul the Non-Caterer.

Whenever I found myself glancing at Raul, his eyes invariably met mine. He'd grin, and I would look away and pretend I hadn't been stealing glances. It happened more than once—I'd be looking at Raul, not realizing what I was doing, and he'd catch me. It embarrassed me every time.

Raul and Cole slept in one of the third-floor guest rooms at our house since there were so many other family members staying at Uncle Loring's, and I ran into Raul several times a day on the stairs. He probably thought I was *trying* to run into him. He knew I didn't have a bedroom on the third floor, so why else would I come up there unless it was to "accidentally" bump into him?

I couldn't look at him without picturing him on his knees, smiling as he wiped up that spill. And every time our eyes met, I was certain he was still laughing over what I had said.

I wanted him to be offended that I had mistaken him for one of the caterers. At least somewhat insulted. I could've handled that. I was convinced he enjoyed watching me squirm, and it annoyed me.

After lunch on Sunday afternoon, when the rest of the household was napping, watching the football game in Dad's home theater, or gossiping on the terrace, I made myself a cup of tea, grabbed a leftover croissant from breakfast, and headed up to the third floor. I didn't run into a soul. Worried about dropping my mug and croissant, I kept my eyes on them as I opened the little library door and then eased it closed with my foot. I turned to face the room and there, standing in front of me with an open book in his hands, was Raul.

Surprise coursed through me and I flinched, sending the contents of my mug sloshing over its sides, onto my hand and the hardwood floor at my feet. The pain wasn't excruciating—I don't care for my tea blistering hot—but I gasped nonetheless, and Raul took a step toward me.

"You all right?"

"Yes, yes," I said through my teeth. I blotted at the tea on my wrist with the paper napkin I had wrapped around the croissant. The roll fell to the floor and Raul knelt to retrieve it. Spilled tea was all around him.

"Want to hand me your napkin?" He smiled up at me as if he had just delivered a punch line.

"No!" I said crossly. I bent down to wipe up the spill myself.

He cocked his head and stared at me, smiling all the while. "So *you're* the one who's supposed to be offended?" he said playfully. "I thought it was me."

"Yes, *you* should be offended," I shot back, wiping up the tea with savage strokes.

I stood up and so did he. He handed me the croissant.

"I didn't know it mattered that much to you," he said.

"It's not that it matters to *me,* it just matters."

He blinked. "Wow. Okay. Sorry."

I huffed. "How about if I do the apologizing instead of you?"

"If that's what you want."

"It is. I'm sorry I assumed you were part of the catering staff. That was rude and—"

"I didn't think it was *that* rude."

"Can I finish?"

"Sorry."

"Will you please stop that?"

"Oh. Right. Sorry."

For a moment we just stood there. I was the first to crack a smile.

The moment I did, his face relaxed into an easy grin. He'd been playing me. Again. I still felt like a fool, but for some reason it didn't bother me as much the second time.

"I really am sorry, Raul." I tucked a strand of hair behind my ear. A nervous habit.

"Apology accepted."

An odd silence followed.

"Did you want to be alone in here?" he finally asked.

No one had ever asked me that before. I was always alone in the little library.

I wondered how he could tell he had intruded on my private space. Did Cole tell him? No, probably not. Cole probably told him the room was just a closet of antiquated books no one cared about. Or he'd said nothing at all because the room itself didn't matter to Cole. It struck me as odd that Raul had bothered to look inside. I had never stumbled upon any of Cole's other friends in the little library. Raul was the first. He still held a book in his hand, *Robinson Crusoe* by Daniel Defoe.

"You can stay if you want." I had wanted to be alone, but I wasn't going to kick him out.

He understood and turned toward the nearest bookshelf to replace the book.

"I'll go. This room's yours," he said.

I felt my face color. "Did Cole tell you that?"

Raul shrugged. "I could just tell. I've seen you coming up here all weekend." He pointed to the book he had just replaced on the shelf. "My father read *Robinson Crusoe* to me when I was ten. Ever read it?"

I hadn't. I'd never been intrigued by a story about a rich man marooned on a lonely island for the better part of his life.

"Great book," Raul continued. "There's a lot of great books in here. Papa would probably burst into tears if he could see this room."

Raul looked at the shelves with their ancient offerings. I took in the room with fresh eyes, seeing it as Raul did. Dull oak shelves, sleepy beige walls, oval rug in a wan hue hard to describe, and row after row of books, their spines in muted shades of blue and burgundy and brown. In that moment, the room morphed in my mind and became an extension of Abigail's faded library. I hadn't thought of the two rooms as being alike in any way, but they were. In my mind, I saw them blending together, indistinguishable from each other. Mausoleums to former lives, most of them fictional. I sucked in my breath.

Raul turned to look at me. "Were you going to say something?"

"No." My voice was barely above a whisper. I collected my thoughts and composure. I needed to reclaim the room as something lovely, not morbid. I blurted out the first thing that came to mind. "Perhaps you and Cole can bring your dad here sometime so he can see it."

Raul smiled. "My father passed away three years ago."

"I'm sorry."

"Now there's an apology you really don't have to give."

"But I am. I'm sorry he's gone."

"Yeah, me too." Raul moved past me toward the door and put his hand on the doorknob.

I took a step toward the nearest bookshelf and reached for *Robinson Crusoe*. I withdrew it and thrust it toward Raul. "Did you want to borrow this?"

Raul looked at the weathered copy. It was more than a hundred years old.

"I don't need to read *that* copy." He laughed.

"I know you don't need to, but would you like to?"

He looked at the book and then at me, and I think he may have looked at the spot on the floor where the tea had spilled.

"Maybe next time." Raul opened the door and left. I heard his footsteps in the hall and then on the stairs as he took them two at a time.

I stood there with *Robinson Crusoe* in my hand, looking at the empty doorway for a full minute before I reshelved the book.

I took the croissant and what was left of my tea and went next door to the Writing Room instead. I sat at my little wicker table with its glass tabletop, sipped my tea, and looked at my black-and-white prints of Paris. The flying buttresses at Notre Dame. The Latona Fountain at the palace at Versailles. The Eiffel Tower at sunset. The sloping lawns at the Château de Sceaux.

There wasn't a person in any of the pictures. I had chosen these prints myself and had always found them pleasurable to look at. I really hadn't noticed before that the photographs were empty of people. Paris landmarks without so much as a retreating figure in the background. Not one living, breathing soul.

I stared at the photographs I loved so much, alone in my Writing Room, until my father came looking for me.

My cousins were heading back to Stanford. It was time to say good-bye.

I grabbed my empty mug, the uneaten croissant, and the sodden napkin and started to follow Dad down the stairs. But I turned back, stepped into the little library, and reached for *Robinson Crusoe*. I tucked it under my arm and closed the door behind me.

I came back to Santa Barbara from Uncle Loring's party with a sizable headache, a slightly bruised ego, and a hundred-year-old copy of *Robinson Crusoe*. The first two made my transcription work tedious the first afternoon back at Abigail's. I had to ask Esperanza for Tylenol an hour into my work. Abigail was attending the opening of a library up the coast, fortunately, so I didn't have to explain my moodiness. The pressure in my head seemed to expand, despite the Tylenol, the moment I read in the diary that the spectacle in Salem had begun.

Everything was about to change for Mercy.

And she didn't even know it.

Twelve

5 February 1692

Goody Trumball, who lives the next farm over, came today to help me press apples for cider. She and my mother were especially good friends. Goody Trumball came to the Village as a new bride fifteen years ago, and my mother was the first to befriend her. Mama let Goody Trumball cry without shunning her when she was sad for the home she left in Topsfield. And then, added to this woe, poor Goody Trumball could not give birth to a live child for many years. Four of them died. I remember two of these dreadful occurrences. I wasn't there in the birthing room either time; I wasn't there at the Trumball cottage at all. But twice I was awake when Mama came home from the Trumballs' to tell my papa that another dead child had been laid in Goody Trumball's arms.

Mama spent day after day with Goody Trumball, sitting with her as she wept. She brought me along to tend to the Trumballs' fire and bake bread and do the washing. I did all those things, but I also listened to my mother whisper to Goody Trumball not to give way to despair. Goody Trumball was grateful for my mother's condolences, but I remember her saying once that my mama did not know how it was to bring a dead child

*into the world. I stopped my sweeping when I heard her
say this. In a hushed voice—I almost could not hear
her—my mother told Goody Trumball she was wrong.
Before my brother Thomas was born, and when I was
three, my mother gave birth to a daughter who never
took a breath. My sister was born pink and unable to
breathe. She turned blue and then gray and then she died.
This was a year before the Trumballs moved to the home-
stead next to ours. My mother knew how it was.*

*Then one summer my mother and Goody Trumball
both gave birth to babies that lived. Thomas was born
in July, and Goody Trumball's first son, Charles, was
born in August. Goody Trumball gave birth to another
son the following year. Those were happy times. Mama
and Goody Trumball spun wool and talked of Village
news, and I had the little lads all about me as we played
on the floor by the fire. Mama and Goody Trumball
talked of having more children, hoped of them, but none
came.*

*Thomas and my mother fell victim to the pox when
Thomas was four. They suffered for days, and I was not
allowed in the cottage to tend to them. Papa sent me to
Maine so I would not also fall ill. I hated him for it.
Hate is a terrible word, a terrible passion. My hate was
like my own pox. I wanted to be with my mama and
Thomas, and Papa forbade it even when he knew they
were dying. It was a long time before I understood that
Papa did what he did to save me. I do not like to think
of the day Mama and Thomas died, both within an
hour. I do not like to think of that year at all.*

Since that horrible time, Goody Trumball has taken

an interest in me and seems keen on letting me know I can come to her with womanly concerns. She thinks it quite odd that I write stories, but she likes watching me write. I showed her how to write her name with a stick in the dirt. Her name is Patience, but she has none when it comes to forming her letters.

As we pressed the apples today, Goody Trumball told me Elizabeth Hubbard is also afflicted with the strange fits. That makes four girls.

I asked Goody Trumball if she thought the girls have brain fever.

She said no one knows what ails them.

I did not want to talk about the afflicted girls anymore. I asked Goody Trumball what she thought of John Peter Collier. She smiled at me and said she thought he was quite handsome.

Back in Santa Barbara, I sat back in my chair and leaned my head against the padded frame. The February 5 entry had been long and tedious to transcribe. Mercy had scrunched her letters close together, no doubt to conserve the paper in her diary, but it made reading her ancient words difficult. The ink was blotchy in places. It was easy to imagine she had cried as she wrote about losing her mother and little brother.

Abigail had left the library at some point while I was working, but as I stretched in my chair, I noticed she had returned and stood near me. Her eyes rested on the computer, where Mercy's three-hundred-year-old thoughts lay across the flat screen in Times New Roman font. Abigail wasn't close enough to read them. At least, I didn't think she could read them. Her eyes weren't focused on the words themselves, just their illuminated presence.

Abigail knew the diary. She knew when I missed a thought or flubbed a sentence, so I knew she'd read the diary before, many times. But I never saw Abigail read it.

She saw I was looking at her. "Esperanza has dinner for us on the patio," she said placidly. "Hope you don't mind eating outside."

I saved the file and stood up. "No. Not at all."

Abigail turned without a word, and I followed her out of the room.

We stepped into the entryway, and as we headed toward the dining room and the expansive set of french doors that led to the patio, I noticed that the doors to the sitting room were closed.

Abigail was silent as we moved through the hall and dining room and out onto the flagstone patio. Esperanza was filling water goblets when we reached the iron and glass table. A slice of lemon and several raspberries floated among the perfectly round globes of ice in our glasses. Abigail motioned to one of the place settings with her head. My invitation to sit. She then took the chair opposite.

"Spinach salad with cherries, balsamic vinegar, and gorgonzola," Esperanza said, placing a salad plate in front of me.

I thanked her. She set a plate in front of Abigail and then disappeared through a doorway that led back into the kitchen.

Abigail picked up her napkin. "It's such a lovely evening." She said this as if she were speaking to the evening itself, complimenting it on its beauty.

I said yes, it was.

"Would you say grace tonight, Lauren?"

"Um. Sure." I fumbled through a casual prayer of thanks for the meal and a generic blessing upon our families. Not nearly as eloquent as Abigail's rote table graces, but she had caught me off guard.

When I opened my eyes I saw that Abigail was smirking.

"What?" I asked, slightly embarrassed.

"You pray to God as if you are old chums."

I couldn't tell if she was amused, envious, or aghast.

"Is that a criticism?" I plunged my fork into my salad.

"No. A warning, my dear." Abigail picked up her fork and knife and sliced a tender spinach leaf in two.

I held my fork in midair. "A warning?"

"I just don't want to see you get hurt." She slipped her fork into her mouth and began to chew.

My fork was still suspended a few inches from my lips. I had no idea what she was talking about. "Get hurt how?"

She finished chewing, stared at me for a moment, and then gently lifted her shoulders. "Never mind."

But I did mind. "What do you mean?"

Abigail pursed her lips and sliced another spinach leaf in two. She said nothing.

It dawned on me that Abigail was telling me something about herself, not about me. Not even about God. After spending nearly a month with her, I was finally beginning to understand that this was how I would discover who she was and why the diary mattered so much to her—via scattered moments at her dinner table.

Deep down I knew she meant having a casual relationship with power could be dangerous. I'd just missed an opportunity to peel back one of her layers. Instead of saying, "Get hurt how?" I should have said what my Dad would have said had he been at Abigail's table.

Tell me.

I wondered if it was too late to say it anyway.

Abigail opened her mouth. "How was your uncle's birthday celebration?"

It was too late.

"It was a nice party." I slid my fork into my mouth, wiser.

"That bad?"

I finished chewing. "No. Not that bad. Just not my kind of thing."

Abigail reached for her water glass. "And what is your kind of thing?"

I thought for a moment. "I guess I prefer smaller crowds. Less activity. Less booze. Less food, less bling."

"Bling?"

"Flashy jewelry. Diamonds. Stuff like that."

Abigail smiled. "Stuff like that."

I didn't think Abigail used the word "stuff" very often, but I was pretty sure she knew what I was talking about. I told her so.

"Excess alarms you," she said.

"Annoys me," I corrected her.

She tipped her head. "I wonder why that is so?" But she didn't wait for my answer. "You didn't see some of your high school friends while you were home?"

I worked a slippery cherry onto my fork. I had the strangest feeling Abigail knew I didn't have any close friends from high school. Knew that I really didn't have close friends at all. That I often preferred being alone to being with people. That I was a loner and always had been.

Like her.

The cherry tumbled back onto my plate. "No."

"Must have been a lonely few days, then."

I pursued the cherry across a layer of olive-oiled spinach. "My cousins were there."

And Raul.

"And a couple of their friends," I added, tossing Bria and the cell phone into the mix.

"Oh. How many cousins do you have?" I sensed Abigail was thinking of her singing cousin Dorothea and that the memory was sweet.

"Four. My dad has one younger brother and he has four sons. We've pretty much grown up together."

"Four sons," Abigail's voice was wistful, like so many others have been when Loring's sons are mentioned.

"Yes."

"And you're the only girl."

"Yes."

Abigail smiled. "I see now where your muscle comes from."

I was five four and barely weighed 110 pounds. "What?"

"You'll be a perfect CEO." Abigail skewered a cherry in one deft movement.

Words failed me. I wanted to argue with her, but I didn't know where to start. The fact was, I would make a good CEO if I wanted to be one. I just stared at her.

There was a second or two of silence while Abigail chewed. Then she looked at me. "You transcribed February 5 today?"

"Yes."

"So sad what happened to Mercy's mother and her little brother."

"Yes, it was."

"It was just her after that. Just her and her father in that little cottage."

The equation she was drawing between me, her, and Mercy was plain.

Three daughters. Three fathers. No sons.

I saw nothing but the vaguest of similarities. Mere mathematics.

Besides, Abigail and I didn't grow up without our mothers like Mercy did.

I decided to remind Abigail of this. "It would've been terribly hard on Mercy's mother, had she been alive, to witness what became of her daughter. I imagine it was hard enough on her father."

Abigail gave me a strange look and then nodded.

She had forgotten there were things about Mercy I didn't yet know.

Thirteen

14 February 1692

I have been out of ink and out of walnut shells to crush to make more. Papa has been to the harbor and back several times, and he brought me ink from Boston. It is very fine ink, as black as night. Papa seems pale and weak to me, but he insists fresh air and labor are making him well. I wonder if he would rather live at the harbor and not be constrained to travel so much when his brother's ship is in port, but he will not leave this cottage where he loved my mother.

Something odd occurred at the meetinghouse during the sermon today. Prudence Dawes would not stop staring at me. She would look at me and then John Peter and then me again. When our eyes met, she did not look away. I smiled at her. I did not know what else to do. She did not smile back. She just slowly turned her head to face the front.

When the meeting was over, John Peter and his mother met Papa and me at the door as we walked outside. John Peter asked if we would care to sell them eggs every week as the family that had been selling eggs to them moved away. Papa said of course we could and that he could bring some over on the morrow. But John Peter

said no, he would come get the eggs himself. Papa looked
surprised. So did John Peter's mother. So did I, I'm sure.
One of John Peter's sisters could surely come get eggs.

But then Papa looked at me, and I think he knew
why John Peter wanted to come get the eggs himself.

As we made our way home, Papa did not say anything until we were almost at the cottage. And when he
did speak, it was not to me, but to God, I think.

"'Tis the way it should be," he said.

I think he will miss me when I marry someday. I
think he sorrows at the thought of being alone in the
cottage.

18 February 1692

John Peter was back again to fetch eggs. I daresay he
asks his mother to cook eggs every night. He asked if he
could read my stories sometime.

"Who told you I write stories?" I said. I could
scarcely speak. I do not tell this to people. Papa has asked
me not to, and it is not something I wish others to know.

"You did," was his answer, "when you were ten."

Eight years ago. I don't remember telling him this,
but he does.

He held the basket and watched me gather eggs from
our henhouse. I told him I could gather the eggs and hold
his basket, that I do it all the time, but he said, "'Tis no
trouble for me to hold the basket."

I brushed up against him when I stepped away from
the roost. 'Twas not what I planned: I merely misjudged
the distance between us. I am usually alone in the henhouse. I begged his pardon.

He told me he is not free to pardon where no offense is taken. Then he reached out and laid a hand gently on my hair. I nearly toppled with the weight of that gentle touch. He pulled a piece of straw from my hair and tossed it to the ground.

I looked down at his basket. It was full.

"I shall have to get a bigger basket," he said.

"I shall have to get more chickens," I said.

We both laughed.

My heart won't be still.

If I were in the meetinghouse for the sermon and the tithing man saw my pounding heart, he would whack it.

20 February 1692

I do not know what to make of the news Papa has brought home tonight. Dr. Griggs has made a diagnosis in the case of the afflicted girls: witchcraft. The doctor can come by no other explanation for their fits. Everything he knows to do, he has tried. Nothing has healed them. He has declared they must therefore be under the spell of a witch. When Papa told me this, my mind conjured a picture of a Mary Glover, even though I know not what she looks like. I saw her standing at a barrel of soaking laundry as men accused her of strangling the children, making them fly and bark like dogs. What was she thinking when they said these things? Could she have done what they said she did? Did she in truth do the Devil's bidding? The thought makes me shiver.

Papa is skeptical that the girls in our Village are bewitched, but he cannot explain the fits. No one can. And now that the cause has been determined, the girls

will be pressed upon to name their afflicters. How does
one know something like that?

    The little bird with the broken wing is back. Winter
is far from over. He must know this now.

I dreamed again of Mercy. This time I dreamed she was at my writing
desk back home, just like I pictured when I was there. She was writing in her diary—the one I spend my afternoons with—bending over
it with her feather pen. I could hear the soft scratching of the quill on
the parchment.

I was afraid that if I spoke to her, she would disappear, so I said
nothing. I just stood and watched her. She wore the dress from my
fourth-grade play. Her brown hair was swept back with the ponytail
holder I had worn. I could see its hot pink hue just under her white cap.
Her facial features were indistinguishable. She had eyes and a nose and
a mouth, but they were out of focus. I couldn't make them out. The
room was different, the way dream rooms are. The walls were still painted
yellow, but there were more of them, like the room was expanding, creating more space for itself.

My pictures of Paris were there, but they were full of people, and
the images were alive. The people in the pictures moved, going about
their Parisian business, oblivious to their onlookers.

The photographs made me uneasy. For some reason I didn't want
Mercy to see them. I moved away from the walls and they receded, but
the photographs seem to grow larger. Mercy would surely see them.

Then I heard a noise, something beating against the window. I
turned. Mercy had heard it too. A bird flew into the window above the
desk, over and over.

Mercy stood and leaned over the desk. She grabbed the window
latch and struggled to release it, calling to the bird to wait and she would

help it. But the bird kept flinging its body against the glass. And Mercy couldn't open the window.

I knew I should help her. I knew that window stuck sometimes and you had to push down on it before lifting up.

But I just stood there.

Mercy continued to struggle with the window, calling out to the bird in a frantic voice to wait. To stop. To give her a moment.

And the little bird hit the window over and over with its body.

When blood appeared on the glass, Mercy screamed, and I awoke. It was a few minutes before dawn.

I got out of bed to the aroma of strong coffee. A light was on and Clarissa's bed was empty. She sat at our cramped desk area, tapping madly away on her laptop.

She had pulled an all-nighter. She looked up at me.

"Can you proof this when I'm done? It's due today."

"Sure." I grabbed a clean mug from the microwave cart that housed our coffee maker and poured a cup from the pot. It was as black as tar.

"Will this kill me?" I asked.

"Hardly. It will keep you awake, sister."

I took a sip. It tasted medicinal, earthy and wild. I forced myself to take another drink.

"Yeah, you look like you could use it," Clarissa said, smiling as she typed.

"What do you mean?"

"You were having a nightmare or something just now."

"I was?"

"Weren't you? You were thrashing around and whimpering."

My mind conjured the bloody window, the dead bird, and the pitch of Mercy's scream. I wrapped my hands around the mug, eager for its warmth.

"I guess it was a nightmare," I said.

"Chased by a madman with a knife?"

"No."

"I don't have that dream either," Clarissa said. "I always dream I'm on fire. Like I'm in a burning house or something. I hate that dream."

I pulled my fingers away from the hot mug.

"So were you falling off a cliff?" she continued, still drumming away at the little keys on her laptop.

"No, nothing like that."

Clarissa whirled. The tiny diamond stud on her left nostril caught the light from her desk lamp and winked at me. "Oh no, you didn't dream you were, like, walking down Rodeo Drive in your underwear?"

Ah, a rich-girl joke.

"It was nothing like that, Clarissa." I sank into her canvas beach chair and took another sip of the industrial-strength coffee.

"Well?"

I toyed with a string on the chair's cushion with my free hand. "I dreamed I was in my parents' house with this girl who's been dead for three hundred years, and a bird was flinging itself against the window. I woke up when it started to bleed."

"A dead girl? You dreamed up a dead girl?" Clarissa couldn't care less about the bird.

"She wasn't dead in the dream," I said. "She was alive in my dream. But she's been dead for three hundred years. It was that girl whose diary I'm transcribing."

"The witch?"

"She wasn't a witch."

"But I thought you told me she was hung as a witch in Salem."

"But she wasn't a witch. That's the whole point. Hardly any of those people were."

Clarissa was quiet for a moment. "How do you know she wasn't?" She turned around and began to type again.

"She wasn't."

"So why did people think she was?" *Tap, tap, tap.*

"I don't know yet. I'm only two months into the diary."

Tap, tap, tap.

"Don't you wonder why, though?" Clarissa said. "I mean, she must have done something weird or quirky or strange."

I looked at Clarissa's purple-streaked hair, her glistening nose stud, and the tattooed cherub on her forearm and said nothing.

"There. Done!" Clarissa pressed a couple of keys on her laptop, and her printer began to hum.

I sat there, waiting to see if Clarissa really wanted to know how I thought Mercy ended up at the end of a noose. But she just gathered up the pages from her printer and handed them to me.

"Do you know how many of my friends are totally jealous that I have an English major for a roommate?" she said.

She grabbed her bathroom bag and headed for the door, apparently uninterested in an answer to that question also. But she turned back toward me before leaving the room. "Anytime you want to go strolling down Rodeo Drive in your underwear, just holler. I'd do it in a heartbeat. That would be a total blast! Can you imagine?"

Clarissa laughed and disappeared.

Fourteen

24 February 1692

Betty Parris has named Tituba, their servant from the islands, as the one who bewitched her. No one is much surprised. Tituba is not English. She comes from a different world called Barbados, where it is summer all year and where magic is not feared. But why would Tituba cause Betty to suffer so? She is the Parrises' slave, and she cares for the Parris children when Rev. Parris is away and Goody Parris is unwell. What end would Tituba desire?

26 February 1692

The afflicted girls now say Goody Goode and Goody Osborne also torture them! Sarah Goode is indeed a strange woman, but she is not evil. She carries many burdens. Perhaps I would mumble and make strange faces if I had to beg for food and clothing in the dead of winter for myself and my child. And Sarah Osborne is ill.

My cider is cloudy and sour. It is not setting well.

29 February 1692

Papa came home from the Village fearful and angry. Men in the Village have made formal complaints against the

women accused. The town magistrates John Hathorne
and Jonathan Corwin have issued warrants to arrest
Tituba, Sarah Goode, and Sarah Osborne. They will be
taken to Ingersoll's on the morrow and publicly examined.

Papa says we are to go.

My father called me with a business proposition, as he called it. He asked if I would assist one of his staff members in writing a proposal to develop a multifaceted art gallery.

"Ben's a whiz at technical writing, but this project needs to appeal to a group of investors who speak the language of art, not commerce," Dad said. "You speak both. The wording in this proposal will sway them one way or the other. I want them to be swayed to build. I need a good writer on this one."

I had been sitting in my car in Abigail's driveway when my cell phone rang, about to pull away, and my mind was somersaulting on the names of three women—Tituba, Sarah Osborne, Sarah Goode. All I knew of these women was the little I remembered from Arthur Miller's play and Mercy's agitated thoughts.

I only half heard my father's request.

"You want me to write what?" I said.

"I want your help. I'm not asking you to write the whole thing, Lauren. I just want your insight on this one. Ben will be able to tackle the technical beauty of this project, but I need a writer who understands aesthetics."

I've never thought of my dad as a good liar. He doesn't lie. He doesn't have to. I wasn't going to accuse him of lying to me, but he was withholding something. He had at his command a host of artistic people who understood aesthetics and could write.

I slowly eased out of Abigail's driveway and onto the road. "I don't understand why you're asking me. You're surrounded by expertise."

"I'm asking you because you can do this. And because the investors are members of a family who appreciate art and literature. I know they'd like a proposal crafted for them by my daughter who also loves art and literature. It would give us an edge over anyone else's design. It would be a wonderful debut project for you, Lauren. You're perfectly suited for it."

I do believe he was complimenting me, but "perfectly suited" seemed a bit of a stretch.

"How so?" I asked. "I don't know anything about land use, Dad."

"I don't need you for that. I have architects and civil engineers on my staff. Ben will take care of the technical part of the proposal. I just want you to help him interpret our research data and make sure the proposal fits what this family of investors will appreciate. It's not the technical ingenuity that's going to sell them. It's the aesthetics and attention to the artistic elements. We're looking at creating a gallery dedicated to art and literature. It's going to be quite different. I know this kind of project will resonate with you, Lauren. You can't tell me it won't."

I pulled onto a twilight-lit thoroughfare. "How come you didn't mention this when I was home for Uncle Loring's party?"

"I barely saw you. Between entertaining the other guests and running errands for your mother and aunt, I had only a few minutes to myself. And you were always nowhere to be found, I might add."

I was hiding from Raul, Dad, because he made me feel like a fool, and for some reason I actually found him attractive.

Dad continued. "Besides, we weren't sure last week we were going to move forward on this one. But now we are. It's a fabulous project, Lauren. You'll love what this gallery will house."

"How many hours are we talking?" I said, still unconvinced.

"That depends on you. I'd say ten to fifteen tops for the whole thing if all you do is edit and tweak. More if you want to have more input, and I think you will. You could do it in a couple weekends. I know you don't work for Abigail on weekends. You could do it here at the house.

Or there, if you insisted. But all the drawings, models, and schematics will be here."

Uneasiness crept over me. I wanted to do the project, and I didn't. Dad was right about my interest. That unnerved me as much as anything. I didn't want to be tricked into a budding career as Dad's up-and-coming, sonlike heir.

"Is this part of a bigger plan, Dad?"

He paused only for a moment.

"Everything is part of a bigger plan. Don't think for a minute it's not. You don't think I know you've got a bigger plan in attending a state school? You don't think that Abigail has a bigger plan for this transcription you're doing? Everything small is a part of something bigger. That's just how it is."

"So you admit you're tying to woo me into coming to work for you," I said, slightly miffed at his mini-lecture.

Dad laughed. It was gentle, not unlike Raul's smooth laughter, like he was amused at my innocence or naiveté.

"I'll pay you thirty dollars an hour," he said, "and you can give it all away to charity if you want."

He had admitted nothing.

"Come home this weekend and look at the plans and the research data," he continued. "If you're not impressed, I'll find someone else. No hard feelings."

I flinched as if I'd been pinched. Find someone else. He'd find someone else.

That thought annoyed me.

"This weekend?" I said.

"You have other plans?"

No. No, I did not.

"I can come," I said.

"Good. I'll tell your mother. She was just saying she hardly saw you at the party."

"There were a lot of people in and out of the house," I said, turning into my dorm parking lot.

"I didn't even get a chance to ask you how your work with that diary is going." He seemed genuinely interested.

"It's going well."

"Tell me."

"It's fascinating. Haunting, sometimes. Today I transcribed Mercy's entry about the first arrests. Three women were accused initially."

"Was she one of them?"

"No. One was a West Indian slave named Tituba. The two others were older women, one named Sarah Goode and the other named Sarah Osborne."

"And these are the actual people mentioned in history books?"

"Yes. They were women Mercy Hayworth knew. She was shocked at their arrests. She couldn't believe they were witches."

Dad was quiet.

"Dad?" I checked my phone to see if we were still connected.

"I'm here. Sarah Goode. Yes. There was a Sarah Goode who invented the Hide-A-Bed."

Hide-A-Bed? "Dad?"

"Not your Sarah Goode, though. This was one was born in 1850."

"Dad, what are you doing?"

"Googling her name."

I gasped.

"Oh, here's yours. Here's the record of her trial and execution."

"Dad!"

"What?"

"I'm not supposed…" But I didn't finish. How could I tell him I'd promised Abigail I wouldn't look at any information on the Internet until I was done transcribing the diary?

"Not supposed to what?"

"Nothing." Curiosity overpowered me. "What does it say about Sarah Goode?"

"The grammar is terrible. Couldn't they spell? Ah. She appeared as a wolf. That's *wolfe* with an *e*."

I shivered. "That's impossible. She wasn't a witch."

"It says her name was in the devil's book. That's *booke* with an *e*, too. And they spelled *devil*, d-e-v-e-l-l. She had three birds—two black, one yellow—and the birds hurt the *Children*, capital *C*. Doesn't say which children. I never saw such poor sentence structure. How can you decipher this stuff? Is the diary like this?"

I didn't want to hear any more.

"No, the diary isn't like that," I said.

"Well, there's just the one Sarah Osborne. Her name comes up in the first page of hits. This one says she maintained her innocence throughout her trial. And she was searched for a witch's teat, whatever that is. The slave Tituba testified Sarah Osborne was a witch."

"She wasn't."

"Osborne died in prison. You know, you really should ask Abigail what she plans to do with the diary when you're done, Lauren. You should protect your interests."

My interests. "I'll ask her sometime."

"So what's this girl's last name? The girl whose diary you've got?"

If I told him Mercy's last name, he would do an Internet search right then, and I would be unable to resist asking him to tell me everything.

"Dad, I promised Abigail I wouldn't do research on my own until the diary was finished."

"Why?" He sounded amazed.

"Well, knowing too much might affect the way the diary comes across as I'm transcribing."

"That doesn't make any sense, Lauren. You already know how it ends. She gets hanged. Besides, you're just transcribing. I don't see why Abigail would have you make that kind of a promise."

"I don't know. She's old. She's eccentric. This diary is very important to her. Old people sometimes do things that seem a little extreme."

"All the more reason to find out what her plans are. I want you to promise me you'll find out."

"I promise. I'll ask her. When the time seems right."

We were both silent for a moment.

"So you're coming this weekend?" Dad finally asked.

"I'll drive down Saturday morning."

"Okay, then. Thanks, kiddo."

"Sure, Dad."

We hung up.

The windows were down in my car, and I heard the chirping of birds as they sang the end of the day. In my mind I saw three birds. Two black, one yellow.

Fifteen

As I packed a few things to take home with me, my dream from a few nights before filled my thoughts. I saw my empty Paris pictures suddenly teeming with people. In my mind, I heard Abigail asking if I had met up with any high school friends while I was home and I heard my own voice saying no, I hadn't.

I pictured Robinson Crusoe—I had begun to read the book— alone on his island with nothing but goats and a mimicking parrot for company. King of his own little universe, but with no subjects to adore him or even usurp him.

Alone.

I decided to prove to myself I had friends.

I turned to Clarissa, who sat cross-legged on her unmade bed, eating ramen noodles raw, crunching them like peanuts while she read from a textbook.

"You working this weekend, Clarissa?"

"Of course." She didn't look up.

"Want to get out of it?"

Her eyes met mine. A curl of raw noodle was hooked over her bottom lip. "Why?"

"So you can come home with me for the weekend." I couldn't look at her as I said it. I folded a bra in half and waited for her response. I was prepared for anything.

"Really?"

She sounded incredulous. I couldn't tell if it was because she had no desire to come and didn't know how to tell me or because she was shocked at being asked, since I had never asked her before. She was my roommate our freshman year too.

"No big deal if you don't want to come," I said quickly.

"I'd have to be back by six on Sunday. Can't get out of that one. I work seven to midnight."

"So you'll come?" Now I sounded incredulous.

"If you want me to."

"I do. I want you to come."

"You've never asked me before."

"I know," I said.

We just looked at each other, wordless, for a few moments. We both knew we had absolutely nothing in common except an address. She had never asked me to her parents' house, either. They lived 150 miles away in Bakersfield.

"Sure. I'll come." Clarissa stood and brushed noodle fragments off her holey cutoffs. "What do I need to bring?"

I shrugged. "Nothing special. A swimsuit if you want to use the pool. We can go out Saturday night if you want."

Clarissa snorted. "Yeah, but we don't need any clothes for that, 'cause we're strolling naked down Rodeo Drive. Forget the underwear!"

I stuffed some pajamas in my bag. "Very funny."

She yanked a canvas tote off a bedpost and stuffed the oversized T-shirt she slept in inside it. "It *would* be funny. It'd be hilarious. You'd get your name on the society page." She whipped her head around to look at me. "But you've probably been there lots of times!"

"Yeah, sure. Lots of times."

Clarissa laughed and threw a pair of sequined flip-flops in her bag. "So do you have a butler and maid and everything?"

"Yeah, and a shoeshine boy and a chauffeur and a scullery maid and a footman."

Clarissa smirked. "C'mon. What've you got?"

"A couple gardeners."

"Really? That's it?"

"We have a housekeeper." I sighed. Eleanor was more like a doting aunt.

"Does she bring you your dinner on plates with those silver dome things on top?"

I began to wonder if I'd made a mistake asking Clarissa to come. "Only on your birthday," I quipped.

"I always thought that would be cool, to have your dinner arrive all hidden away like that." Clarissa tossed in her toothbrush and a makeup bag. "Well, I'm ready."

I didn't tell her the dome lids weren't there to make you feel special. They just kept your food warm.

"Don't you want to call to see if you can get off work?" I asked.

"I can call from the road. I'll say I'm sick. I could use a break."

"You're going to call in sick?"

"Yep. I am sick. Sick of working all the time."

Clarissa tossed the rest of her dry ramen noodles into the trash.

I grabbed my bag and *Robinson Crusoe,* and we left.

❧❧❧

My parents' house is situated on a hill shared by two Hollywood execs, one Academy Award winner, a Golden Globe nominee, and seven or eight people like my dad—men and women who shape the local economy and beyond.

It's Mediterranean in style with a red tile roof over its creamy beige vastness. Long, sloping lawns, plenty of palms and bougainvilleas, heavy oak doors everywhere you look, and wrought-iron gates and fencing.

"I can't believe you live here," Clarissa breathed as we got out of the car.

"It's just a house, Clarissa."

"Yeah, right." She grabbed her bag and flashed me a wicked smile. "God, I wish you had some brothers!"

I reached for my own bag. "I've got four cousins. All boys." I doubt she picked up on the edge to my voice.

"Get out of town. Really?"

"One of them is too young for you, Clarissa. He's only seventeen."

"Who says that's too young?" She winked at me.

"I do," I whispered under my breath.

This is what money does to people.

My parents were pleased to finally meet Clarissa. My mother wanted to know if we'd eaten breakfast, and as soon as she heard Clarissa and I had split a granola bar on the way down, she headed for the kitchen to ask Eleanor to make something for us.

"I'm not really that hungry, Mom," I called out to her.

"I am!" Clarissa yelled and Mom smiled back at her.

"So, what's your major, Clarissa?" Dad asked as we followed him into the breakfast nook.

"Political science. I want to work as a lobbyist in Washington. This country needs some fresh vision. It's totally falling apart."

"Do you have anything against free trade?" Dad asked casually and I felt my heart miss a beat. *Please, please, Clarissa, don't say you do.*

"I have nothing against free trade. I don't care how money gets made. I care how it gets spent."

"Interesting," Dad said. "Please have a seat." He motioned her toward the table and cleared away scattered pages of the *L.A. Times.*

I was all for changing the subject. I was trying to think of something to talk about when I heard movement in the doorway behind me.

It was Cole. He wore a pair of gray sweatpants and a sleeveless T-shirt, and his hair stuck out in all directions. It was obvious he'd slept at my parents' house and that he had just gotten up.

"Lars! What are you doing here?" he asked. Before I could answer, he saw Clarissa and backed up a step. "Whoa. Sorry. Didn't know there was company."

"Hi! I'm Clarissa. Lauren's roommate." Clarissa thrust her hand forward. A tangle of bracelets jangled. She was smiling from ear to multi-pierced ear.

"Hey. I'm Cole. Lauren's cousin." He shook her hand and then turned to me. "What do you know? We both brought our roommates."

"Raul's here?" I asked.

"Yep. He's out running, I think."

"You guys drove five and a half hours to come here? Why?" I couldn't believe Cole and Raul were there. Again.

"Last weekend I met up with a buddy of mine from high school who's moving today. I told him I could help. Your parents said I could stay here 'cause my folks are in Singapore and there's nothing to eat at my house. Raul wanted to help too. We flew."

"You flew."

"Yeah. Raul has his pilot's license. We came in a Cessna. It only took a few hours."

"You flew."

"Yeah." Cole laughed.

"In a plane."

He gave me a withering look. "That's usually how it's done. I don't see what the big deal is, Lars. Lots of people our age have their pilot's license." He turned to my dad. "Is it okay if I use your Expedition today?"

"Sure," Dad said. "The keys are in the breezeway. It needs gas, though."

Cole started to walk away. "I got it, Uncle Bryant." He turned back around to face Clarissa. "Nice to meet you, uh…"

"Clarissa," my roommate said, and I swear she fluttered her eyelashes.

"Clarissa." Cole took another step and then swung back around. "Hey, you guys heading back tonight?"

"No," Clarissa said quickly.

"Do you want to go to a party with us?" Cole continued. "We're going to a beach party in Malibu. Should be fun. My ex-girlfriend's throwing it."

"That'd be great!" Clarissa said before I could respond.

"Cool. We'll be back here by seven."

Cole disappeared and Clarissa turned to me. The stud in her nose glistened in the sunlit room. So did her pearly white teeth.

***

It was seven thirty that night before I saw Raul.

I made sure I was in my dad's office looking at schematics when Raul came in from running that morning, and I tried to beg off from going to Malibu when he and Cole returned from helping Cole's friend move. But Clarissa wouldn't hear of it.

She spent the day lounging by the pool, chatting with my dad about why communism didn't work and helping my mother fix a glitch on her laptop. At lunch, Eleanor brought her a salmon steak seared with garlic butter under a shiny chrome dome as she basked on the patio. I'd asked Eleanor to do it.

I didn't tell Clarissa why I was hesitant to go to Malibu; she had no idea it had anything to do with Raul. She just assumed I had no clue what it was like to have fun, since I so rarely presented her with evidence that I did. And it wasn't that I didn't want to see him again. I just wished I had met him under different circumstances.

Clarissa dragged me downstairs when Cole called for us. She wore a gauzy, lime green baby-doll blouse, flared jeans, her sequined sandals, and huge silver hoop earrings. She looked fabulous and hip. I had on yellow capris and matching jacket that for some reason made me look model-skinny.

"That outfit looks really hot on you," Clarissa said, as we made our way downstairs. She stopped me on the landing, reached behind me, and undid my barrette. My hair fell about my shoulders. "And your hair looks good down around your face. You shouldn't wear it back all the time, Lauren. You look like somebody's grandma."

She tossed the barrette up to the top step and sailed down the stairs.

Raul and Cole waited in the tiled foyer. Raul stood right about where I had commanded him to mop up a spill. He looked up at me and smiled.

"Hi! I'm Clarissa! I'm Lauren's roommate." Clarissa walked right up to Raul and beamed at him.

"Raul San Domingo." His accent decorated his words like music.

"Raul, you remember Lars?" Cole said.

"Yes. Yes, I do." Raul smiled at me.

"Lars! That's a cool nickname. How come you never told me that was your nickname?" Clarissa punched me lightly.

I looked away from Raul's brown eyes. "No one calls me that but my cousins."

"Ready?" Cole motioned toward the door, and Clarissa dove forward to walk with him. I could read her. She wanted to sit by Cole in the car.

I fell into step with Raul. What else could I do?

"I didn't know you had your pilot's license," I said.

"Well, I don't see how you could've known."

I caught a whiff of his cologne. It was subtle and clean. I didn't recognize it. Ahead of us, Clarissa chattered at Cole.

"That was nice of you to help Cole's friend move," I ventured.

He just nodded.

Then he turned his head to look at me. "I like your hair down like that," he said.

"Oh!" Clarissa turned to face us as we stepped out the front door and into the cool night air. "I've been hiding her barrettes for months, hoping she'd just give up on them. But she keeps buying more."

"Yeah, Lars has always been a bit old-fashioned," Cole said, jangling my dad's keys and opening the vehicle door for Clarissa.

I felt my face flush. "Thanks a lot, Cole."

"Don't mention it."

"It's true! She's always reading old stuff. I mean *really* old stuff," Clarissa said, as she stepped inside the vehicle. "What've you got lying around our dorm right now?"

I didn't answer. Raul opened my door for me.

"Oh yeah," Clarissa continued. "*Robinson Crusoe.* Wasn't that written, like, a zillion years ago?"

Raul looked at me. "You're reading *Robinson Crusoe?*"

Before I could say anything, Clarissa assured him, that yes, I was reading *Robinson Crusoe,* and it wasn't even for a class. Then, as soon as Raul and Cole were inside the vehicle, she told them I spent all my free time with an old woman, working on the diary of an accused Salem witch.

"A witch?" Cole sounded disgusted.

"She wasn't a witch," I said quickly, ramming my seat belt latch into its buckle and catching my finger. I winced and shoved the finger into my mouth.

Raul was staring at me.

"Well, she said she wasn't," Clarissa said.

"You have a diary from the Salem witch trials?" Raul asked.

I withdrew my pinched finger from my mouth. "It's not mine. I'm just transcribing it."

"The whole thing is kinda creepy if you ask me. I'll be glad when she's done with it. And anyway, we're going to toss out the old-fashioned ways, aren't we, Lars?" Clarissa turned to face Raul and me in the back-seat. "We've got it all figured out. Lauren and I are going to walk down Rodeo Drive in the nude!"

Cole burst out laughing. Raul just rewarded me with half a lop-sided grin.

The rest of the evening was the Clarissa Show. She was in her ele-ment. I was not. Raul was quickly embraced by Cole's friends, as was Clarissa. I landed in a quiet spot like I usually do at parties and spent the first half of the breezy evening hanging onto my hair, which, with-out its reins, whipped about my face with gusto.

At some point in the evening, Cole, Raul, and a couple other guys walked past me on their way to start a sand volleyball game. I sat in a deck chair by the fire pit, listening to a girl I had just met tell me and another girl how many times she'd been stung by a jellyfish last summer. I was nodding, only half listening to her, when I heard Raul's distinctive voice and my head lifted. He looked down as he swept past me. Moon-light and torchlight splashed about his shoulders. He smiled at me as he walked past, amused, it seemed, that my hair had gleefully hurled itself into my eyes and mouth. I dipped my head and yanked my hair away from my face. When I looked up, his back was to me and he was walk-ing away.

I watched him trudge through the sand toward the net. Ahead of him and off to the right, Clarissa stood in a clutch of people who seemed to devour her every word. She threw her head back and laughed, spilling the beer she held in her hand. Someone reached out to steady her.

"The welts went from my hip to my ankle," the girl next to me said. "I looked like something from a horror movie."

I grasped as much of my hair as I could in my fist and wondered how I was going to tactfully escape from Jellyfish Girl. I slipped one foot back into a flip-flop. The other sandal was half buried in the sand. I reached down, grabbed it, and shook it gently. Sand rained down around my toes. I slipped on the other flip-flop and raised my head. Raul stood in front of me.

"Hey."

"Hey," I said back. A wisp of hair sashayed across my forehead. I let it.

Raul squatted in the sand as Jellyfish Girl explained that the meat tenderizer the lifeguard gave her did absolutely nothing for the pain, but he was a total babe, so it was okay.

"What are you doing?" he asked softly. Jellyfish Girl kept going with her play-by-play. His grin said, *Are you nuts? This is a party. Why are you sitting here?*

"Nothing," I whispered back.

"Want to play some volleyball?"

There haven't been many moments in my life when I wished I had natural athletic ability, but that was one of them. I sucked at just about every sport but foosball, and that's not even a sport.

"Thanks, but you don't want me on your team," I whispered back.

He just smiled and said, "Come on."

"I'm serious. I'm terrible at volleyball."

"Then you can play on the other team."

I smiled back. "Very funny."

From the net several yards away, Cole shouted at Raul to hurry up.

"You can watch." Raul stood. He held out a hand to help me up.

I hesitated only a moment. I reached for his hand, and seconds later I was following him to the volleyball net. A few people had gathered to watch the match, but there was nowhere to sit but on the sand, and I felt awkward standing there alone. I stayed for ten minutes or so, unable to keep my eyes off Raul, but he seemed engrossed in the game, or at least very busy. He was a good player. A couple times the ball skittered off into the crowd, and I fetched it for the players, providing seconds of usefulness.

When Clarissa shouted at me to "come meet this guy who knows Tom Cruise!" I looked to see if Raul was watching me leave.

He wasn't.

I lost track of him after that. I spent the rest of the evening keeping a drunk Clarissa on her feet and out of trouble.

We got back to my parents' house a little after two in the morning. Raul and Cole headed to the game room to play video games. Cole didn't ask Clarissa and me to join them. It was obvious Clarissa was in no shape to do anything but go to bed. I led her upstairs.

Clarissa slept in late the next morning and missed the guys' departure back to Palo Alto. I drove them to the municipal airport in Santa Monica twenty minutes away. Along the way, Cole and Raul talked about the party, how much fun it was, and how they'd clobbered every mismatched team that tried to beat them in sand volleyball. I just steered and listened.

"Tell me what you think of *Robinson Crusoe* when you finish," Raul said as he got out of my car. He handed me a slip of paper. "It's my e-mail address."

Cole mussed my hair, told me I should go find a barrette or something, and thanked me for the ride to the airport.

"Bring Clarissa to the next Sorry," he called as he walked away from the car. "She's kind of fun."

Raul lingered just a second longer. "That was nice what you did for Clarissa last night."

"What?"

"I saw how you spent the rest of the evening watching out for her. She's lucky to have you for a friend."

No words would come.

He smiled at me and left to catch up with Cole.

I didn't stay to watch them take off.

Sixteen

1 March 1692

I went to the tavern with Papa to see what Tituba, Goody Goode, and Goody Osborne would say to the charges against them. So large a crowd gathered that we had to move the whole assembly to the meetinghouse.

I wish I had not gone. It was akin to a nightmare, what I saw.

There, in front of the entire Village, while Goody Goode shouted her innocence, the afflicted girls began to scream and writhe, twisting their limbs in terrible ways and seeming to choke as if being hung. People rushed to soothe and calm them, and all the while the girls cried that they were being tormented by Goody Goode, though she laid not a hand on them. And when the magistrates bade Goody Goode explain why she did such things, Goody Goode, her eyes ablaze with fear, said it was not she who afflicted the girls, but Goody Osborne!

Then Goody Osborne was brought in and the girls were taken to the back of the meetinghouse so as not to be tortured by her.

The magistrates asked Goody Osborne with what evil spirit she had familiarity, and had she indeed made a pledge with the Devil, and many more questions. She denied all the charges.

The afflicted girls fell into fits behind her. It was like a nightmare again.

Then Tituba was brought in.

They asked of her the same questions. I could see that Tituba was afraid and desired to give the magistrates whatever they wanted so it would go well with her. They wanted to know if the Devil appeared to her. She told them she thought perhaps he had. The room went silent. They asked her to explain. She said she saw a dark man in the lean-to who bade her to serve him but she said she would not. The dark man told her Sarah Osborne and Sarah Goode hurt children at his bidding and he would have her do the same. He threatened to kill the children if she did not do his bidding. She was asked if anything else appeared to her, and she said she had seen a hog and black dog with the dark man.

And a yellow bird.

And a red cat. And a black cat.

Then Tituba told the magistrates she rides on a pole through the air and Sarah Goode and Sarah Osborne ride with her.

I, who have an imagination, could see that Tituba was creating a story such as the magistrates, the towns-people, and the afflicted girls wished to hear. The magistrates desired details and would not be satisfied without them. She, who is of a mind to do as she is told by her master, obeyed.

The girls then fell into more fits, Elizabeth Hubbard being in as agitated a state as ever seen. Tituba joined them, falling into a fit herself.

Goody Osborne, Goody Goode, and Tituba were led back to the jail.

I fled the meetinghouse. I did not even care to see John Peter, though I know he was there. Everyone was there.

I am in my writing tree. Papa stayed in the Village to confer with the menfolk. He will be home soon and will have news.

I do not want to hear it.

Abigail was not in the room with me when I stopped for the evening a little after seven. The transcription work that day had been mind numbing. I had to ask Abigail several times to help me decipher words that had faded to ghostly near nothingness. It unnerved her to look down at the diary's pages. I could see it in her eyes and expression. But she did what needed to be done to help me and then quickly looked away.

At one point she told me just to go with my instincts, that I was certainly a better judge of what Mercy was trying to say than she was.

That didn't make any sense to me. I had no longstanding familiarity with the diary. I asked her what she meant by it.

"You are practically the same age as Mercy was," she said.

I told her that didn't mean anything. Clarissa, my roommate, and I were the same age and had absolutely nothing in common.

Abigail laughed lightly and began to walk away from me. "I wouldn't be so sure about that."

Abigail didn't even know Clarissa. The little she knew about her I had told her. "We're completely different," I called to her.

Abigail reached the library door. "That doesn't mean you don't have anything in common."

Then she was gone.

That was an hour ago. She hadn't come back.

The diary entry for that day had been frustrating to read. I couldn't understand what made those girls do what they had done. How could they throw themselves into fits like that? Were they brilliant actors? Were they truly delusional? Were they physically ill? Mentally ill?

I itched to get on the Internet and do some research, but Abigail didn't have Internet access, and I knew I wouldn't go back to my dorm and do any sleuthing on my own. I had promised her.

Firstborns and Duroughs are promise keepers.

But I also knew I wouldn't rest that night if I didn't have at least a vague idea of what had gone wrong in Salem. I had a sociology test to study for, and I didn't want these troubling thoughts interfering with the long night of studying I had ahead of me.

I saved the file and walked to the library door. I opened it, planning to look down the long hall to see if there was a light on in the kitchen, thinking I might find Abigail there.

Instead, my eyes met a thin ribbon of light under the sitting room doors across from me.

I crossed the hallway and tapped on the door. Several seconds ticked by before Abigail answered me.

"Come in, Lauren," she said.

I opened the door. Abigail sat in a high-back wing chair facing a long, empty sofa. She held a cup of tea in her hands. A single lamp burned next to her on a marble-topped table.

"All finished for today?" She didn't look at me. Her eyes were on the empty sofa.

"Yes."

"Well, good night, then."

"Actually I wanted to ask you something before I head out."

She slowly turned her head to look at me. "Yes?"

"It's about the fits those girls had. Do you know if they were they real? Did they really have symptoms the doctors could not explain? Or were they pretending?"

Abigail turned back to face the sofa. "They'd be as monstrous as witches themselves if they were pretending. That's what you mean, isn't it?"

I hadn't thought of it that way, but it made sense. If those girls were putting on an act, it was incredibly evil. Perhaps that was exactly what I meant.

"Wouldn't they be?" I said. "I mean, we know how this turns out. Those girls were responsible for so many deaths."

"Are they the ones responsible?" Abigail's eyes rested on a satin-covered throw pillow, perfectly fluffed by nonuse. "They never touched the hanging rope."

"They set everything in motion," I answered.

Abigail said nothing for a long moment.

"You want to know if their behavior can be explained any other way," she finally said.

"Yes."

She turned to face me again. "And you haven't gone looking for explanations on your own?"

"I told you I wouldn't."

She smiled. "So you did."

I expected her at this point to invite me to sit down with her. She didn't. She just faced the sofa again.

"A graduate student published an article thirty years ago suggesting the afflicted girls might have eaten moldy grain. There is a plant fungus that, in one of its stages of development, contains a chemical compound similar to one found in LSD. But of course, if these girls from different households were ill from it, then all of Salem should have been too. Certainly the other members of the girls' families. Plus, as other colleagues pointed out in the same magazine, the girls' symptoms came and went. A hallucinogenic poison does not know when court is session, but that's when the girls fell to the floor writhing."

"So they were faking it," I said.

Abigail took a sip of her tea before answering. "If you are asking me if I think these girls were victims of a mind-altering fungus, I would say no."

"And there are no other explanations?"

"Encephalitis would explain some of their symptoms. Before the trials started, that is."

"But not after?"

"Well, what do you think?" Abigail met my gaze.

"I…I don't know much about encephalitis."

Abigail's smile was wan. "But what do you know about people, Lauren?"

I said nothing. I didn't know how to answer her.

"I'm not expecting you to answer that. Look, let's not get ahead of ourselves. Besides, you have a test to study for. I'll see you tomorrow."

She brought her teacup to her mouth. We were done.

I said good-bye, left her, and drove home. Clarissa was out when I got back to the dorm.

I studied for my test until nine thirty, checked my e-mail, then worked on my dad's project until I could stand it no longer. I googled "encephalitis."

Abigail was right. An acute inflammation of the brain would explain the seizures, the disorientation, the fever.

But it would not explain how Betty Parris and Abigail Williams fell to the meetinghouse floor in agony, screaming they were being tormented by the ailing Sarah Osborne.

Nothing medical seemed to explain *that*.

I got into bed and read a chapter of *Robinson Crusoe*, but I couldn't concentrate on the words. I turned out the light.

Clarissa didn't come in until after two.

I wandered in and out of sleep.

Seventeen

3 March 1692

Papa bade me go with him again to the meetinghouse. I pleaded to stay at the cottage, but Papa said one cannot pretend that what one does not like does not exist.

Today, Ann Putnam told the magistrates that the shape of Dorcas Goode, the daughter of Sarah Goode, appeared to her and demanded she sign the Devil's book.

The child is four years old!

Tituba then said she has seen names in the Devil's book.

I do not think Tituba knows how to read. How does she recognize names?

No one asked her this.

John Peter came for eggs after the proceedings. He asked what I thought of the events at the meetinghouse.

I did not know what to say. I do not know what he thinks.

I told him I fear the Village has lost sight of God and His tender provision.

He paid more than he should have for the eggs. He would not allow me to take less.

6 March 1692

Still it goes on, this endless exercise. The Village is mad with interest in the Devil's ways. Who among us remembers it is God's ways we are to embrace? Townsfolk see the shape of Sarah Goode in their barns, in their cottages, in their dreams. She comes to them with knives and threats. Ann Putnam now says she saw the shape of Elizabeth Proctor among a company of witches and that Goodwife Proctor proceeded to bite and choke her. I do not know what to make of any of it. Elizabeth Proctor's husband, Goodman John Proctor, owns a tavern and is wealthy. She is not what anyone would call strange. And she is with child.

I did not go to the meetinghouse today.

Papa did not ask me to.

7 March 1692

Tituba, Goody Goode, and Goody Osborne have been sent to Boston in chains to await their trial.

I have no zeal within me for stories.

13 March 1692

Mercy Lewis, Mary Walcott, and Mary Warren have joined the ranks of the afflicted. Ann Putnam has accused Martha Corey of witchcraft. Goody Corey is not a foreigner like Tituba, not odd like Goody Goode, and not ill like Goody Osborne. She is a godly woman. She is like any woman of good standing in the Village. And yet the charges are heeded.

*Betty Parris has been sent away to live with family
in Salem Town to ease her afflictions.*

*I told Prudence Dawes when I saw her at Ingersoll's
that it was wise for Betty to have been sent away. I think
Prudence mistook my meaning. She looked at me as
though I had said Betty was the cause of all the trouble.*

The end of the week came swiftly. By Thursday I was halfway
through March in Mercy's diary. I finished the March 13 entry a
few minutes before six, and Abigail, who knew I was going home again
that weekend to work on my dad's proposal, told me I could stop there.
But she wanted me to eat dinner with her anyway.

I correctly assumed she was in the mood to talk that particular
afternoon. She wouldn't have asked me to stay if she weren't.

I waited to see what was on her mind before telling her what was
on mine. She had only taken one bite of her *brie en croûte* before launch-
ing into book talk. I should've guessed it would be about a book.

"What are you reading for pleasure these days, Lauren?"

I felt my face color. I hoped she didn't notice. "Um...*Robinson Crusoe.*"

She did.

"Well, that's nothing to be ashamed about, Lauren," she said, cock-
ing her head, waiting for me to spill the reason reading *Robinson Crusoe*
made me blush.

"I know it's not."

She waited and I chewed.

"You've not read it before?" she said.

"No." I took a sip of water.

"I'm surprised." Abigail blotted the corner of her mouth with her
napkin. "You're such a fan of British literature."

I shrugged. "For a long time I just didn't think I would enjoy reading about a man marooned alone on an island."

"Mmm. And now you think you would?"

I coughed on a flake of phyllo dough and looked up at Abigail. She was smiling. "No. Not really," I said.

"Someone recommended you read it?"

"Yes." I took another sip of water.

"A professor?"

I set the glass down. "A friend."

"You know, I've always thought that Mr. Crusoe was a bit elitist for all he learned about life on that island. Even when he had no one and nothing, he set himself up as master of all that he saw. He taught the native he named Friday to call him Master instead of Friend, when what he really needed at that point was a friend, not a servant."

I didn't know if Abigail was really that annoyed with the fictional hero or playing the devil's advocate.

"Well, I don't know that he thought of himself as master of everything. I think his attitude of subduing the island was more about survival. Doesn't the island deepen his relationship with God?" I said. "Doesn't he begin to see himself as the created and not the Creator?"

"And yet he introduces Friday to Christianity and keeps him as a slave."

"I guess Defoe was just keeping it real," I ventured. "That was the custom of the day, to own servants. I do think Crusoe wishes he had listened to his parents instead of running off to do whatever he wanted. He seems repentant about that."

"Oh, I'm not saying Mr. Crusoe didn't wish he had listened to reason before he left England. It's just that he repents as a lord and not a pauper. He learned his lesson, but he saw himself as a privileged man in a hostile environment, not a broken man in the everyday environment of need."

I hadn't read enough to know if she was right. I wondered what Raul would have said had he been there.

"I used to think that way," Abigail said, her voice soft.

"Pardon?"

"I used to think I was a privileged woman in a hostile environment."

"Why did you think that?" I kept my voice soft too, coaxing her to continue.

"Because I was raised like you were, in a home where money was as abundant as expectations. What couldn't be controlled with money seemed grossly unfair. Hostile, even. But that was just the ordinary world I'd come up against. That was everyday life, and everyday life is full of choices. The privileged have very few truly difficult choices thrown upon them, Lauren. So when we're called upon to make them, we've no history of success or failure."

I didn't quite agree with her there. It's a ridiculous notion that the rich have no troubles. But I wanted her to keep talking. I was certain she was reminiscing about the man she wished she had married. "What was it you came up against?"

"I had to make a choice. I made a poor one."

"What did you choose?"

She hesitated for only a moment. "I chose the easy way."

"The easy way?"

"The way that left me alone."

Esperanza appeared at that moment to take away the brie and replace it with scallops in a sherry sauce.

I waited until she left. "Who said that was the easy way?"

Abigail raised her head and smiled. "Who, indeed?"

She said nothing else. She thought I was being facetious, but I wasn't. I really wanted to know. Why had Abigail not married the man she loved?

I could only think of one reason a rich young woman wouldn't marry the man she loved: he had no money, and that woman feared losing her social standing, the respect of her family, or perhaps even her wealth. So she chose ease over love.

This is what Abigail had done. I was certain of it.

"Abigail, what was his name?" I asked.

She cut a scallop in two. "It doesn't matter." She didn't look at me.

"Yes, it does."

Abigail pierced the scallop with her fork. "Not anymore."

But I could see it did matter. Anyone could see it.

For several long minutes, we said nothing to each other. We ate our scallops, the breeze toyed with our napkins, and a lone bee buzzed about the floral centerpiece.

"The transcription work was hard today," she finally said, letting me know we were done rummaging around in her past.

"Yes."

The bee flew away.

"There are more entries like that one, I'm afraid," she said. "Time has not been overly kind to the diary."

Or to you, I thought. "I hadn't heard of someone appearing as a shape to someone else. Those sentences threw me, especially since they were so hard to read," I said.

"That was called spectral evidence. Many of the Salem convictions were based on spectral evidence. By autumn of 1692, it was no longer allowed, but by that time it was too late."

"And spectral evidence was...?"

"It was one person saying he or she saw the specter or the shape of someone else, sitting in the rafters above their cooking fire, prancing about their kitchen, or hovering over them as they slept, sticking them with pins and knives."

The thought sent a shiver down my spine. "Like ghosts?"

Abigail inhaled deeply. "Well, yes, sort of like ghosts, only those whose shapes were seen about the village terrorizing innocent people, those people were still alive, many of them sitting in prison in chains at the time."

"No one else saw these shapes, though?"

"Apparently only the bewitched could see the shapes. No one else."

I was beginning to understand. "So no one could refute them."

"No. No one could. And it went on for months. By the time spectral evidence was finally banned in late November, Mercy was already…" Abigail's voice trailed off.

Silence filled the air around our table and uneasiness enveloped me.

I knew what was coming in the pages of the diary. Not the exact details, but I knew how the story would end. Abigail didn't have to finish.

I knew assumptions were going to be made about the girl I spent my afternoons with. Accusations were coming. Mercy would be asked to choose. There was no easy way. Confess or face execution. There would be a trial. A conviction.

A hangman's noose.

I pushed my plate away.

Eighteen

15 March 1692

Papa brings home news every day. Goody Corey was taken to the Putnam house to determine if she is indeed the one torturing Ann Putnam. It is said when Goody Corey walked into the Putnam house, Ann fell to fits and horrible writhing and screamed that Goody Corey suckled an evil yellow bird between her fingers.

And then Ann screamed she saw a man roasting on a spit in the fireplace. Mercy Lewis, who is a servant at the Putnam house, said she saw it too. And she also fell into fits.

And now Goody Nurse is accused! Goody Nurse is wise and good. We should all laugh to think Goody Nurse is in league with the Devil. But nay, Abigail Williams screams Goody Nurse torments her and she is believed. Is not Goody Nurse also tormented by such horrible accusations? How can so many good women in the Village be witches?

John Peter comes to get eggs, and we do not talk of what is happening in the Village. But since nothing else is happening, we barely speak.

Today he asked if I was writing stories.

I told him I have no heart for happy stories when all around me is madness.

He held my gaze before he turned to go back to his own cottage. For a moment I thought he might reach out to touch my face. There was no straw in my hair this time.

I don't know how I know he almost did this. His hand, the one not holding the basket of eggs, stayed close to his body. But I believe he almost did.

21 March 1692

A warrant has been issued for Goody Corey's arrest. She was examined today, but I did not attend. Papa, I think, has begun to see these unseemly meetings distress me. He told me Goody Corey maintained her innocence and the girls who accuse her displayed their awful evidence. They claimed to see a man whispering evil words in Goody Corey's ear. They moaned in agony.

I do not know what to think. Goody Corey has always been kind to me and Papa.

I am fast running out of ink. Papa does not speak of going to Boston. I will have to find some walnut shells to crush.

28 March 1692

Elizabeth Proctor has been accused of witchcraft. So has the child Dorcas Goode. The Village may as well accuse Lily, my milk cow, of bewitching young girls.

Papa is coughing again. Tonight he did not eat.

T hat weekend, I brought the schematic design for the art complex my father wanted my help with back to the dorm. Clarissa, who had no interest in the project the weekend we were at my house, had asked to see it. I think she was really interested in spending another weekend at my parents' home in hopes of seeing Cole again.

My rich, single cousin.

When she asked to see them, I told her I could probably bring the drawings back to the dorm. She gave me a funny look. I'd had many restless nights dreaming of yellow birds and screaming girls, but even though my thoughts were scattered, I knew what she was really after. Another beach party at Malibu. More face time with Cole. Another silver-domed meal served to her on the patio.

But Clarissa would have been disappointed had she come. Cole wasn't home. There were no beach parties. And Eleanor had the weekend off; we went out to eat. No silver-domed meals on the patio.

But Dad did let me take the drawings back to Santa Barbara. I think he liked that I wanted to show them to Clarissa.

When I got back late that Sunday afternoon, I spread the drawings out on our dorm room floor. Clarissa knelt over them and asked me if I had seen Cole and Raul while I was home. I wondered if she really cared at all about what she was looking at.

"No," I said.

She paused for a moment and then pointed to the drawings. "So what exactly is this? I thought you said it was an art gallery."

"It's a group of buildings, really. Like a family of galleries all in one place, connected thematically and centered on a garden in the middle of the complex. But it's not just art that will be on display. There will be a viewing library of rare books, and a museum of antique musical instruments, and a gallery of rare china and furniture."

"Well, okay. But I don't see what makes it different than other museums. Didn't you say it was unique?"

"The difference is the artifacts in this complex will be used, not just displayed. There will be readings of the rare books, concerts with the instruments, and meals served with the antique china and furniture. This building here will resemble a manor house or mini-palace. Everything will be displayed as if it's in current use, because in some respects, it will be. The garden in the middle of all the buildings will be a replica of one of King Ludwig's gardens, with all the same plants and flowers."

I pointed to a separate wing off the replica of the manor house. "And here are classrooms for lectures on art history, music, literature, design, textiles, pretty much anything from the last three centuries that contributed in an artistic way to cultural expression."

Clarissa's eyes swept across the drawings. "Cultural expression of the aristocracy, you mean?"

I looked down at the drawings. "Not necessarily."

"I don't see anything here that reflects the working class," Clarissa said simply. "Unless you plan to have maids in black dresses and white aprons serving those fancy meals on the antique china."

I hadn't thought much about what the complex *wasn't* about, only what it *was*. And even then, I hadn't spent any time pondering its limitations. "I don't think there's anything wrong with showcasing fine art," I mumbled.

"Nothing wrong with it all," Clarissa said, getting to her feet. "You should just know what you've got there. That's the culture of the upper class. Will the blue-collar crowd even be able to afford the admission?"

I felt my face grow warm. I couldn't find the words to tell Clarissa that the complex wouldn't be open to the public except during membership drives. Nor that membership would exceed several thousands of dollars a year per person.

"You think it's a bad idea," I said instead.

"No. It's a great way for the fortunate to spend their money and celebrate all they've been able to enjoy over the years." Clarissa dusted off her knees.

"You're kidding, right? You think this idea sucks."

Clarissa threw me a look and laughed. It was laced with a sarcastic edge. "If I showed you a drawing for a museum that celebrated the cultural history of the migrant farm worker, would *you* say that idea sucks?"

"Of course not."

I answered before I knew what she was trying to convey to me, what kind of equation I had drawn. When it dawned on me a second later, I grimaced.

"So why assume I think this project sucks?" she continued.

I said nothing.

"I can appreciate your little experiment, Lauren, but it doesn't seem to be doing you any good."

"My little experiment?"

"Living here in the dorm with me. Your token commoner."

I gasped. "I've never thought that about you."

"You just did. And really, it doesn't bother me that much, so don't get all depressed about it."

"But I didn't…" I couldn't finish. When I didn't continue, Clarissa did.

"I was kind of ticked at you our freshman year. I knew you could live anywhere, go to any school. But after a while, I kind of admired you. It seemed like you were really trying to understand what it's like to make your own way in life. But you're no different now than you were a year ago when I met you."

Clarissa was standing over me. I rose to my feet, annoyed. "What do you mean?"

"You make all the same assumptions about people."

"What assumptions?" I felt a muscle in my neck twitch.

She paused for a moment. "You know what? Let's just drop it." She reached for the coffee shop apron hanging on her bedpost. She had to be at work in fifteen minutes.

But I didn't want to drop it. "What assumptions?"

Clarissa slipped the black apron over her head. "I think we should just let it go."

She grabbed a pair of earrings from her nightstand and her wristwatch. There was no way I was letting her leave thinking what she was thinking.

Even though I wasn't quite sure what she was thinking.

I knew it had something to do with me coming off like a rich snob, an image I loathed. And she couldn't even see that she was acting like a jealous middle classer who only pretended she didn't envy the rich.

"Clarissa, do you remember how you fawned over my house last weekend? How you gushed over having our housekeeper serve you a meal on the patio?"

She narrowed her eyes. "Are you telling me you don't think you have a really nice house? That you don't like having your meal brought to you on your patio?"

"What?"

"You don't like those things?"

"That's not the point."

"You think because I'm not rich like you, I shouldn't like a really nice house and a really nice meal?"

She wasn't getting it at all. "Clarissa, you practically started hyperventilating when I said I had four male cousins."

Clarissa laughed. "Hyperventilating?"

"We were in my driveway and you said you couldn't believe I lived in a house like that and you wished I had brothers. When I told you I had four male cousins, you got all pumped."

Clarissa slipped on a long, dangling earring and shrugged. "So?"

"So, you assume things, too! You assume marriage to a rich guy would be better than marrying a guy who doesn't have money."

My roommate whipped her head around to face me. "Marriage? Who said anything about marriage?"

"I… You… I saw the way you were around Cole! You wanted to sit with him in the car on the way to the beach party. You wanted to see him this weekend. That's why you said you wanted to see these plans. You…"

"You think I want to *marry* Cole? A guy I barely know? For his money?" She laughed ruefully and grabbed her car keys. She only had one dangling earring on; the other she still held in her hand. It was as if she couldn't wait to get away from me.

Clarissa thrust open the door to the main hallway. "Thanks, Lauren. You've just proven my point."

I took a step toward her. "What point?"

But I knew already.

"You haven't learned a thing since you've been here." She stepped into the hall. "You still think you're better than everyone else."

She shut the door hard behind her.

I looked at our closed door for a moment, unable to decide what to do next. Unable to process what Clarissa had said. I looked down at my bare feet, at my toes crinkling the edges of King Ludwig's garden.

I was standing on the paper tribute to nobility.

Nineteen

3 April 1692

*Winter seems to be loosening its white hold on us. Today
I worked the garden. I love planting the seeds for summer's
harvest. I love imagining all the wonders that take place
below ground where no eye but God's can see. I wrote a
story about the corn seeds and pea seeds meeting each other
across the buried rows and producing yellow peas and green
kernels.*

*Writing the story relieved my mind for a few moments
of the happenings in the Village. It seems Mary Warren has
been healed of her strange afflictions. She said her fits have
ended and the prayers of the Village have made her well.*

But none of the other girls claim to be healed.

*Papa thinks Mary can no longer play this awful
game and has decided to end her part in it.*

A very small part of me thinks she is brave.

*The rest of me thinks you cannot hold in high esteem
someone who stops doing evil. It is like rewarding the thief
who stops stealing. What about all the people he stole
from before he stopped?*

*Papa is tutoring a young man today. The man's
spelling is atrocious. He spells his own name wrong. Sad,
really. Most of the girls in the Village can't spell their
own names. Most care not. That is sad as well.*

8 April 1692

John Peter came for the eggs today and brought news from the Village. Warrants have been issued for the arrests of Rebecca Nurse's sister, Sarah Cloyse, and for Elizabeth Proctor. They are being taken to Salem Town for their examinations. I do not know why. There will no doubt be a larger crowd there.

I've heard Sarah Cloyse is thought a witch simply because she defended her sister.

Prudence stares at me whenever I walk near her. I saw her talking with John Peter after the midweek lecture. He looked as though he wished to be somewhere else, but Prudence kept talking. He caught my eye, and then Prudence did, and I had to look away. His eyes spoke interest. Hers, spite.

She fancies John Peter. Who can blame her?

I wonder if she knows John Peter comes to my cottage for eggs when he could—and should—send one of his sisters.

I think perhaps she does.

But I don't want him to stop coming. I don't want one of his sisters to come.

I must stop for now. Papa needs something warm to drink to settle his cough.

10 April 1692

Sarah Cloyse, who is in chains and in jail, has been appearing all over the Village, torturing people. The shape of Sarah Cloyse is here, then there, and her shape is always biting, pinching, and tormenting.

Do you suppose it is possible to imagine something into existence? When I write my stories, I write them as though they are true. I know they are not, but there are no words that say these words are but a story. What if I wrote a story and then became convinced it was true? What if I truly believed I had grown yellow peas and green kernels? What if I were somehow able to convince other people I had grown yellow peas and green kernels?

I wonder if perhaps the afflicted girls set aflame a terrible fire that has so fascinated the Village that everyone who wants to believe it true need only close their eyes. All they have to do is imagine the corn is green and the peas are yellow and it is so. This would make the girls not evil, but rather something else. Tricked. Perhaps by evil itself and they do not even know it.

11 April 1692

I did not go to Salem Town for Sarah Cloyse's examination. Papa did. He did not say much when he arrived back at the cottage. It was the same spectacle as before. Accusations. Denials. Screaming girls.

Clarissa barely spoke to me in the days that followed our argument. She didn't appear to be mad at me, nor did she seem hurt. It was more like she had given up on me. Given up on finding common ground on which to base our friendship.

I stayed up the night we argued, finishing *Robinson Crusoe*. I wanted to apologize.

When I finished the book at eleven, she still wasn't home. I knew she got off at nine thirty, and I began imagining that she was staying out with friends to avoid coming back to our room. The longer she stayed away, the worse I felt.

I made a pot of cinnamon streusel decaf and sat down with a mug and my father's ancient copy of *Robinson Crusoe*. I had slipped Raul's e-mail address inside the cover after he gave it to me, and I took out the scrap of paper as I sipped the coffee.

It perplexed me that Raul wanted to know what I thought of the book. Was he genuinely interested in my opinion? Was he flirting with me? Was he teasing me?

I had taken the scrap of paper out and looked at it many times over the previous two weeks, thinking about what it would be like to initiate a conversation with him. There was something about Raul that set me off kilter, more than just my mistaking him for one of the caterers and his playful attitude about it.

I hadn't told Clarissa about *that* little event before our argument, and I certainly wasn't going to tell her after it either. It would've only confirmed that she was right and I was wrong. That I made elitist assumptions about people.

I hadn't been mesmerized by a guy in ages. I couldn't remember the last time I had daydreamed about a man. And it made no sense to me that I was daydreaming about Raul.

I didn't care much for how he reacted to my mistake the day I met him.

I didn't care much for his fancy shirts and fancy plane.

I didn't care much for *Robinson Crusoe,* probably because Abigail didn't.

And I didn't like how thinking about Raul made me feel—vulnerable and exposed.

I was fairly certain he wasn't particularly attracted to me. He liked my hair down, and he liked to tease me. He was kind to me. But then, he was kind to everyone.

He did like books, though. He had that on my cousins.

And as I sat there drinking coffee, waiting for Clarissa and thinking about Raul, it occurred to me that he probably would be quite attracted to Mercy Hayworth. She was a book lover, as well as kind, reasonable, smart, and compassionate. At that moment I began to picture John Peter looking like Raul. Whatever image I had conjured in my head for John Peter fell away and Raul's likeness was nailed in its place.

I couldn't shake the image away.

At eleven thirty, annoyed with Clarissa, I snapped open my laptop and typed Raul's address into a new e-mail.

I agonized over what to say to him, finally deciding on this:

Hey, Raul.

Been busy but finally finished *Robinson Crusoe* tonight.
I can see why it's a classic. The language and detail is quite remarkable for that time period. But I never quite developed a fondness for Crusoe. Abigail, the lady I work for, told me she felt Crusoe never lost his imperialistic mind-set, even when he was reduced to nothing. It was hard for me to see past that once she mentioned it.

I think my favorite parts were those places where Crusoe had to admit he was merely human after all, flawed and weak just like everyone else.

It was a good read. Thanks for recommending it.

Hope you had a good weekend.

Lauren

I hit Send and waited at the computer until midnight to see if Raul was at his computer too and would respond.

But a few minutes after twelve, and when no new messages had arrived, I shut off my computer, turned Clarissa's desk light on for her, and crawled into my bed.

I woke up when she came in a few minutes before one, but by then I was mad at her for staying away. It didn't occur to me that she often stayed out late. I pretended to be asleep.

For the next three days, I only saw her from a distance in the dining commons or asleep in her bed. She wasn't awake when I left for class, and she wasn't home when I went to bed at night.

To make matters worse, I had heard nothing from Raul in response to my e-mail. Not a word.

By Wednesday night, I couldn't stand Clarissa's silence anymore. I waited for her to get in that night. It was after midnight when she stepped into our room.

"Clarissa?" I could see her shape moving in the semidarkness.

"Sorry. Didn't mean to wake you." Her voice was sincere but curt.

"It's all right. I was waiting up for you. I want to apologize for what I said the other night."

She paused a moment. Then I could see her pulling off her hooded sweatshirt. "Apologize for what?"

So she was going to make it hard for me. So be it.

"For thinking you were only interested in Cole because he has money."

Clarissa kicked off her shoes. "Lauren…"

"What?"

"I am *not* interested in Cole. I liked going to your house. I liked talking with your dad about economics. I liked your mom. I liked your housekeeper and the way she made me feel while I was there. I liked Cole. I liked the party at Malibu. But I am not interested in Cole or anyone else. I have two more years of college and three years of grad school ahead of me. Cole is a fun date and you have a beautiful house and I had a great time while I was there. Get over it."

I sat up in bed. "That's what I'm trying to apologize for! For jumping to conclusions."

"You didn't hurt my feelings, Lauren."

"But I feel bad."

"That's what your conscience is for," she mumbled.

"What?" I had heard her, though.

"You want to apologize so you can feel better about the way you think." She stepped out of her jeans.

"I want to apologize because I was wrong."

"You don't have to apologize to me for being wrong."

I couldn't help raising my voice. "What do I have to do then?"

"You don't *have* to do anything. You're not accountable to me for how you think or what you do. Go to sleep. I'm going to go brush my teeth. And I don't want to talk about this when I get back."

She was gone for a few minutes. When she came back, she said nothing. She just switched off her light and got into her bed.

Not too long after that I heard steady breathing from the bed across the tiny space we shared. She really wasn't bothered by any of this.

I lay awake for another hour at least.

And when I finally did fall asleep, I dreamed I was eating yellow peas.

Twenty

14 April 1692

Papa went again to Salem Town to hear Elizabeth Proctor's examination. He came home in a foul mood, coughing and muttering. Everyone, it seems, sees yellow peas and green kernels. Papa said Goody Proctor could scarcely answer the charges against her, so astonished she appeared at the scope of them. Her husband, John, stood up to protest such ridiculous proceedings, and as soon as he did, the screaming girls named him a tormentor as well! Papa said Goodman Proctor will spend the night in chains, accused of being a wizard. I am glad Papa issued his complaints to me and not the magistrates.

19 April 1692

She who was afflicted is now an afflicter. The shape of Mary Warren is now flying about the countryside torturing people. Goody Bishop too. Afflicted girls carried on throughout the sermon today. I do believe Papa was of a mind to take a strap to them and whip the foolishness out of them. Would that it were only foolishness.

More names have been added to the list of the accused besides Mary Warren: Goody Corey's husband, Giles, Abigail Hobbs, and Bridget Bishop.

*Prudence told me Abigail Hobbs is a beastly wench
and no one likes her.*

*I wanted to say, "But that does not make her a
witch."*

I hated waiting to hear back from Raul. I hated that it mattered that
he respond.

I didn't want to be on the edge of my seat, waiting for his response
to my e-mail, but that's exactly how I felt. I'd never checked my e-mail
as much or as often as I did that week.

It didn't help that Clarissa spent as much time away from the dorm
as ever and that my dad was hounding me to get Abigail to state her
intentions for the diary. Between Clarissa, my dad, and Mercy's haunt-
ings—I dreamed of her almost every night—I was a distracted mess.

Abigail could sense I was bothered by something, and I knew she
wouldn't continue to accept my lame excuse for my grumpiness. I told
her I had midterms to prepare for. That was true, but my irritability had
nothing to do with midterms.

Raul's short response came Thursday, four days after I'd e-mailed
him. I didn't routinely check my e-mail before heading to Abigail's, but
I did all that week. Three e-mails waited for me that afternoon: one
from Raul, one from my dad, and one from the leader of one of my
study groups. I purposely read the other two first, even though Raul's
had arrived ahead of them. The study group had moved the location of
our next meeting from the library to the Coffee Cat. My dad wanted
my finishing touches on the proposal for the gallery project by that
weekend. And Raul's said simply this:

Lauren: Sorry you didn't like the book that much. I have to
admit I've never looked at any book that close. Pretty deep

thoughts you had. Robinson Crusoe was the first chapter book my dad ever read to me. I just remember it being full of adventure hey lauren this is cole when are you and clarisa coming down again Sorry about that. Cole is hovering over me.

Your aunt and uncle are back from Singapore. Cole and I are flying down this weekend to see them. Maybe we'll see you?

Hey, have you read *Moby Dick*?

Raul

raul sez he'll take you for a ride in the plane if you read moby dick by tomorrow

Cole is a liar. I said by Saturday.

I grinned at the idea of reading *Moby Dick* in two days' time, but the lighthearted moment melted away as I reread the entire message three times, dissecting the sentences to uncover any hidden meaning. What exactly was Raul saying about my opinion of *Robinson Crusoe*? Did he think that I was being nitpicky? that I read into the story stuff that had never crossed his mind? And was he insinuating that he *wanted* Clarissa and me to come down that weekend, or was he just telling me why he and Cole were going?

I had no desire to go cloud-hopping in his plane, joke or no joke. And it wasn't because I didn't like flying. It bothered me that I was attracted to him, a rich kid with a plane. Someone the Durough gatekeepers would approve of.

I didn't want to go for a ride in Raul's fifty-thousand-dollar toy. I knew I was going to be late to Abigail's, but I had to type out my reply then and there. It took fifteen minutes to fine-tune.

Raul:

I liked the book. Really. I just didn't love it. And I'm flattered you said my thoughts were deep. They're not. To tell you the truth, I don't know that I would've come to the same conclusion about Crusoe if I hadn't talked about the book with the lady I work for.

I've been doing a lot of thinking lately about class and privilege and what we find easy to believe about people we don't really know. That might explain why I keep feeling the need to apologize for assuming you were part of the catering staff the weekend I met you.

I am coming home this Saturday to work on a project for my dad, and I can ask Clarissa if she'd like to come home with me. I don't know what her plans are. So maybe we will see you and Cole.

But I'll have to decline the airplane ride. I've already read *Moby Dick.*

Lauren

I read my own message three times too. Then I saved it into Drafts so I could send it later that day.

Or perhaps the next.

Abigail was waiting for me when I arrived twenty minutes later than usual. She opened the front door, not Esperanza. And I didn't need to ring the bell. She opened the door as I walked up the winding path.

"Is everything all right?" Her tightly wrinkled face was creased with concern.

"Yes. I'm sorry I'm late. I had some things I needed to tend to. I should've called."

"I was worried. It's not like you to run late."

"I know. I'm sorry."

Abigail stepped aside to let me in and then closed the massive door heavily behind us. She said nothing as I headed for the library doors. The entryway was half lit and quiet. The doors to the sitting room were closed, and no stray sunlight fell upon the tiles.

I set my purse down and Abigail busied herself with retrieving the diary, just as she did every afternoon. I knew my father would ask me that weekend if I had spoken to her about her plans for the diary. He had mentioned it in his e-mail that day and in a phone call earlier that week, and he'd even brought it up to my mother, because she had called me about it too. I didn't think my mom was too concerned about Abigail taking the credit for transcribing the diary; she didn't care for the subject matter and would have been fine with the diary being published with Abigail Boyles as its editor. But since it bothered my dad, it bothered her. She had to live with him and his disappointments.

I fired up a wordless prayer for boldness and smarts. Then I cleared my throat and said Abigail's name.

"Yes?" Abigail laid the diary on the desk in front of me and began carefully removing her gloves, finger by finger. She looked up at me, and I saw fear in her eyes. Or maybe dissatisfaction.

Or maybe a double dose of both.

It suddenly seemed like a terrible time to ask what her plans were.

"Are you going to tell me you're quitting?" she asked.

The question was off her lips in a second, but it seemed to rattle around in my head for much longer. I said what people always say when they don't know what to say.

"What?"

"Are you quitting?"

"No." I didn't even try to hide the surprise in my voice.

Abigail looked at me for a long moment. She tossed the gloves onto the table, took a few steps, and sank into the armchair she often sat in while I worked. "You've been acting so distant lately, and then today you were so late, and I know you don't *need* this job…" Her voice trailed away.

"I have no intention of quitting, Abigail."

She inhaled deeply. "But something is on your mind."

"Well, yes."

"What is it?"

I sat in the chair next to hers. "I'd like to know what your plans are for the diary."

"My plans." It was a question, but she didn't phrase it like one.

"Yes."

"You think I have plans for the diary?"

I shifted my weight in my chair. "Don't you?"

"What is it you want to know, Lauren?"

Again I fidgeted. "Are you thinking of having it published?"

Abigail inclined her head. "I have made no plans to publish the diary."

I was trying to guess what my dad would want me to say next when she asked me what *I* would do.

"Pardon?" I said.

"What would you do with it?"

"I…uh… My father says it should be published."

Abigail's eyebrows arched slightly. "He does, does he?"

"Yes."

"And what does your father know about the diary?" I saw a flash of doubt in her eyes.

"Only the little I've told him. That it's a first-person account—a very well-written first-person account—of the Salem witch trials. Is there another book like it?"

Abigail laughed gently and inclined her head. "No. I don't think there is."

"Well, then. That's reason enough to consider getting it published."

She tipped her head. "Indeed." But I got the feeling she didn't really agree with me.

"Is there some reason you wouldn't want it published?" I asked. "I mean, everything about Mercy's conviction and execution are matters of public record, aren't they? It's not like you'd be exposing some deep, dark family secret that's been buried for centuries."

Again the little laugh. Not quite a laugh, really, but there's no other word for it. "Very true."

I didn't know what else to say at that point. Several seconds of silence passed.

"Is there a reason you'd like to know what my plans are, Lauren?" she finally asked.

I hesitated. Isn't there a reason for everything? "Yes."

"You want credit for your work."

"Do you think I don't deserve it?"

She immediately shook her head. "Not at all. You're doing a wonderful job. You deserve as much credit as can be given to you."

"Thank you."

Another long pause.

"If the diary is ever published, your name will be on it as editor, Lauren. Certainly not mine. Does that answer your question?"

I nodded wordlessly.

She stood. "Well, then. I'll make us some tea."

And she left the room.

It wasn't until she was gone that I realized how worried she had been that I would quit.

As if I couldn't be replaced.

Twenty-One

21 April 1692

Rebecca Nurse's other sister, Mary Easty, is accused of witchcraft. I know Mary Easty. She surely is no witch. I cannot envision her torturing anyone. She is one of nine new souls who have been accused. Nine more people. Papa went to her examination. He said Mary proclaimed her innocence with such grace and dignity that the magistrates turned to the accusers and asked if they had named the right woman. They assured Mr. Hathorne with shrill cries and much moaning that Goody Easty was the woman who tormented them, among so many others.

Papa is not so much angry now as fearful. He told me I shall no longer attend any of the examinations. He did not give reasons, but I think he wishes me to appear too terrified to attend. He may also fear I shall raise my voice to the madness and find myself in chains. He told me it is dangerous to kick against the will of the people without something in your hand to prove your argument. But what is there to hold? What proof have the accusers? Anyone can say they see someone's shape when no one else can see it. Who can argue with them? But that is not holding anything in your hand. That is suggestion and raw acceptance.

I wonder what would happen if someone collapsed to the ground, writhed in pain, and accused Ann Putnam or Betty Parris of bewitching them. What would the magistrates say then? I should not desire anyone to do this, but I do. Though it would not solve anything.

I am nearly out of ink. And I am out of vinegar.

I've reminded Papa twice that I could use a little vinegar from Ingersoll's Ordinary to make more ink but whenever he goes to the Village, talk of witches and examinations and specters consume him and he forgets.

I asked John Peter if he would trade some eggs for vinegar, but he would not take the eggs as payment. He would not take payment at all. He gave it to me.

30 April 1692

The most dreadful thing has happened.

Rev. George Burroughs has been accused of witchcraft. I can scarce believe it. Rev. Burroughs left Salem Village parish for Maine years ago. He does not even live here.

Ann Putnam has claimed Rev. Burroughs's dead wives appeared to her and spoke to her, and his shape stood right there among them. She said their blood cried out for vengeance, that Rev. Burroughs had murdered them. Ann was in a room full of people when she had this vision and all who saw her were astonished. Ann said George Burroughs's specter then turned into a cat.

Papa is furious.

He told me Ann's father and Rev. Burroughs were at odds with each other when Rev. Burroughs was the

minister here and that they disagreed over something hav-
ing to do with money.

    I have never seen Papa so angry. It set him to cough-
ing, and he has not stopped though I brewed him a draft
of ginger, tea, and honey.

    Papa said Rev. Burroughs will have no idea whatso-
ever why men are coming for him to escort him back to
Salem.

    I wonder if Papa will say anything in his friend's
defense. I want him to and yet I don't. He holds nothing
in his hands except contempt.

    And contempt is not enough to sway the will of
people who assume too much and have no wish to do
otherwise.

I had no idea if Clarissa would want to come home with me that weekend, especially if she knew that not only would Cole and Raul be
there, but Cole had practically asked her to come. She wasn't at the
dorm when I arrived back on campus from Abigail's that Thursday. Not
that I really thought she would be. I did homework until eleven thirty,
and when I could no longer keep my eyes open, I went to bed.

I didn't hear Clarissa come in.

On Friday morning when my alarm went off, Clarissa was in her
bed across from mine, wrapped like a burrito in a jumble of loosely
woven blankets. One leg stuck out, hovering in midair, half on the bed
and half off. Her toenails were painted a deep shade of purple, and a
sizable toe ring was snagged on a loop of one of her blankets. She didn't
have class until ten on Fridays, and I wasn't going to wake her just to
ask a question.

I toyed with the idea of leaving her a note inviting her to come home with me, but then decided to just visit her at the coffee shop later that day. I didn't want her to think I was still trying to make myself feel better. My asking her to come wasn't a peace offering so I could ease my conscience, though I knew that's what she would think. I had told the boys I would ask her to come. It was that simple.

I attended my four classes that day, dropped by the dorm to unload my book bag, and then headed to the coffee shop.

The place was a sea of students, books, and open laptops. And it was noisy. Conversations flew about the room, and every few minutes there was the loud pounding of metal on wood as saturated espresso grounds were emptied by hurrying hands. Clarissa was behind the counter, filling cups and calling out names.

"Tall dark roast with steamed milk for Tyrel!" she yelled.

The man named Tyrel reached for the drink she put on the counter. "Thanks, Clarissa."

"So when are we going to Morocco, Tyrel?" Clarissa asked as she sprayed a plume of whipped cream onto someone else's mocha.

"Can't this week. Midterms." Tyrel winked at her and began to walk away.

"You better not keep me waiting too long, Tyrel. I might have to go with someone else." She placed the mocha on the counter. "Super tall raspberry mocha for Claire!"

Then she saw me.

"Lauren. Hey."

"Hi, Clarissa."

"You ordered something?"

"No. Just wanted to see if you wanted to come home with me this weekend. Cole and Raul will be there, and Cole asked if you were coming. Would you like to?"

She didn't look up from the espresso machine. "I'm working this weekend."

"Well, um, you could come down after you get off, if you want. It's not that long a drive."

"I've got a double shift. I'm working Saturday afternoon at the bookstore and Saturday evening here. Sunday afternoon and evening too. Gotta pay the bills."

She grabbed the stainless steel receptacle of spent espresso grounds and whacked it on the side of a wood-framed trash bin.

"Oh. Okay."

"But thanks for thinking of me."

"Clarissa…"

"Don't say it."

"Say what?"

"Whatever it is you were going to say."

I sighed and said it anyway. "You're not trying to punish me, are you?"

She laughed heartily. "I don't have to. You do a fine job all by yourself. It's okay to be who you already are, Lars. In fact, I bet most therapists recommend it."

I stared at her. "Yeah, but it's not okay to be who people say you are when you know deep down you're someone else." I wanted to add, *And I'm not going to act like I'm better than everyone else just because you think that's what I believe.*

Clarissa looked up at me and blinked. Then she turned to the clutter of people waiting for their afternoon jolt of caffeine and cream. "Skinny white chocolate latte for Denise!"

She turned back to me. "I'm not quite sure where you're going with that thought, but hey, you don't owe me any explanations. Sorry I can't come. Tell Cole I'm sorry I can't come."

"All right," I said, even though I *did* want to explain to her what I meant.

"Hey," she said, as if I had already turned to leave. I hadn't. "I've got a prof who's interested in that diary you're working on."

"The diary?" I felt a tiny spark of devotion to the diary ignite inside me, a jolt of protective hesitation.

"Yeah. He's writing a book on the effects of stigma on culture and economics. He was lecturing today on the historical significance of the Salem witch trials and the role stigmatization played. I stayed after class and told him you were transcribing a diary from one of the women who stood trial. He got all excited. He wants to talk to you. Tall vanilla non-fat for Pete!"

"He wants to talk to me? What about?"

"About the diary, of course. What else?" She dumped two shots of espresso into a cup and pumped a tiny stream of hazelnut syrup into it.

"Well, when?"

"I dunno. After midterms, probably. He wants your cell phone number. Can I give it to him?" She spooned steamed milk into the cup.

"Um. I don't know. I guess so. I might need to talk to Abigail first."

Clarissa rolled her eyes. "She doesn't own you or that girl who got hanged, whatever her name is. You don't have to ask Abigail's permission."

"I know, but…"

"So I can give it to him?"

"Give what?" Surely not the diary.

"Your cell phone number, Einstein."

"Oh. Yeah. Sure." But I didn't want to talk to some professor about Mercy. She was still alive to me. It was October now, but I was with her in April. Abigail had already told me the hangings ended in the fall of 1692. I still had several months to spend with Mercy. She wasn't yet a statistic of stigma and hysteria. She was a young writer in love.

"Great. Tall hazelnut latte for Lauren!"

I looked at Clarissa, wide-eyed.

"You look positively panicked, Lars. Lighten up. He just wants to talk to you."

She pushed the cup toward me and then turned to the next order.

Perhaps it was a good thing Clarissa didn't come home with me. I didn't see Cole or Raul at all on Saturday, though I knew they were just a few miles away at my aunt and uncle's in Beverly Hills. I hadn't e-mailed Raul back to let him know Clarissa wasn't coming. I guessed because I hadn't, Cole assumed she wasn't. And apparently neither one of them wanted to see me. Fine with me.

I spent the morning putting my last editorial touches on the proposal. I added a paragraph at the end about how the complex could become a truly multicultural venue by offering memberships via scholarships to median- and low-income individuals with interest in fine arts. Such an altruistic gesture would endear the complex to the community and inspire others to develop an appreciation for the arts.

I knew Dad would probably call me later that week after reading it to ask me what in the world *that* was all about.

I was fine with that too.

With the draft printed out and safely tucked away in my dad's study, I put on a swimsuit, grabbed *A Tree Grows in Brooklyn* from the little library, and stretched out on a chaise by the pool.

Mom found me a few minutes after one o'clock and told me we'd all been invited to Uncle Loring's for dinner to see their pictures from Singapore. Then she asked me to go shopping with her for a new dress to wear to the ballet the following week. She didn't need a new dress, but I went anyway. While we were at Nordstrom, she saw an outfit on a mannequin, a linen-looking thing with three-quarter-length sleeves in a honey-hued coral, which she said would look divine on me. She insisted I try it on.

I had to admit it looked good with my skin tone and the toast color of my hair. She bought it for me.

That's what I put on a few hours later when we went to Uncle Loring's for dinner. There was no use trying to tell myself I didn't want Raul to see me in it.

But he and Cole weren't there.

My aunt told me they'd been gone all afternoon and were having dinner with some of Cole's friends. She didn't know when they'd be back.

We ate tri-tip on the veranda, devoured a baked Alaska after that, and then watched two hundred images of Singapore fade in and out on Uncle Loring's widescreen TV.

The food was excellent, the pictures lovely, but I was out of sorts. I usually didn't mind socializing with my parents and aunt and uncle. I didn't mind being the kid among the adults. That's how it always was for me growing up. But it really bothered me that night.

And I knew why. Cole and Raul weren't there. And they hadn't wanted me with them wherever they were. Not without Clarissa.

I wandered into the kitchen a little after nine thirty, more bored than hungry. I toasted an English muffin and was slathering it with chunky peanut butter when I heard the garage door open from behind one of the kitchen walls. I knew who it had to be, but I had no idea why they were returning so early. I hurried with the peanut butter, wanting to be out of the kitchen and looking like I was having a wonderful time with the others when the guys came in.

But I was putting the knife in the sink when Cole and Raul entered the kitchen. I could hear that Cole left the engine running on my uncle's Porsche. They hadn't come home to stay. They came to pick up something. Me, perhaps?

I turned to face them.

"Lars! Hey. How's it going?" But Cole didn't wait for an answer. He brushed past me and dashed out of the kitchen and into the interior of the house. Cole had come back for something, but it wasn't me.

I looked at Raul. He wore a sapphire blue shirt, silk. The sleeves were messily rolled up to his elbows like it was made of ordinary flannel.

"Hello, Raul."

"Hi, Lauren."

"Guess you heard Clarissa couldn't make it."

"Oh. Yeah, sure. Well, you didn't e-mail back that she was going to come."

"Right. I didn't."

Silence.

"Did you get your project done?" he asked.

Well, at least he remembered why I was even there. "Yes, I did. Thanks for asking."

More silence.

"So have you really read *Moby Dick*?" He eased into a smile.

I smiled back. "I really have."

"Did you like it?"

"It was full of adventure."

He cocked his head and grinned. "You're mocking me."

"It *was* full of adventure. And way too much detail on how to butcher a whale."

"So you liked it, but didn't love it."

"I appreciated its deeper meaning."

Raul smiled like he'd just figured out something about me he hadn't yet known. "Ah, the soul's quest to understand God."

Cole dashed back into the kitchen, carrying a black and silvery white Xbox 360 and several controllers, which threatened to fall to the floor. Raul rushed to help him.

"Thanks, man," Cole said as he swept past me. "See ya, Lars."

I watched Cole disappear into the garage.

Raul turned to me, looking apologetic. "We're playing *Halo 3* at his friend's house."

"I see."

"Would... Do you want to come watch?"

His eyes were kind, but I detected the signs of a mercy date.

Mercy.

"No, thanks anyway." I picked up my muffin. "Have a good time."

"Yeah. Sure. You too."

"Bye," I said.

"Bye."

His hand was on the door to the garage when he said my name.

"Yes?" I looked up from grabbing a napkin.

"That's a really good color on you."

And he was gone.

Twenty~Two

6 May 1692

*George Burroughs has been arrested and now sits in the
Salem jail. Papa wants to go to his examination, and this
time he wants me to attend with him. All the hearings
are taking place at Salem Town now. Papa fears he would
not be able to hold his tongue were I not there in the room
with him. As long as I am there, he will think twice
about shouting a protest such as put John Proctor in
chains. He worries what would become of me if he were
arrested and I was left alone at the cottage.*

*We are both of us torn by the weight of knowing
all these people cannot possibly be witches. If we speak in
their defense, we become accused. If we say nothing, we
condemn them falsely with our silence. What would God
have us do?*

8 May 1692

*Papa has decided to write a letter to the magistrates
Hathorne and Corwin and fill it with as elegant and
insightful words as can be found to persuade them who
have been so easily persuaded by less grand words.*

He is praying for the opportune time to give it to

Hathorne. He is afraid no matter what he says or how he says it, he will be jailed and I will be alone at the cottage.

I wonder—and I shudder to even write it—where is God in all this?

I have been praying that the eyes of the deceived may be opened, or that my eyes may be opened if these people be indeed servants of the Devil.

But my prayers go unanswered.

9 May 1692

Papa awoke with a fever today and could not attend Rev. Burroughs's examination. I begged Papa to let me stay with him today, but he pleaded with tears in his eyes to see to what could be done for George Burroughs. He tried to raise himself from his bed, as though he might run to the meetinghouse himself and defend George Burroughs. Papa would have crawled to Salem in the mud to speak on his behalf if he had the strength. But he does not. He reminded me that I do.

"Who will care for you while I am away?" I said. But Papa just said, "What need have I today that God cannot rightly meet? But who will stand for Rev. Burroughs in that place of deception, daughter?" And I said in my heart, "And where is God in that place of deception, Papa? If God is here with you, why can He not also be with George Burroughs?" But I did not say it. Papa asked me to carry his letter to the magistrates and pray that God would show me the providential time to give it to Magistrates Hathorne or Corwin.

I am shaking as I write this. And my heart is shaking within me. For I was in that meetinghouse today, and I saw what happened. There was much need for God there. And I fear God was shut out of doors. The people do not want answers to their fear. They want reasons for it.

I sat with Goody Trumball. She fidgeted the whole time. I perceived she is also of a mind that what is happening in our Village and in Salem Town is a spectacle from hell. I knew there had to be others. They are afraid to speak out, just as Papa and I are. The magistrates asked question after question, willing the reverend to confess to partnering with the Devil, but Rev. Burroughs would not.

Rev. Burroughs is not the most holy man I know. He is large and loud and can be driven to arrogance, which is why I cannot believe he is a wizard. He is far too human.

The magistrates asked when Rev. Burroughs had last had communion, as if they already knew it had been so long he could not remember. They asked if his children had been baptized, knowing, surely, they had not. Then they asked about his wives, since they had appeared to people and claimed to have been murdered by him. Here Susannah Sheldon, a young maiden I have known since a young girl, screamed that Burroughs's dead wives were standing right in front of her, wrapped in sheets and calling out that Burroughs had murdered them. Others said Rev. Burroughs lifted a whole barrel of molasses with naught but two fingers. And that he held a heavy gun with one finger. And this six or seven years past! The Devil's enabling, they said. During the questioning,

*the afflicted girls, or so they are called, began to scream
and writhe. It was a dreadful sight. The magistrates
ordered the girls out of the room so they could restore
order. And when order was restored, Burroughs was
taken back to jail.*

*I came home and realized I still had Papa's letter in
my pocket.*

10 May 1692

*Papa is still feverish. John Peter came for eggs today and
told us Rev. Burroughs has been transferred to the jail in
Boston.*

He also told us Sarah Osborne has died in prison.

C larissa didn't ask about my weekend. Perhaps she was waiting for
me to volunteer information, but what was there to say? I saw
Cole and Raul for all of five minutes, and I'm almost certain Cole's
spontaneous decision to play *Halo 3* at a friend's house Saturday night
would have trumped doing something else with Clarissa and me had
she come. I had the feeling Cole forgot he even asked about her. So I
didn't mention the weekend and neither did Clarissa.

Abigail seemed quiet and preoccupied that following week and as
uninterested in my weekend as Clarissa, though I'm sure for very different reasons.

When I arrived at Abigail's house Tuesday afternoon, I was greeted
by Esperanza, who had a pensive look on her face as she opened the
door. She showed me into the tiled entry, and I could hear Abigail's
raised voice coming from behind the closed library doors on my left.

"We've been through this before, Graham," Abigail said, her voice laced with anger and frustration. "I am not going to let the family inheritance be slowly gambled away. I know that's exactly what you'd do with it."

"Miss Boyles is on the phone," Esperanza said quickly. "An unexpected call. Perhaps you don't mind waiting for her in here?"

She motioned to the sitting room. The doors were open today. Crisp autumn sunlight fell across the parquet floor and glinted off the crystal orbs on the chandelier. It was a lovely room, but I would have preferred waiting in the kitchen or the dining room or the patio. The sitting room seemed to exude a keen longing. Not the kind of longing that made you impatient for Christmas, but the kind that filled you with emptiness. The kind that made you feel alone.

I turned to ask Esperanza if I could wait for Abigail in the kitchen, but she was closing the sitting room doors behind her as she left. Whatever Abigail was saying, I wasn't meant to hear it. I didn't know who Graham was, but it was evident Abigail was ticked at him, he wanted money, and Abigail didn't want to give it to him. I could barely hear her voice now—just muffled sound waves and snippets of inflection. I couldn't make out any of the words.

I moved away from the closed doors and gazed about the room. The sofa and armchairs looked pristinely uncomfortable. Each pillow was perfectly situated, and the upholstery bore no wrinkles, pulled threads, or the sheen of having been sat upon. The thick wool rug in the middle of the room looked like it had just been rolled off the boat from China. There wasn't a scuff mark, a smudge, or any other evidence of human touch on the walls or baseboards.

Along a wall of multipaned windows was a mahogany table decorated with framed photographs. Intrigued, I walked toward it, suddenly glad to be in a room where a bit of Abigail's past lingered.

The first photograph was a sepia-toned eight-by-ten of a man with a handlebar moustache and wearing a suit, sitting in a Queen Anne chair. Behind him was a woman with dark curls wearing a white dress and matching white shoes with button closures. She held a small bouquet. Neither smiled. Abigail's parents, no doubt, on their wedding day, looking like they couldn't stand the sight of each other. Perhaps they loved each other very much and the photographer had told them to stand still and not move a muscle, which meant no smiling. But looking at those dour faces, it was easy to imagine Abigail grew up in a cheerless home.

The next photograph, also in sepia, was of a black-haired young girl in a sailor dress, who was also no doubt sitting quite still but whose tiny features bore a smile under wraps. I recognized the shape of the eyes and the lift of the cheekbones. This was Abigail at five or six. She looked happy.

The third photo was also of Abigail, now a few years older, sitting on a porch railing with another girl with lighter hair. Dorothea, perhaps? The two girls wore matching ruffled dresses and carried unopened parasols. Their heads were bent toward each other, and they looked content to sit that way for hours.

The fourth was another bridal photo, this one black and white and with the look of the 1940s. The man in the photo wore an army uniform and the woman, a white peplum suit with a matching netted hat. In her arms she carried a nosegay of teacup roses. She and the man both smiled from ear to ear. The woman looked like an older version of the honey-haired girl sitting with Abigail. The fifth and last photo was of the same woman holding an infant in her arms. The woman was smiling at the camera, and the baby was smiling at the woman. I picked it up.

Dorothea had had a child.

I wondered at that moment if the baby in Dorothea's arms was the guy in Maine who expected to inherit Abigail's estate. Abigail told me the day I met her she had only one living relative. Just the one. And it was a man who lived in Maine.

Abigail had also said she had a mind to will that man her books and nothing else because he saw so little value in them.

And it occurred to me with a tantalizing jolt that this was who she was talking to, at that moment, in the library.

Graham.

Her cousin Dorothea's child.

Her only living relative.

And clearly someone she did not admire.

I had the photo of Dorothea and her baby in my hand when the sitting room doors opened and Abigail came into the room.

"Sorry I kept you waiting, Lauren," she said, looking at what I held in my hands, not at me. She walked toward me.

"No problem." I kept my voice casual, like I hadn't just figured out something curiously tragic. I set the photograph back on the table where I found it. "Is this Dorothea?"

"Yes." Abigail's tone revealed nothing.

"And her child?"

"Yes." And this time Abigail's voice seemed to falter. She looked at the photograph, and I could see hushed pain in her watery eyes. I had touched a place that still ached.

I wished I had said nothing, so great did the anguish appear to yet be.

"I'm sorry, Abigail. I didn't mean to pry."

She took her time answering. "You didn't pry. You merely asked a question. Yes, that's my cousin, Dorothea. Her husband, Joseph, died in the war, and she died within a year of giving birth. She never got over losing her husband. And Joseph never even saw his child. He left for Africa when Dorothea was six months pregnant."

"I...I really am so sorry, Abigail."

"It was a long time ago." She inhaled heavily, and I could see her gathering up her composure to move away from a past that still stung. Her eyes lingered on the photograph I had replaced.

I pointed to the photograph of the two girls. "And this is you and Dorothea?"

"Yes. At the beach house. We spent a few weeks every summer at my aunt and uncle's summer place on Pismo Beach." The muscles in Abigail's face relaxed as her mind floated back to sandy beaches and salty air. For a moment, she looked young and nearly happy. But then the muscles around her eyes and mouth tightened again, and when she turned to me a second later, her gaze was polite but stiff. "Ready to work?"

"Um, sure."

I moved away from the table and followed Abigail toward the double doors. Her rubber-soled shoes squeaked on the wood floor, and she seemed to hurry into the entryway so the squeaking would stop. We moved wordlessly from one room to another, from the room of the dead to the room where time lay in pages everywhere I looked.

As Abigail retrieved the diary and I took my place at the writing desk, I laced my thoughts together. Abigail had probably promised to look after Dorothea's baby, and she tried, but Graham grew up to be a man who cared only about money. Perhaps Abigail's aunt, Graham's grandmother, raised Graham, but she and her husband didn't have the money Abigail's father did. Maybe they didn't care for Graham the way Abigail wanted him cared for. And Abigail felt like she had failed Dorothea somehow. She wanted to do more for Dorothea's child, but something prevented her. Just like Mercy wanted to speak out on behalf of the wrongfully accused, but saw no clear avenue by which to do it.

Abigail set the diary in front of me.

"I've had a busy day, Lauren, and I'm not feeling well. I hope you don't mind if I don't join you for supper tonight. Esperanza is making a salmon quiche. It's very good. But I think I will retire for the day. I...I need to lie down."

Abigail hadn't lost her indomitable polish, but I saw cracks in her armor for the first time. She didn't just grieve for a lost love; she grieved a lifetime of loss. I wondered how much I had accurately guessed.

"Can I do anything for you, Abigail?" I had never been more sincere.

She smiled at me. "Thank you, no."

Abigail walked slowly away, leaving me alone with Mercy.

Twenty-Three

14 May 1692

*Papa felt better today. He went to the Village as he had
ledgers to balance and letters to write for people. I went
with him to make certain he would not collapse from
weakness along the way. He tucked his letter inside his
satchel before we set out.*

*There was word from Boston that the new governor
for the colony, Sir William Phipps, has arrived from
England. I pray this man will put an end to this horrible
situation.*

We came home. Papa still has his letter.

19 May 1692

*There was book work to be done for Uncle's ship so Papa
rode his horse to Boston, though I implored him not to.
He is still not entirely well. When he came home this
evening, tired and hungry, he told me Mary Easty had
been released from jail and then just as quickly rearrested
when her accusers protested.*

*John Peter came for eggs today, but he did not stay
because Papa was not home.*

But he looked as though he wanted to.

23 May 1692

*Prudence Dawes is seventeen today. I found a lovely stone
by the creek. It was smooth and near-white, and I wrote
her name and age on it. I spent some time making the letters. I thought the result was rather beautiful. She did
not seem to be taken with it. She thanked me but what
came out of her mouth were just words born of polite-
ness. I believe it is not the stone she does not like but the
fact that it was I who gave it to her.*

28 May 1692

*Papa should not have gone into the Village today. He was
pale and weak, but he went nonetheless. I do not think
Governor Phipps will put an end to anything. He has
issued a commission for a Court of Oyer and Terminer,
which Papa tells me means "to hear and determine." The
court will hear the complaints against those accused of
witchcraft and will determine their innocence or guilt.
Sir William has assigned seven judges to sit on the court,
including John Hathorne. I am afraid for everyone in
chains. I asked Papa what would happen to the ones found
guilty, and he would not answer.*

The call from my dad came on Thursday. I expected to hear from
him Sunday night or Monday morning at the very latest. When I
had heard nothing by Wednesday, I began to believe he had no problem at all with my added paragraph to the gallery proposal. Surely he
had read the finished product. When I left Sunday afternoon, Dad told

me he planned to look at the completed proposal—my part of it at least—later that evening after an hour at the driving range.

He had seen the rough draft the weekend before and seemed pleased with the way I described the scope of the project. He was particularly happy with the descriptors I used to portray the different galleries.

"The matriarch of this family is going to love that," he had said. "Actually, the other women will too."

I'd asked him what he meant by "other women," and he said this family of investors included a grandmother, two brothers, a sister, and a granddaughter, all passionate devotees of culture and fine art.

"You've captured images with your language that will appeal to women," he said.

"Meaning what, exactly?" I'd replied, aware I was his daughter, not his son. I didn't want to hear that I appealed to a feminine eye and mind-set, which typically had no forte for hard facts and bald analytical truths, but I waited for him to say it anyway. Isn't that what he meant?

"It means you've done a great job." He had handed the rough draft back to me. "An excellent job."

Eleanor had called us to dinner. He changed the subject as we walked into the dining room, and I let him.

I knew my father expected no big changes to the final draft. And my suggestion that the investors fund an endowment to make the galleries accessible to art lovers of any social class wasn't a monumental change to the project's dollar amount. What was another half million to billionaires?

No, my change altered the scope of the project, not its bottom line. Broadened it. Enhanced it. Added a deeply philanthropic layer to what would certainly become an icon in West Los Angeles' art community.

These were the bald, analytical truths I was prepared to use in defense of my tiny additional paragraph.

And I waited to use them.

On Thursday, when I finally heard from Dad, I had lost some of the steam I needed to convince him it was a good idea. It was about eight in the evening when he called, and I had been home from Abigail's for half an hour. I was alone in the dorm, as usual.

"What's this added paragraph all about?" Dad stated the question simply and without a trace of displeasure right after I said hello.

"It's not all about anything. It's just a nice, magnanimous gesture that will further cast this project into a unique light. People who love art don't usually want to keep it to themselves."

"Yes, well, scholarships are for colleges and learning institutions. The galleries are for appreciation and enjoyment."

"But you said yourself there will be lectures, book readings, concerts. This project is both. It's part entertainment, part education."

"Okay. Point taken. But we make buildings happen, we don't tell people how to run them."

"Suggesting a broader use for buildings you've made possible isn't arrogance, it's more like…enhancing the scope of the investment."

"But what you're suggesting doesn't translate into a return to the investor. Memberships create a return on the investment. You're talking about giving a sizable amount of money away."

"Well, who's to say that kind of generosity won't actually attract members who believe in living a philanthropic life? We both know this is a not-for-profit project. This family will always be giving money away to maintain it."

"But I don't usually suggest how an investor runs his investment."

"Well, maybe you should from time to time."

"Lauren."

"What?"

"Where are you getting all these ideas?"

He sounded animated and curious, like it excited him that I was sparring with him over a business idea. I looked down at my feet and noticed I had begun to pace my tiny dorm room.

"It's just one idea, Dad. One idea. And I think it's a good one. There's nothing wrong with the galleries without it, but there's nothing truly wonderful, either. It's just a place for the upper class to maintain their distance from everyone else. I don't think that's what art and music and literature are for."

"So you think you can help bridge the gap between the classes with this, eh?" His tone was almost wistful. Is there a nice word for "mocking"?

"I'd rather shorten the distance than build a bridge, Dad."

He laughed gently. "But, Lauren, there will always be rich men and poor men. Even the Bible says that."

"I'm not talking about redistributing wealth. I'm not talking about changing what people *have*. I'm talking about changing how people think. I've been mulling over this for months."

"Tell me."

How to explain it? It was still a process in my head, these things I was trying to work through. "We use the dumbest things to measure someone's worth, Dad."

He was silent, but I could almost hear his thoughts.

You won't change that with an art gallery.

Twenty-Four

1 June 1692

Papa is again abed with a wrenching cough, and I am very nearly glad of it. He needs me home with him, so I have not been dispatched to bring him news from the Village.

But news comes regardless.

Goody Trumball came by the cottage with a crock of pea soup for Papa—it was very good—and told us Bridget Bishop will be the first to be tried in the new court.

3 June 1692

I am not of a mood for stories or diaries today. Bridget Bishop was found guilty.

She is to be hanged.

She is a very odd woman and I am a bit afraid of her, but odd does not mean evil. John Peter came by the cottage with this dreadful report. He said if Goody Bishop had confessed to witchcraft they would have let her live and simply driven her from the Village. But she would not, and so they believe she is a witch who refuses to confess instead of an innocent who will not lie to the court to save herself.

I am bewildered.

John Peter stayed and talked with Papa for a while and brought him ledgers and letter requests from Salem Town so that he can work. He cut firewood for the stove and mucked out the barn.

I think Papa likes John Peter. I am glad of that.

It is good to be glad of something today.

10 June 1692

Bridget Bishop is dead.

I did not go to her execution as Papa needed me home with him. I would not have gone were he well. But though I did not go, I saw Goody Bishop's swinging body in my mind all afternoon and no amount of hard work or prayer or story hatching would chase it away.

Who thought of such a horrid way to take a life? To snatch away one's very breath as the mind and body are wrenched away from each other.

Papa consoled me in a whisper that it is far less dreadful to hang than to burn.

But you are dead either way.

17 June 1692

Papa's illness lingers. I have been too occupied with his care and maintaining the cottage to write. Always before, Papa has fought off the disease that wracks his lungs, but it is different this time. It is like a monster with talons. Papa coughs up bright crimson blood. He

is at war with the monster, and I fear he will not win.
He grows weaker by the day.

John Peter has taken over the care of the animals in
the barn while I tend to Papa.

I finally let him read some of my stories.

He told me they were wonderful and that I should be
writing books.

I laughed. He did not.

30 June 1692

Papa is so weak and frail. I pray every day that God will
reach down from Heaven and heal him, but a little voice
inside me says God is reaching out for Papa in a different
way—to embrace him into His bosom.

I am afraid of what my life will be like without
him. He is too weak to speak, yet he asks me every day if
I have written to Samuel to alert my cousin of his ill-
ness. I do not wish to write the letter and so have a part
in bringing about what I dread.

Goody Trumball helped me shell peas today. Rebecca
Nurse, Sarah Goode, and three others have all been sen-
tenced to die.

I think I knew several weeks into the transcription that Mercy's father would not live to see his daughter's execution.

Abigail told me without really telling me.

She didn't outright say that Mercy's father, Eli Hayworth, was already dead when Mercy met the knotted rope. But when I transcribed the June entries—when I realized, as Mercy had, that her father was dying—I remembered the quizzical look Abigail gave me weeks earlier when I mentioned it was perhaps a blessing Mercy's mother had suc- cumbed to the pox years ago, because it had no doubt been hard enough on Eli to watch Mercy climb the gallows.

Abigail knew Eli Hayworth had already died of whatever had been eating away at his lungs by the time Mercy was hanged. That explained her puzzled look at my comment. But she hadn't corrected me. Like everything else about Mercy, Abigail wanted me to discover this detail as I read the diary, as her story unfurled around me.

Still, I found myself disheartened when I finished the June entries and knew beyond all doubt that Mercy's father was dying.

She was going to be alone.

She was about to face, alone, an inquisition as undeserved as any. As Mercy prepared herself for her father's passing, all she knew was that she would soon be alone. She thought it was only grief and loneliness that awaited her.

That seemed terribly unfair as I saved the document and powered down the computer for the day. Mercy thought the worst thing that could happen was that her father would leave her.

I'd grown envious of Mercy's relationship with her father. They seemed so in sync with each other. It was inconceivable to me that Mercy could have hidden anything about herself from Eli Hayworth, or that she would have wanted to. Mercy's bond with her father seemed the kind shared by kindred minds. The kind that makes someone look at a parent and child and say, "The apple doesn't fall far from the tree," or, "They're peas in a pod, those two."

Or "like father like son."

I pushed myself away from the diary, moody and contemplative. Abigail and I had eaten early, a light Florentine omelet that was very good, but it was after seven and I was hungry again. All I had in my dorm room was a package of stale Oreos—stale because Clarissa had gotten into them and hadn't bothered to seal up the package after her rampage. I wondered if Esperanza had left out any of the oatmeal cookies she'd made earlier in the day. I wanted one for the ride home.

I stepped out of the library and into the tiled entry, intent on heading to the kitchen, but the sitting room doors were open across from me, and I could see a fire blazing in the fireplace on the far wall. Surprised, I tiptoed in, fully expecting to see Abigail sipping a cup of tea and at last enjoying a room that needed to be enjoyed.

But it was Esperanza I found kneeling by the hearth, feeding hand-torn scraps of paper into the snapping flames.

She looked up at me. "Are you leaving? Do you want me to turn on the porch light for you?" She started to get up.

"No. I know where the light switch is. I was just… I was wondering where Abigail was."

"Do you need something?"

"No. I just saw the fire and thought she was in here."

Esperanza turned back to her task. She thrust a handful of torn paper into the blaze. "She's upstairs, on the phone."

"Oh."

"If you must speak to her, I can interrupt, but I'd rather not if I don't have to. It's a long-distance call. She didn't want to be disturbed."

My eyes flew instinctively to the photograph of Dorothea and her baby. "You don't have to disturb her," I said.

"Good," Esperanza said, "because I really don't want to." Then she added to herself, "Not when she's talking to *him*."

I don't think she realized I'd heard her.

"Is it Graham?" I asked

Esperanza swiveled her head to face me. "What do you know about Graham?" Her dark eyebrows crinkled to curious angles.

"Um. Not much."

"Has she told you about him?" Esperanza looked dubious. No, more accusatory. I shouldn't have said anything.

I felt my face color. "No, not exactly."

"What you mean, 'not exactly'?"

I decided tell the truth. I am not a very good liar. "I've only guessed at who he is."

Esperanza blinked at me and waited.

"She mentioned to me once that she has just one living relative, a man in Maine." I continued. "That's Graham, isn't it?"

Esperanza looked away. "We should not be discussing this."

"Why not?" I took a step toward her.

"Because I work for her and so do you. She may not pay all your bills, but she pays mine." Esperanza tossed the rest of the paper shreds into the fire and stood as the flames welcomed them greedily.

"Why is no one allowed to talk about him?" I asked as gently as I could.

Esperanza waited a moment before answering. "Because that's the way Abigail wants it. If it makes her happy not to talk about it, then fine with me. She hasn't had much happiness."

I knew this already about Abigail. I knew she had lived a thwarted life, and I itched to know what had happened to her. I wanted to know what she had chosen. I think, deep down, I wanted to avoid making the same mistakes.

"What happened between her and the man she wishes she'd married?" I asked. "Do you know?"

Esperanza exhaled deeply, watching me as she contemplated my question. She might have shared at least part of the answer had we not at that moment heard footfalls on the carpeted stairs beyond the sitting room.

Abigail.

Esperanza said nothing. Neither did I.

We waited in silence as Abigail closed the distance between us and then stepped into the sitting room. I turned to face her.

"All done for the evening, Lauren?" She looked tired. Pale.

"Yes."

"And you are finished with those papers, Esperanza?"

"*Sí.* They are all burned."

"Thank you, Esperanza. I'll take my sherry now. Then you may go home."

Esperanza left the room, and Abigail nodded toward the fireplace and the smoldering scraps of paper.

"Someone might try to steal my identity," she said.

"Okay."

Abigail grinned wryly. "I'm only kidding, Lauren. My shredder is broken."

A weak smile formed on my lips.

Abigail turned to lead me out of the room. "Who'd want to steal this life?" she quipped.

My tepid smile vanished.

Abigail walked me to the front door. As I stood on the threshold, I saw Esperanza carry a tiny bell-shaped glass on a tray into the library. The liquid inside the glass was a bronzy autumn color. Esperanza's eyes met mine just before she disappeared into the library with Abigail's sherry.

Abigail and I said good-bye. As I walked to my car in the circular drive, I thought about waiting for Esperanza to come out. Her car was parked just ahead of mine. Perhaps she could tell me in a few short sentences what had happened between Abigail and the man she loved.

But Abigail chose that day to stand at the door and wave to me as I left. There was nothing I could do except drive away and wave back.

It wasn't until hours later, when I was in bed, listening for Clarissa's footfalls down the hall, that I realized Mercy couldn't have been completely alone when her destiny became clear. Not completely alone.

John Peter had to be there.

Raul's face filled my mind as John Peter's name rushed to the forefront of my thoughts.

John Peter was there.

Twenty-Five

10 July 1692

I have been too busy and distressed to write. Goody Trumball brings us meals, though Papa cannot eat but a bite or two. John Peter still comes every afternoon to care for the animals and muck out the barn. Today he stayed to weed the garden and tend to my apple trees.

Papa asked me in a whisper to read him the story I wrote about a ship that sailed to the end of the world and found that it was really the beginning.

I read it to him twice.

19 July 1692

John Peter came to take care of the animals and brought us the latest news from the Village. Five women were hanged. Rebecca Nurse, Sarah Goode, and three others. Their bodies were thrown off Gallows Hill among the rocks. They were not even buried. Papa took my hand and asked me, if the same fate should fall to Rev. Burroughs, that I attend the execution and pray it would go quickly for his friend. He said it as if he would not be waiting at home for me afterward.

Then he asked me to burn his letter.

I asked him why, but he would not answer.

28 July 1692

Papa is with the angels. With Mama and Thomas.

He was borne away to Heaven as I slept at his side, and I did not hear him leave. When I gave in to exhaustion sometime in the middle of the night, he was with me. When I woke up at dawn, he was gone.

John Peter found me stretched out over my papa's frail body as I cried. He stayed with me until I was able to ride back with him to his mother's house. Then he and Goodman Trumball attended to my father's body. I do not remember being at his house. I remember a summer rain began to fall as I rode with John Peter on his horse. I remember laying my head against the wide expanse of his back and that his muscles moved beneath my cheek as he led his horse through the rain. I remember sitting in a chair and someone drying my wet hands with a soft cloth. It might have been John Peter who did that. I think his mother brought me a cup of cider.

I do not remember anything else of that day.

Papa was buried the same evening. An angry sun came out after the rain and set the earth to steaming. He could not stay above ground.

I do not remember that, either.

I have written to my cousin Samuel, but he is at sea. I do not know how long it will be before he learns my papa is dead. Papa told me before he died that Samuel must come with his new bride to live at the cottage so I will not be alone. It is not proper for an unmarried girl to live alone. But I do not wish to share the cottage with anyone else, not even Samuel. Not yet. I only want to grieve in solitude.

I am glad Papa is breathing the air of Heaven with lungs that are not diseased. But I miss him. He has been gone from me five days.

29 July 1692

I laid out table settings for two tonight.
  I laughed at first.
  Then I wept.

I pushed my chair away from the diary, blinking back tears that I didn't want to fall on pages already smudged from long-ago grief.

Abigail had returned to the library at some point while I worked, and she moved toward me. In her hands she held a tissue. "Here," she said.

I took it and dabbed at my eyes. "Guess where I'm at in the diary today?" I said. My voice cracked.

"I know where you are." Abigail took a chair across from me at the writing table instead of her usual one behind me.

"And I even knew it was coming." I laughed, but fresh tears tumbled down my cheeks. I mopped at them, surprised and angry that they refused to stop.

Abigail said nothing. Her face revealed nothing. It was as if she felt nothing.

"So how did you know I'd need this?" I waved the wet tissue.

"Because I needed one the first time I read it." Her voice was flat.

I looked up at her. "When was the first time you read it?"

"The day my mother gave it to me. I was thirteen."

"Thirteen?"

"You think that's too young."

"Well, sort of. She just handed it to you one day?"

Abigail's features softened. "I had to wash the chocolate off my hands first."

I dabbed at the last stray tear and smiled. "I'm serious."

Abigail inhaled, as if to grab a remnant of oxygen from that long-ago day when she first saw Mercy's diary.

"It was my birthday. My mother invited me to her bedroom. She had a little safe in her closet. She told me was going to give me something special for my birthday. I thought it was going to be one of her diamond necklaces, or maybe the ruby ring I liked, or the sapphire earrings her parents had given her. But it was the diary she handed me."

Abigail stopped and I waited.

"I was disappointed," she continued. "Not terribly so, because I loved books and was taken with the idea that the diary had been written by an ancestor of mine during colonial times. But still, I wasn't overjoyed."

"You wanted the ruby ring instead?"

"No, not exactly. I was just frustrated at the reason my mother gave it to me then. She told me she was supposed to wait until I was nineteen, like she had been when her mother gave it to her."

"Mercy's age?"

"Mercy died a month before her nineteenth birthday."

"So why didn't she wait?"

Abigail blinked slowly and then locked her eyes on mine. "Because she was dying."

My voice hung useless in my throat.

"So I was mad," she continued. "Ticked, I think your generation would say. I ended up with all those jewels anyway. She didn't bother to give them to me ahead of time, like she did the diary. The diary was the only thing of hers she actually handed to me before she died, so I saw it as proof that life isn't fair. And then, of course, I read it that day and was sure of it."

"You read it in one day?"

"I wasn't as patient as you. If I got to a part I couldn't decipher, I skipped it and went on to the next part I could read. I stayed up most of the night."

I imagined Abigail as an adolescent, reading the saddest parts of the diary alone in her darkened bedroom. What had run through her young mind as she read of ghostly apparitions, screaming girls, and swinging bodies?

"Did you know before you began reading what happened to Mercy?" I asked. "Did your mother tell you?"

Abigail looked at her withered hands folded in her lap. "She told me…" Abigail's voice fell away and she chewed on her lower lip, obviously deep in thought. I didn't think she was trying to remember what her mother said. She was trying to decide how to tell me.

Or how much.

"What did she say, Abigail?"

Abigail raised her eyes to look at me. "She…she said the diary would make me sad, but that I was to remember that underneath all the sadness, the diary told a love story. That was the part I was to remember, and that's what I was to tell my daughter, if I had a daughter, when I gave *her* the diary."

I blinked. "A love story."

"Yes."

A love story? I saw no hope for Mercy and John Peter's love for each other. None. I had two months of Mercy's entries left to transcribe, and I knew in that time she'd be accused, tried, and hanged.

She'd be dead.

That didn't seem like a love story to be remembered.

"Is that what you think it is? A love story?"

Abigail looked past me, into the room across the hall, whose doors stood open that day.

"Yes, I do," she said. "I think, when you are done, you will too."

I let my eyes wander down to Mercy's aging words. There weren't that many pages left to transcribe. August and September, just two months. I suddenly wanted nothing more than to finish it.

I wanted to stay up all night and finish it, as Abigail had done.

I was about to ask if I could rearrange my work hours so I could spend the weekend at her house and finish the transcription, when her voice broke the silence.

"Lauren, I need to go away for a couple days. I need to take care of a few things."

"Oh." I couldn't hide the disappointment in my voice. I didn't try.

"This doesn't need to interfere with your work on the diary. You can either not come the next few days, or if you wish, I will give you a key and you can work your normal hours. Esperanza will only be here a few hours a day. I'm giving her most of the week off, so she won't be cooking meals. She deserves some time to herself. "

"Oh. That's okay," I said, my mind already whirring with how easily I could finish the diary if I could stay as long as I wanted.

"I hope this doesn't cause problems for you."

"No. Not at all. I'll be fine, I'm sure."

She studied me for a moment. I was too eager for her to go and it showed. I attempted to back-pedal a bit. "I'll do what I can while you're away and just save any questions I have until you return."

Another long moment passed between us where she simply studied me.

"Lauren, I want you to know that I trust you. And I'm glad I can trust you. I know you won't let the laptop or the diary leave this house while I'm away if I ask that they not. And I am indeed asking you. Being able to trust you means more to me than I can say."

It was my turn to be silent. It had never occurred to me to remove the diary from the house. I would never have taken a chance with such a priceless relic. But taking the laptop out? I might have thought of that. It annoyed me that Abigail had thought of it first and was forbidding it.

"I know you're anxious to finish the diary," she continued. "I don't blame you. But you'll have questions when you're finished, and I ask that you wait until I return to find out the answers. I assure you everything will be perfectly clear in the end. I would like you to trust me on this as I trust you."

We sat and stared at each other as she waited for me to seal our covenant of trust.

"Why will I have questions?" I said. "I don't understand."

She ignored my question. "When you finish the diary, wait for me. Anything unclear to you I will make clear. I promise."

"How long will you be gone?" I asked.

"Three days. Maybe four. I plan to return on Monday. Tuesday at the latest."

"All right."

"All right to everything?" she said.

"Yes." I sighed. "I'll wait for you."

She rose from her chair, placed her hand in her pocket, and withdrew a key. She placed it on the writing table next to the diary.

"You may stay in the guest room at the top of the stairs if you wish."

I closed my hand over the key. "Thank you."

Abigail started to walk away. I wondered if she was heading to Maine. To Graham. To bail him out of some kind of trouble, perhaps?

I called her name and she turned.

"Is everything all right? Do you need help with anything?"

The corners of Abigail's mouth rose slightly. "No. Everything's not all right. But it's my problem to deal with. Thanks for asking, though. I'll see you when I return."

"Good-bye, Abigail."

As soon as Abigail was gone, I stood, covered the open diary with a plastic sheet, and gathered my things, including Abigail's key. I tossed the wet tissue into the trash and ran my hand lightly and lovingly across the diary as I stepped away from the table.

I was both anxious for and dreading the time I would spend with Mercy while she still lived. I couldn't wait for class to get out on Friday so I could rush over to Abigail's and work as much as I wanted.

No one showed me to the door.

I walked out into the autumn twilight and switched on my cell phone. I'd turned it off while I worked. Two voice mails waited for me.

The first was from my dad.

The second, from Clarissa's economics professor.

Twenty-Six

The professor's message was short and to the point. He'd learned from my roommate that I was working on the transcript of a diary written during the Salem witch trials. Clarissa had told him the diary's author was one of the women accused of witchcraft. He would very much like to talk to me about my work.

That's what he called it—my work.

Professor Turrell gave me his home phone number and e-mail address in addition to his number and e-mail on campus.

He sounded interested. He also sounded unconvinced the work I was doing was authentic. There was something in his tone that made me nervous. I didn't want to talk to him. Not yet.

Maybe not ever.

I drove to the dorm and made a mental list of all the reasons I could postpone calling him back.

I hadn't read the whole diary yet, so my "work" was incomplete at the moment.

I should ask Abigail's permission before speaking about the diary to a man writing a book. Even if he was a college professor.

I had no insights on how the Salem witch trials affected the colonists' economy.

I owed this man nothing.

My cell phone trilled as I composed the list. I reached for it with one hand while driving with the other. It was my mother.

"Didn't you get Dad's message?" she asked when I answered. No *hello*. No *how are you*. She sounded agitated.

"Sorry, Mom. I was working. I just got off."

"Well, he's been waiting all afternoon for you to call him back." She sounded on the verge of tears.

From somewhere behind her, I heard my dad say, "Julia, just give me the phone. It's not that big a deal."

"Yes. Yes, it is. It is a big deal." My mother began to cry. I negotiated a turn with one hand while trying to cradle the phone in the crook of my neck.

"Mom, what's going on?" I grabbed at the wheel as I swung wide, nearly hitting the curb.

"I knew something like this would happen. I knew it." Mom wasn't into theatrics, but something had her shaking with dread. And she wasn't talking to me anymore.

"Mom, please!" On impulse, I pulled into a grocery store parking lot and took the first available spot.

"Just let me have the phone, Jules." My dad's voice was near hers. I heard the phone exchanged from hand to another.

"Lauren."

"Dad! What's going on? What happened?"

"Nothing's happened. I just have to have surgery."

"Tell me," I said, hardly aware of having said those words, that way.

"I've got three blocked arteries. The doctors want to do a bypass. They told me it can't wait."

A wave of alarm sliced through me. For a brief moment, I saw Mercy weeping over the body of her dead father. I tossed the unwanted image from my mind.

"Dad," I finally managed to say, "when did all this happen?"

"Over the last fifty-two years."

"I'm serious."

"So am I. This has been waiting to happen for fifty-two years. It doesn't matter that I'm at the gym four days a week. It's just the way I'm wired, apparently."

I was still trying to process the idea that my father was ill. I couldn't wrap my brain around the thought. I had never known my dad to be sick. He got the occasional cold or sore throat, but he never spent a day at home in bed. It'd been years since he'd seen a doctor.

"When did you find out?"

"Today. I'd been feeling kind of crappy. Your mom made me make an appointment. I put it off as long as I could, so she's mad at me, of course."

"When are you having surgery?"

"Tuesday."

In five days.

"Do you want me to come?" I asked.

"On Tuesday? Your mother would probably appreciate it."

"I mean now."

"You don't have to come now. I'm going to have a very boring weekend sitting at home and trying not to take care of things at the office. Don't come for me, not this weekend. I wouldn't mind seeing you on Tuesday, though. I wouldn't mind that at all."

There was an inflection in his voice I hadn't heard before. He sounded afraid.

"I'll be there."

A moment of silence passed between us. Neither of us seemed to know how to segue into another topic following that one.

"Got a big weekend planned?" he finally asked.

"Abigail's going out of town. She left me the key to her place so I can work on the diary as much as I want. I'm almost finished."

"Still haven't convinced her to get it published, eh?"

"I think she needs to see it finished before she decides. I think there's something about how it ends that makes her unsure what to do."

"But I thought you knew how it ends. The girl gets hanged, right?"

I winced. "Yes."

"So?"

"I don't know, Dad. But I'll finish it this weekend, I think, and then maybe I'll know."

"Then, by all means, stay and finish it. When I see you on Tuesday, you can tell me all about it."

"Okay, Dad."

"Hey. Maybe I'd like to read it."

"Maybe."

"Think she'd let me?"

"No, actually. Not yet."

"Why not?"

In that little niche of time, while I sat in my car and talked to my dad, I saw for the first time that I was part of—for lack of a better title—a trinity of mortals. Me, Abigail, and Mercy. Until the diary was done, until I understood whatever it was that Abigail wanted me to understand, there would just be the three of us. Three women. Three daughters. Three searching hearts. Three destinies to be forged.

Just us three.

"Because it's too soon," I said.

My father said nothing for a moment.

"Well, when it's published, I'll read it," he said finally. "She won't be able to stop me then."

"If."

"When."

My mother asked for the phone back, so we said our good-byes. Mom asked me when I was coming, and I told her I'd be there Tuesday. She told me to drive carefully and to go to bed. I sounded tired.

But when I got back to the dorm a few minutes later, I didn't feel tired.

I felt alone. Completely isolated. I was in a circle of three that somehow cut me off from everyone and everything, even my father's illness.

Though it shamed me to admit it, I was relieved my dad didn't want me to come that weekend, that I would be able to finish the diary after all. Yet within the sense of relief was a thin layer of despondency. I would have been glad for Clarissa's silent company just to shake the chill of such strange solitude.

But she was gone, of course, and my room was tomb-like. I had no desire to go to the library or a coffee shop or anywhere else I would be with people but still alone.

I didn't want to be like Abigail who had no one or Mercy who had everything taken from her, including love.

I didn't want to wind up like either of them.

So I did something spontaneous and not like me at all.

I powered up my laptop, opened my e-mail inbox, and clicked on Raul's address.

My heart rate quickened as I began to type.

Hey, Raul:

Sorry to bother you. Just got some somewhat scary news from home and felt like telling someone. My dad has to have open-heart surgery on Tuesday. He makes it seem like it's a simple thing, like getting your wisdom teeth pulled, but I'm afraid for him. And for me. And my mom.

Hope you don't mind me dumping on you. Clarissa's not here and I just found out.

Been busy with school stuff and the diary. I've almost finished it. Such a sad story.

Hope you're having a good week.

Lauren

I read it twice, then changed "Lauren" to "Lars" and sent it. And immediately wished I hadn't.

I sat there for several long moments, looking at my screen,

wondering why I had done such a rash and irretrievable thing. I stood up, kicked off my shoes, and yanked my pajamas out of my dresser drawer. I was standing in my underwear when my computer chimed, letting me know I had a new e-mail message.

In near slow motion, I walked over to my laptop and peeked at the screen.

Raul had e-mailed me back.

> Hey, Lars.
>
> Good to hear from you. Sorry to hear about your dad. If it makes you feel any better, the stats are on your dad's side. I'm in the cardiovascular program here at Stanford, and I'm studying what doctors can do now with open-heart surgery. It's not as bad as it used to be. I'm sure your dad has a good doctor and will come through okay.
>
> But my prayers will be with you and your family nonetheless. Let me know how it goes.
>
> What will you do when you finish the diary?
>
> Take care,
>
> Raul

Cole hadn't told me his rich friend was going to be a doctor.

I didn't reply.

I didn't know what I'd do when I finished the diary.

Twenty~Seven

5 August 1692

George Burroughs has been sentenced to hang. He and five others. None of them are witches, I am certain of that. But they will hang as if they were.

10 August 1692

There is no word from Samuel.

John Peter does not come to the cottage anymore now that Papa is gone. I know why he does not. He is protecting my name. It is a very dear thing. I should be glad of it, but I am weighed down by loneliness.

I wish Papa had seen to my marriage before he left me.

I miss Papa.

I miss John Peter.

I miss being happy.

17 August 1692

I have not been to the Village since Papa's passing. I do not want the Village leaders to see me and remember that I am alone at the cottage. They will ask when Samuel will be here.

I have not heard from Samuel.

I have no more meat or potatoes or flour.

John Peter's sister, Sarah, brought me honey and some bread. She made the bread. John Peter sent the honey. She told me he was stung a dozen times getting it for me.

She asked about Samuel too.

I think John Peter may have asked her to ask. I can think of only one reason John Peter would want to know when Samuel will be here. He wants to talk to him. Ask him something.

It makes me smile just thinking of it.

The honey is as sweet as Heaven.

19 August 1692

George Burroughs and four others were hanged today. The innkeeper John Proctor was among them. His wife is still in prison, and in her womb, their child grows.

If I had not promised my papa I would attend, I would not have been anywhere near Gallows Hill today. I would not have heard the sound of the ropes pulling taut, the anguish in the throats of the innocent, or the awful silence when the ropes went still. I would have been in my tree writing a story about water nymphs and secret treasure. I would not have to wonder how to cleanse my mind of the five swinging bodies, the relaxed feet, the tilted heads, the slow swinging back and forth. God, help me.

Goody Trumball told me a petition signed by thirty-two persons and which attested to Rev. Burroughs's inno-

cence was brought before the court before his hanging. There would have been thirty-three signatures if Papa had been alive to sign it. I would have signed had I known about it, but Papa would not have wanted me to. And one of George Burroughs's accusers is said to have recanted. But Rev. Burroughs was hanged nonetheless.

As the noose was placed around his neck, George Burroughs looked out upon the crowd. He saw me. For a moment his eyes held mine, telling me to be brave. How did he know I was afraid? Then he opened his mouth and proclaimed his innocence to everyone. And after he had done this, he began to recite the Lord's Prayer. His voice was large and full, and as he spoke, the birds hushed to listen. The mouths of the villagers fell open as though they were struck dumb. Rev. Burroughs recited the prayer of the Lord in full, without hesitation, something we have been told a witch or wizard cannot do.

There was much rumbling in the crowd then, and for a moment I thought perhaps reason had broken through the cloud of deception. Perhaps the people could at last see Rev. Burroughs was not in league with the Devil after all. But then Cotton Mather jumped onto the platform so that all could see him and shouted that Rev. Burroughs had been convicted in a court of law, and that the Devil himself can appear as an angel of light. I looked away when the ropes fell.

The bodies were tossed down into the rocks like the others had been. I did not stay to watch. I felt eyes on me as I turned away. Goody Dawes. Goody Harding. Prudence's eyes. Esther's eyes. I heard Goody Harding whisper to Goody Camden that she knows my cousin Samuel has

*not arrived and it is a disgrace to the entire Village that
I live alone. I pretended I did not hear her.*

I did not see John Peter. But I did not look for him.

*I walked past the cemetery on my way back to the
cottage. Grass is starting to grow on Papa's grave. It is
hard to tell where new earth meets old.*

20 August 1692

*The air is thick with mosquitoes and heat and the
squeeze of death. Goody Trumball came by today with
a leg of lamb for me, and it was all I could do to look
at the bloody mass and take it with a grateful heart.*

*She asked if there was word from Samuel. She knew
I had not heard from him. If I had, I would have told
her the moment she stepped inside the cottage. She asked
because her husband will ask if she asked. Are people so
daft that they think a man on a ship gets letters by post
every nooning? Who can say if Samuel even knows Papa
has died? Perhaps he has not received my letter. Perhaps
his ship has not yet left Liverpool. Perhaps it will be
weeks before my letter finds him.*

*Goody Trumball told me I must stay with them
until Samuel comes. But I cannot leave the animals,
and the Trumballs do not have a barn big enough for
two of everything and two dozen more chickens. And
who is to say someone might not come and claim the
cottage as theirs while it stands empty? What would
Samuel do then, if he arrived to find I had lost all the
animals and left the cottage empty so that anyone could
take it?*

"*You cannot stay here alone,*" *Goody Trumball said,
her voice kind. But I told her I am not alone. I have Lily
the milk cow and Henry the goat and my father's horse
and all the chickens and the birds and the owl that lives
in the barn and all the fairies in the glen that I write
about. She did not want to hear about the fairies. She
bade me to silence.*

"*Do not speak of fairies and writing, Mercy, not
even to me,*" *she said. Her voice was then not so kind.*

She insists I come. What am I to do?

Evening

*Goody Trumball came back today with her husband to
fetch me. Goodman Trumball scarce spoke a word to me.
I told them that Samuel was surely on his way, though I
am sure of no such thing, but Goody Trumball was insistent. "What of the animals?" I said. Goody Trumball
said they would make room for Lily and Papa's horse,
but I would have to leave the goat and chickens. "You
can come at the nooning each day to feed and care for
them," Goody Trumball said.*

*I did not want to leave my cottage. I do not want to
share Goodman Trumball's home or board or the air he
breathes. But Goody Trumball took hold of my hands,
her eyes wet with tears, and told me it is unsafe for me
to be alone. I know not what she meant.*

There was nothing for it but to go with them.

*I had to carry all of Papa's books and Mama's little
wooden chest. Goody Trumball carried my winter cloak,
my woolen stockings, and the coverlet my mama made for*

*her wedding bed. Goodman Trumball carried nothing but
the horse's lead.*

*I carried my diary in the hidden pocket in my apron
with my quills and ink. But I left my book of stories
hidden in the barn. Henry the goat will watch over them.*

*I must sleep on the floor by the cooking fire because
Goody Trumball's two young boys have the ticking by the
back door. Goody Trumball and her husband have a room
of their own.*

*I found a quiet place behind the firs that rim the
Trumballs' property. There is a nest of rabbits here and
a family of sparrows. I am writing in this quiet place. I
shall give it a name so it will be real to me and will be
mine. I shall call it Remembrance so I shall not forget
what it is to be at peace.*

22 August 1692

*Goody Trumball spoke not a word to me today until
Goodman Trumball left the house and took their sons
with him. Then she drew me to the fire and spoke as
though the walls themselves might care to listen.*

*"You know good women sit in chains in Salem," she
said. "Once the accusers point a finger, there is no holding them back!"*

I nodded and told her I knew this.

*She leaned in and whispered, "Prudence Dawes told
her mother that you keep a book of stories, Mercy. She
told her mother it is your spell book! And that you cast
spells on her and Esther Harding to torment them. She
said your shape has appeared in the rafters of her house*

and that your shape has stood over her bed with pins to stab her. Mercy, I fear her mother shall take Prudence to the magistrates. I fear Prudence will tell the magistrates what she told her mother and she shall be believed."

I could summon no words. No thoughts. I could scarce imagine myself doing such things. I would have laughed had I not seen so many people hanging from ropes.

"Mercy, did you hear me?"

"I am no witch," I whispered, though in my head, I screamed it.

"Destroy the book, child!" Goody Trumball inclined her head toward the cooking fire. "Put it into the fire and destroy it!"

I pictured my story book in the flames, glowing, burning, disappearing. All my lovely words gone. I shuddered.

Goody Trumball took my shoulders and shook me. "Mercy! Give me the book. We must throw it into the fire. Do you not see? If there is no book, the charges cannot be proven. They will think Prudence lies. We must destroy the book."

Papa once told me I should burn every stick of furniture in the house to keep warm before burning a book. I should be willing to sit on stones in an empty house before burning a book.

"Mercy!"

"'Tis not here," I said. "I left it at my cottage."

Her eyes grew wide. "Where? Where did you leave it?"

"In the barn. With Henry."

"Henry?"

"My goat."

Goody Trumball closed her eyes as if they hurt. "Is it hidden?"

"Yes."

She opened her eyes again. "When you go there today to feed the chickens and care for the goat, you must take the book out of the barn and bury it away from the cottage. Then when it is safe, you shall bring the book here and we shall burn it. But only when I tell you it is safe. Do you understand?"

I nodded.

"Say nothing of the book to Goodman Trumball unless he asks you, child."

She said nothing else because Goodman Trumball came inside then and saw us sitting by the fire with no sewing or spinning, and he frowned at his wife. I made leave to muck out the barn but I am here in Remembrance with my quill and diary. I cannot let Goody Trumball know I have them. She does not know about the diary.

I must go. I do not know if I can do what Goody Trumball says. I can bury my book, but I do not know if I can burn it. It is all that I have left of my father. And my mother and Thomas.

Of me.

23 August 1692

Always before, the words would come faster than I could write them. But today I cannot order my thoughts.

I do not know if God has stepped in to protect me or if evil has stepped in to slay me.

The book is gone.

I did as Goody Trumball asked of me. I went to the cottage to fetch the book from the barn so I could bury it. But it was not there. Henry was there, and the chickens, but the book was gone.

Did God bend down from Heaven to hide it for me? Did He take it to some hidden place deep in the earth? Or did He burn it Himself with His fiery eye? Are my lovely stories smoke and ash in some holy hearth?

Or did someone take the book?

I do not know. I do not know.

How will I tell Goody Trumball the book is missing?

25 August 1692

I am again at the cottage. Goodman Trumball sent me home. Without Papa's horse. He let me take Lily, though.

This morning before anyone had broken their fast, Goodman Trumball said aloud, as if to a room of observers, that 'twas not wise for his growing sons to have a young woman in the house who be not their mother or sister. And so I should return home and await the arrival of my cousin Samuel from England. 'Tis plain as day he wishes me gone. But he wishes not to part with my father's horse. I care not. I am home.

Goody Trumball wept when I left, but she did not beg her husband to allow me to stay. The Trumball boys stood as still as statues. I offered my spinning top to the younger one, but he would not stretch out his hand to take it.

Again I carried the books and the little wooden chest. I put the coverlet on Lily's back and my winter cloak, too, since Goodman Trumball did not offer to assist me home.

Evening

I write by twilight so I form my letters in near darkness. My thoughts are flying every direction, and I know not what to make of them.

John Peter called on me today. He came on his horse, but stayed on his mount a stone's throw from the cottage and from there he beckoned me.

I came out of the cottage and bade him good day. I was so happy to see him. It was hard to walk out to him, as if he were only a neighbor come to bid me good day. I wanted to run. I offered him a drink from our well, but he just looked at me as if I had said nothing at all.

"Have you any other relatives in the colony, Mercy? Anyone at all?" he asked.

My first thought was that he wished to court me. With Samuel still away, he wanted to know whom he should ask, because he could wait no longer. I smiled at him. I could not help but smile at him. "I have Samuel, my cousin. He is expected home soon from England."

"There is no one else?" He did not smile back at me.

"I have an aunt in Maine, Samuel's mother, and three other cousins there."

"I will take you to them. Can you leave now?"

God forgive me, but I laughed. "I have not seen them in three winters, John Peter."

He swung down off his horse and walked toward me.
I saw so many things in his eyes as he closed the distance.
Affection. Hope. Longing. And fear.

"Let me take you to them, Mercy. Please." He
reached out to touch my shoulder. His fingers moved in
a caress that anyone standing in the clearing beyond us
would not see. The breath within me stilled.

I closed my eyes but for a moment, and when I opened
them, his head was inclined toward me, his eyes shiny as a
brook. "Please let me take you to them," he whispered.

I raised my hand to touch his fingers as they rested
on my shoulder. He took a step closer to me. I sensed his
dread, and in that moment, I knew.

God did not have my book of stories. The magistrates did.

"Are they coming for me?" I asked.

He nodded once.

"When?"

"On the morrow." He placed his other hand on my
shoulder and drew me to his chest. His arms enclosed
me tight. I leaned into that warm place between a
man's neck and chest where a turned head fits like a
glove. I could feel his chest rising and falling beneath
my cheek.

Time could have stopped for me then and I would not
have railed against it. I knew there would never be
another moment like that one, where every hope and longing within me was silenced by one embrace.

'Twas my falling tears that counted off the seconds,
reminding me time had not stopped but marched ever forward. If the magistrates found George Burroughs in

Maine, they could surely find me. And they would know who brought me there.

When I sensed John Peter was about to pull away and lift me onto his horse to flee, I spoke. "The magistrates will know I have an aunt in Maine, John. They will know Samuel makes his home there."

He hesitated only a moment. "Then I will take you somewhere they cannot find you."

Such wonderful words. Such unattainable words. I leaned heavily into him. "There is no such place."

"There are other colonies, Mercy. I will find a place."

"But I am innocent!" I looked up at him.

He cupped my face with his hands. "As was Rebecca Nurse! As was Elizabeth Howe and Susannah Martin! Reason does not reign in Salem, Mercy. Whatever one crazed soul can say about another is believed."

"Then why cannot I be believed as much as another?"

"Because 'tis easier to believe ill of someone than good."

I did not argue. I knew the moment he uttered it, 'twas true.

"Gather your belongings," he said in a voice as soft as bare feet on a dirt path. "I will come for you tonight when the moon is high. We will use darkness for cover. I will take you south instead of north. I will find a safe place." He touched my cheek, his fingertips brushing across wetness. I leaned into his hand.

He moved his palm to rest under my chin and tipped my face toward his own. He leaned over me and bent his head so that our cheekbones whispered against each other. His lips, warm and soft, met mine.

It lasted only a second, as gentle a kiss as the kind my mother lavished on me when she lived. And all the love I felt in my mother's kisses I felt in that kiss, and every dream I had ever spun between princes and princesses burst through the confines of story and met me in that moment. This was that divine pairing I saw between my papa and my mama and few others. This was that interlacing of body and soul that spoke of a deeper oneness I had but tasted. I know I will never love another.

John Peter stepped away from me—his hand on my chin the last part of him to leave me—and made for his horse.

"Do not be afraid," he said as he took to the saddle. "I will come for you."

"I will be waiting," said I.

He sped away, and I watched him go until the sound of his horse's hooves melted into the afternoon.

Even now, as night begins to swallow day, I can still feel his touch on my cheek, his lips on mine. I pray God will go with us tonight. I pray Papa would send me away on John Peter's horse were he here. I pray there is a place that is not consumed with madness.

I must prepare more ink. The hour grows late.

Twenty-Eight

I didn't want to stop reading. I didn't even want to take the time to transcribe the entries.

I would decipher several paragraphs and then realize I had typed nothing; I'd merely uncovered more of the story and devoured it. Countless times I had to go back and transcribe onto the laptop what I had already moved on from.

Mercy's penmanship in the diary had been exquisite up to that point. Any trouble I'd had reading her words had been because of age and wear, not from of any lack of skill on her part. But she had been in a rush with the August entries, and they were long, and perhaps she had tried to conserve her ink and paper. The sentences were crammed together, and the script was smaller than in her previous entries. I began working a little after eight on Friday night, but by 3:00 a.m. Saturday, my head ached from eyestrain.

Alone in Abigail's house, I went into the kitchen to look for Tylenol or Advil, fully intending to climb the stairs in search of the guest room Abigail had offered. But when I had taken something for my headache, I looked up at the dark staircase and the second floor, where Abigail's long, lonely life seemed to stretch into the next neighborhood, and I changed my mind. I went back into the library and its horde of books. I curled up on a leather sofa by the french doors that led to the patio and covered myself with a throw, hoping to rest for a few minutes.

But I fell asleep.

A hand touched my arm and my eyes flew open.

Esperanza stood over me. It was morning.

"Why didn't you sleep in the guest room? I changed the sheets for you."

I blinked and sat up, allowing the throw to fall away. "I wasn't planning on sleeping. I just stopped to take a rest."

"A rest? A rest from what?"

I looked over at the diary, open to August 25, 1692. Esperanza followed my gaze.

"That?" Her brown eyes widened.

"I'm almost done. I didn't want to stop."

Esperanza stared at the diary with something like disgust in her eyes.

"Have you read the diary, Esperanza?"

"No." Her answer was quick. "I don't want to read about witches."

I shifted my weight on the sofa and the leather squeaked. "But Mercy wasn't a witch."

"I don't want to read such a sad thing. Abigail used to read it, and it always made her sad. The world is sad enough. Especially her world." Esperanza started to walk away.

I jumped up. "Why did she stop reading it?"

"She doesn't talk to me about the diary, so I don't ask. Come. I make you breakfast."

I followed Esperanza out into the tiled entryway. I really wasn't hungry, but I had Esperanza all to myself. I didn't want to waste this moment.

"What happened to Abigail? Do you know why she didn't marry the man she loved?"

Esperanza looked back at me but kept walking toward the kitchen. "Why do you ask? This is the second time you ask me."

"Do you know?"

"I wasn't here when it happened, you know. I was just a baby. My parents were still living in Mexico."

"When what happened?"

"The war."

I almost skidded to a stop. "The war?"

"Sí." Esperanza kept walking.

"So was he in the army? Did he die in World War II?" Even as I asked, I knew that couldn't be the reason Abigail didn't marry him. She made it clear she'd made a choice. A choice she regretted. But perhaps she chose not to marry him *because* he went away to war. Maybe she was afraid to love a man who might die. So she said no. He left, met someone else, survived the war, and lived happily ever after with a woman who hadn't been afraid.

"He wasn't in the army." Esperanza stood at the fridge, opening its gleaming pewter-colored door and pulling out eggs.

I sat on a stool at the island in the middle of the kitchen. "But you said it had to do with the war."

"Like I said, I wasn't here. I just know what my mother told me, and she came to work for Abigail when I was ten. So it had been ten years already since the war." She placed a small skillet on the stove.

I leaned forward. "What happened?"

Esperanza tapped an egg on the side of a glass bowl and a stream of silvery white and yellow fell out of it soundlessly. "Well, Mr. Boyles had a gardener and the gardener had a son. Abigail and the gardener's son were friends. And then more than friends."

"And her father didn't approve," I said.

Esperanza broke another egg open and cocked her head. "What makes you say that?"

"Well, did he?"

She shrugged. "I don't know. My mother never mentioned Abigail's father knowing about his daughter and the gardener's son."

"So Abigail and the gardener's son fell in love," I said, trying to recapture the momentum.

"Sí. Well, he certainly fell in love with her."

"He asked her to marry him."

"And she turned him down," Esperanza finished. She whisked the eggs together.

"Because he was poor," I said, "and she was rich, right?"

Esperanza stopped beating the eggs. Her hand froze on the whisk and she looked up at me. "Because he was *poor?*" she asked, astonished.

I opened my mouth and then shut it.

Esperanza pressed her lips into a thin smile and resumed thrashing my eggs to a foamy mix. I had gotten something terribly wrong.

"That wasn't it?" I asked.

She laughed. "You people always think everything is about money."

"What?"

She lifted the whisk and gestured at me. "People with money always think everything revolves around money. Everything. Love, hate, desire, dreams."

I didn't know what to say. I wanted her to be wrong. Especially when it came to me, I wanted her to be wrong.

"So it had nothing to do with money?" I whispered.

Esperanza tossed a bit of water into my eggs. "Ever make an omelet?" she asked, ignoring my question.

I shook my head.

She stared at me for a moment. "Come. I'll show you."

I hesitated but got off the stool and came toward her. "You're not going to tell me now, are you?"

"Turn the heat down on that skillet," she said.

I obeyed.

She opened a drawer, lifted out a black-handled spatula, and handed it to me.

"I tell you what. You finish that diary. When you finish, I will tell you why Abigail said no. And then you can tell me why the diary makes her sad. I think that is why she doesn't read the diary anymore. It reminds her of the gardener's son. And I have always wondered why. You tell me what you know and I will tell you what I know. Deal?"

I took the spatula. "I guess so."

"*Bueno.* Now, the key to the omelet is the water. Only use a little. It makes the bubbles. The bubbles let the omelet breathe. No breath and we suffocate, no?" She brought a hand to her neck. "No breath, no life. No omelet."

Esperanza looked at the skillet and held her hand several inches above its hot surface to test the temperature. "Now we are ready."

Twenty-Nine

26 August 1692

I am ashamed to write what I must write. I can feel my cheeks burning with disgrace as I smooth the page and dip my quill. I am astonished I had the foresight to stow my quill and ink inside my hidden pocket with my diary as I prepared to escape with John Peter. Had I not, I would not be able to write this, though it shall pain me to do so. I would only be able to read what I had written before. And I have done that today, many times, reliving the moment John Peter kissed me. Torturing my heart and soul with that memory. There is pain either way.

I am ashamed because I know now that I am foolish. Last night, when the moon was high and the sound of horses' hooves came into the clearing, I dashed out of the cottage on wings of love instead of realizing John Peter would not chance such a noisy entrance. He would have carefully steered his mount toward the edge of the clearing, whispering gently to it so it would not so much as nicker.

Foolish girl that I am, I ran straight into the embrace of hell.

There were several men on horses, not just one. So stunned was I, so taken by my folly, I scarce heard the charges against me. I remember only snatches of the accusations. A book of witch's spells, which I had written and they now possessed, was their first charge, and the list of my evil dealings grew from there. My shape had appeared to Prudence Dawes and tortured her many times as I demanded she sign the Devil's book. I carried on with familiar spirits, with birds and animals, talking to them and causing them to do my evil bidding. Then they accused me of killing my father, of killing my mother and my brother Thomas, of killing James, my betrothed, so I could marry a demon instead. All of these nightmarish things I did out of allegiance to the Devil and for his benefit.

I should have demanded to know who could lay such charges against me. I should have declared my innocence with grace and dignity. But I was not prepared to hear such despicable things said of me. My eyes sought John Peter. Was he hiding in this crowd of men? Had he come to bear me away to some safe haven? Would he ride in on his horse and lift me onto it, and then gallop away as my accusers fought to grab the reins? I called his name as I moved about looking for him. Someone grabbed my arm. I turned and swung. Another arm came down hard across my chest. I tried to wriggle free. I bit and scratched and called John Peter's name. Then there was a bright stinging at the back of my head and I knew no more.

When I awoke, I was here. I felt the iron chain on my ankles first, then the brackish taste of blood in my mouth, then the chill of a stone floor.

Mary Easty is here. Martha Corey is here, in another room. There are others. They have all been charged with witchcraft.

And so have I.

The others watch me as I write. I cannot tell what they are thinking. Mary Easty said when I am done writing I should hide the diary in the straw where I sleep. She said it isn't safe for me to keep it in my secret pocket.

There is only a little sunlight each day in this cell. It falls across the stone floor in the late afternoon hours. So I am told. I do not know. It is only my first day.

29 August 1692

I am tired. I do not want to write, but I must. I was brought before the magistrates today to be examined. They laid their charges against me. I prayed to God to give me a clear voice and sound mind to answer them, because as I looked at those mere men, I could see they did not wish evil against me. They simply believe what has been said of me is true.

They do not design evil, but they do not recognize it, either.

They brought forth my storybook and bade me explain how I came by such spells. I asked how they came by property that did not belong to them. But they would not answer me this.

"How came you by these spells?" the magistrates asked.

"Read the pages and you will see they are naught but stories," said I.

"Stories of the Devil!" said one.

"Nay, stories of simple things: fairies and woodlands and princesses."

"And talking birds!" said another.

" 'Tis only a story," said I. "Aesop told a story of a talking lion and a talking mouse and no charge of devilment was laid upon him. Christ the Lord told stories!"

"Do not take the name of the Lord in vain, woman!"

"I do not take it in vain. The parables of Christ are stories."

"There are no parables of Christ in this book. Who taught you to write such stories?"

"No one taught me. They came from within me."

"From the Devil!"

"No!"

"Why do you torture Prudence Dawes?"

"I torture no one!"

"The shape of Mercy Hayworth appeared to her above her bed and bade her sign the Devil's book."

"I know nothing of the Devil's book, and I have never been in Goodman Dawes' house."

"And what of your familiar spirits?"

"I know of no spirits."

"You speak unto birds."

And on it went.

I answered every charge and still they came at me with more. And more and more.

When I thought at last they were through with me, I heard noise at the back of the meeting room and then the voice of goodness. I shuddered to hear it.

"She is no witch!"

John Peter.

He was bid to be silent. He shouted all the more. I dared not turn to look at him.

"She is no witch. She is no witch! If Mercy Hayworth be a witch, then so am I. So be all of you!"

My heart quaked within me. I saw the eyes of the magistrates narrow as they glared at John Peter where he spoke far behind me. I could see their thoughts aligning. He who defends a witch...

I could not keep the tears from coming. And still I dared not turn to look at him, not with love in my eyes. He shouted again that I was not a witch. I saw Prudence turn her head from John Peter to me, and then I heard him being escorted out of the room, shouting my innocence all the way.

Prudence dropped to the floor and began to writhe in front of me.

"She bites me! She pinches me! She chokes me!" Prudence screamed.

"Why do you torture this girl?" the magistrates asked.

But I could not speak. Two words tumbled about my head and within my anguished heart, and I would not say them.

John Peter. John Peter.

I cannot write anymore. The light has the left the room.

30 August 1692

Shame is again keeping me warm in this dank cell. Today I was made to strip naked before old women and midwives who poked and prodded the secret parts of my body, looking for a Devil's teat, for some abnormal protrusion where I suckle familiar spirits to nourish them and become one with them. My stomach churns just writing the words. I could barely stand while these women moved about their task, these women whom I have known all my life.

One of them, Widow Treaves, guided me from my mother's womb eighteen summers before, washed the body she now hovered over. She brought forth Thomas as well. And the tiny sister that did not live. The widow's eyes met mine for only a second, and in those gray pools she said to me, "What else can I do? I am bade to look."

They made much of a little brown circle under my arm, a tiny thing the color of tree bark. I have always had it. Mama told me long ago it was a kiss from God given to me as I left Heaven to be her little girl.

One of the old women asked me what it was. I told her. The women looked at one another, clearly measuring the truth of my words. I should have said it was naught but a spot I had long forgot I had. They believed it was a kiss, but not from God.

If this were not agony enough, the women in my cell whisper that John Peter has come under the eye of the magistrates. Prudence will certainly not accuse him; she is enamored of him. But she does not have to accuse him. There were plenty of observers in the meetinghouse who heard him defend my honor. He who defends a witch...

I am awash in troubling thoughts.

I cannot write anymore. I must save my ink.

1 September 1692

My worst fears are taking form. John Peter is to be examined. If the magistrates believe me a witch, there is no hope for him.

If I confess I am a witch, they will let me live. But I am not. How can I say I am a witch when I am not?

*And if I confess, John Peter will be in greater danger. If
I do not confess and yet am found a witch, he will face
the same fate as long as he defends me.*

*And he will defend me. This I know with all my heart.
There is only one way to save him.*

If I can find a way to get a letter to the magistrates...

*I cannot use more ink for my own thoughts. There is
something else I must write.*

God be with me.

2 September 1692

*The deed is done. The letter has been written. I pray the
magistrates care only about its contents and nothing for its
author. I pray that what has so easily been believed before
will be believed yet again. It should not prove difficult.*

3 September 1692

*I was brought before the magistrates today. I should have
been trembling, but I saw they had my letter and their
eyes were fierce with dismay. They believed the letter. Its
words, untidily formed and misspelled so they would not
be recognized as mine, had done what I asked of them.
They fed the madness.*

*It was easy to give the letter to another girl in
the cell with me. I bade her drop it on the floor of the
meetinghouse when she was called to be examined and
to let no one see it dropped. I told her a life would be
saved if she did this. She agreed.*

When I stood before them, the magistrates glared at

me. One of them held my letter in his hands. "Why do you bewitch John Peter Collier?" he asked.

I said nothing.

"By which spell in your book do you bewitch him?"

Again I was silent.

"We have come by a letter, the writer much afraid to state his name for fear you will bewitch him as well. The writer has heard you gloating over your witchcraft and your power over John Peter Collier. You have bewitched him! Confess it!"

I could not answer yes. I could not answer no. So I gave them the answer they truly wanted to hear.

"I am no witch."

And then I did something I knew would seal John Peter's fate.

And my own.

I fiddled with the brown spot under my arm. The magistrates saw it. So did the women who examined me.

John Peter is safe.

5 September 1692

The girl who carried my letter knows Prudence Dawes. She asked me what I had done to Prudence to torture her.

I told her I loved the man Prudence loved.

Evening

What would we do for love?

Would we imagine we are pricked with pins and blades? Would we writhe on meeting room floors, desperate to believe our challenger is indeed evil?

*Would we convince ourselves that what could be true
is true?*

*Would we write letters damning ourselves to save the
beloved?*

Yes.

6 September 1692

*Someone said John Peter demanded to see me, but he is
believed to be held captive by my evil spells, and he was
sent home.*

9 September 1692

*We were sent for. They lined us up and pronounced their
judgments. I am to be hanged. Goody Corey, Goody
Easty, and four others as well. I do not know what else
to write. When I try to form letters, I see only the face
of John Peter.*

*I should have liked to be in his embrace one more time.
But then I would want it again after that. As I do now.*

10 September 1692

*I dreamt last night of the rope tight around my neck.
I could not breathe. I could not take in air to scream.
I felt the hand of evil upon me, pulling on the rope.
I awoke to the whispered shouts of the women in my
cell who share my fate.*

*"Wake up, Mercy," said Goody Easty. " 'Tis only
a dream."*

Sleep would not return to me.

11 September 1692

I am making a list of what awaits me. The list does not begin with the rope.

    1. The Lord Jesus

    2. Mama

    3. Papa

    4. Thomas

    5. My baby sister

    6. Heaven

    7. Peace

    I do not hate Prudence Dawes. If I hate her I cannot set my mind on these seven things. Is Prudence Dawes evil? No, I think not. She has been deceived. She truly believes I am a witch. She can believe it because she wants it to be true. She loves John Peter.

    The magistrates do not love John Peter, but they love believing themselves in the right. And they fear the responsibility that is akin to being right.

13 September 1692

John Peter came to the cell last night. I heard his voice at the window above our heads, the one where sunlight visits us. He called my name. I could not see him, it was too dark and the window too high. I could only see his hand reaching through the tiny opening. I wanted to run to him, but my chains would not let me. I could only reach up to his fingertips and touch them with my own.

    "Are you warm? Are you fed?" he asked. "Have

they hurt you?" His voice was strange, like he was swallowing shouts of rage.

His fingers were warm. I thought of how these fingers reached for the straw in my hair, how they dried my wet hands the day my papa died, how they rested under my chin the day he kissed me.

"Mercy, do you hear me?" he asked.

"Yes, always, John Peter."

"I will not let them harm you!" he said, his voice racked with anger.

I could say nothing. I made my fingers kiss his.

"I will not let them!"

And then there were other voices outside the window, and his fingers were snatched away from mine. I heard him cry out my name as the jailers dragged him from the window.

Mercy.

Mercy.

Mercy.

Sleep runs from me.

17 September 1692

Nine more are to be hanged. There is weeping all around me. And anger. And fear.

I close my eyes and see my writing tree. Lily. Henry. I see the little copse of firs at the Trumballs' cottage, the place I called Remembrance, where I promised I would remember peace.

I don't know what has become of the animals. Papa's books, Mama's coverlet. The cottage.

210 SUSAN MEISSNER

Goody Easty told me the property has been seized. What a strange word. As if my home and its contents were scurrying away in the night and the sheriff apprehended them in an exhausting chase.

There is no word from Samuel. I wonder if he knows I await my execution.

What could he do?

Nothing.

'Twould be best if he came not at all.

I dreamt of John Peter last night. We were on his horse heading south. To the safe place.

21 September 1692

It is cold. I cannot feel my toes. And I am thirsty.

There is but a shaft of cold sunlight left to me so I must write quickly. Our jailers delighted in telling us today that Goodman Corey refused to answer the charges against him. He refused to play to the crowd's intrigue. So they laid great stones upon his chest, willing him to cry out his innocence or guilt. He would not. More and more stones were placed upon him until his bones were crushed within him and he died, unable even to scream out in pain.

Goody Easty told me a hanging lasts but seconds. "Be glad we shall not be pressed to death or burned. Goodman Corey suffered for two days." She is trying to be strong for me. Martha Corey, Giles Corey's wife, is in another cell nearby, and I hear her weeping. I wonder if she has heard everything we have heard today.

Goodman Corey was an old man. Eighty years if a day.

I cannot rid my mind of those two words: *confess* and *live*. The harder I try to sweep them away, the more they stand their ground in my spinning head.

Will I have one last chance to confess? To give the accusers what they want—my very soul?

I am no witch. I shall not live as one.

And I shall not die as one.

Here is a new thought. Here is what I ponder hour after hour in this darkness.

There is no escaping what awaits me. I will hang. God knows I will hang.

But I fear the anguish. I am afraid for Prudence. John Peter...

One thing remains that I can do, even in chains.

The ink is nearly gone. Is there enough? Do I have enough?

Yes.

There is a new girl chained to the wall with me. She has not yet been examined. The evidence against her is weak. Perhaps she will not be found guilty. Her name is Benevolence and she is twelve, the age I was when Mama and Thomas flew to Jesus. I will hand her my diary, if she is willing, and will bid her, upon her release, to see that it is delivered to John Peter. I wish him to know that I chose. That there was a choice, and I chose mercy.

I pray he will forgive me.

And I pray God will have mercy on my soul.

I am ready.

Thirty

I was alone in Abigail's house when I completed the diary. It was early Sunday, between two and three in the morning. I had finished reading the diary well before then, but my mind refused to be a dictation machine and simply decipher and type. I read, digested, pondered, and then typed.

It was the only way to get through it.

I read the final three words a dozen times before committing them to digitized image.

I am ready.

I am ready.

Ready for what? Ready to hang? Ready for something else? What had Mercy done in the last few hours accorded to her? What took the last of her ink?

She could have written another letter. Is that what she meant by, "one thing remains that I can do, even in chains"? Did she pen a letter of forgiveness to her accusers? If so, what happened to it? If she slipped it into the diary, which was given to John Peter, did it fall upon him to give the letter to the magistrates?

Or was the letter written to Prudence Dawes? Perhaps that was why Mercy prayed John Peter would forgive her—her last act of mercy was to write a letter of absolution to the woman responsible for her execution. And John Peter, the man who loved Mercy and for whom she had given her life, had been called upon to deliver it.

What had she been afraid of?

My head spun with wanting to know exactly what happened after Mercy ran out of ink.

After she ran out of time.

The diary didn't say, but I was certain Abigail knew what Mercy had done with her last hours. Abigail knew I would have questions.

And she asked me to wait until she returned to learn the answers. That meant if I wanted, I could probably find the answers somewhere else. Mercy Hayworth's name was no doubt floating around Internet search engines just like Sarah Goode's and Sarah Osborne's. Would I be able to keep myself from looking until Abigail's return?

I didn't know if I could.

I wondered how long it would take to find out what Mercy had done. It likely wouldn't be mentioned in the legal documents relative to her execution. So who could have known about what she had done in the last hours? Someone in the jail cell with her would have known. Someone like Elizabeth Proctor, whose own hanging had been postponed because she was pregnant. Someone who might have told someone else, and the story of Mercy's last deed had carried through the decades and centuries.

The possibilities made my head ache, but this time I was too tired to go into the kitchen and take something for it. I crept over to the sofa like I had done the night before and curled up on noisy leather cushions.

I was afraid to fall asleep, though I was exhausted. I was afraid I would dream of her. And I was sure that not knowing the last few details of Mercy's life would feed the dream machine in my head.

But I couldn't keep my eyes open.

As I lay there, warding off thoughts of hooded men and a wooden platform and a loop of rough rope, I made myself think about what I *did* know. I was fairly certain I had an answer for Esperanza. I knew why reading the diary made Abigail sad, made her think of the gardener's son.

Mercy had given all for love. Her very life.

Abigail had given away nothing. I didn't know why. Maybe it wasn't about money, like Esperanza said, but surely there had to be a question of status. Abigail was an heiress. The man who proposed to her was the son of a gardener. Abigail must have felt obligated to choose between the life she knew and the man she loved. I was convinced Abigail now saw her choice as incredibly selfish and damning, and so every time she read the diary, every time she came to face to face with what Mercy had done for love, Abigail was reminded of the mistake she made.

That much I was sure of.

I let my eyelids close and felt my body relax. I tried to think of happy things like the ocean at dawn, hydrangea blossoms, and walking the aisles of a three-story bookstore with an iced mocha in my hand.

Sleep overcame me within seconds.

I did not dream.

<hr />

I was startled awake the next morning by the high-pitched trilling of my cell phone. I jumped from the couch, unable to remember why I wasn't in my own bed, convinced it was the middle of the night and something bad had happened. I lunged for my phone on the table next to me and answered, not thinking to see who was calling.

"Yes?" I said, groggy with sleep.

"Hi. This is Steve Turrell. I'm a professor at UCSB. Is this Lauren Durough?"

"Oh. Um, yeah."

"Did I call too early? Clarissa said you usually go to a nine thirty church service, so I thought I'd catch you before you left. Sorry if I woke you."

"No. No, I was awake," I lied. "Look, I'm sorry I haven't called you back. I hadn't finished the diary yet and I…"

"So you've finished it?"

"Yes. Last night."

"Is it really a diary written during the Salem witch trials?"

"Yes, it really is."

"And the author herself was one of those accused of witchcraft?"

"Yes."

"Wow. That's amazing. And the woman you work for just has this diary in her house?"

"She's taken excellent care of it. It belonged to an ancestor of hers so it has"—I searched for the right word—"a lot of sentimental value."

"Well, the reason I asked Clarissa for your number is I'm writing a book about the effects of stigmatization on culture and economy. I've always been fascinated by what transpired during the Salem witch trials, even before I started writing the book. I'd really like to see this diary. Would that be possible?"

I cleared my throat for no particular reason. "It's not mine to show. I could give Abigail your number and she could get back with you on that. She's out of town right now. She's pretty protective of it, though."

"But you've transcribed it, right?"

"Yes."

"Well, could I see the transcription in the meantime?"

I looked down at my feet and noticed I was pacing between the sofa and the writing desk. I stopped.

"I think we'd better wait until Abigail returns," I said.

Professor Turrell paused a moment. "Could I ask you about the content?"

"I...I don't know. I guess."

"What's the name of the diary's author?"

I hesitated to say her name. Would Abigail want me to? Would I be divulging something I shouldn't? Mercy was a historical figure. She was surely mentioned in other records and historical accounts.

But I didn't say it. If this man was fascinated by the Salem witch tri-als, then surely he knew more than I did. He might know what I wanted to know. Or he might know where to go to find out.

"Professor Turrell, have you studied the Salem witch trials?" I asked instead of answering his question.

"Yes, I have."

"Could I ask you a few questions too? There's something about how the diary ends that intrigues me."

"Yeah, sure. Do you want to meet? I could show you what I've col-lected so far in my research." He sounded excited. Hopeful.

"I would like that. The sooner, the better."

"Okay. Tomorrow after my last class? That would be a few minutes after three."

"Actually, I'd like to see you today, if that's possible. It probably sounds crazy, but there's something I need to know. It might take me days to find what I need on my own, and I can't wait."

"And it's about the diary?"

"Yes."

"Want to tell me her name?"

"Can I see you today?"

"I can meet you at my office on campus in an hour. Is that good enough?"

"Yes," I said. "Her name is Mercy Hayworth."

"Mercy Hayworth."

"Yes."

"See you in an hour."

Thirty-One

P rofessor Turrell was in his early thirties—younger than I thought he'd be—and rail thin. He wore holey jeans and a faded striped dress shirt that probably looked nice with a tie before the hue had faded from pristine white to ash. His hair was cut short and gelled into chaotically neat peaks on top of his head.

He welcomed me into his office in North Hall, which was eerily quiet, and I could tell he had already gone to some effort to create space on his desk to show me his research.

"Sorry about the mess," he said, as he scooped up a pile of essays from the extra chair in his office and flung them onto a credenza along the wall.

I eased into the chair and watched him toss books from his desk onto the floor at his feet. If I had majored in economics like my dad wanted, I'd have had Professor Turrell for a class or two, and perhaps one of my essays would've been in that clutch of papers resting atop copies of *The Wall Street Journal* and *Forbes* magazine.

"Okay," he said, having cleared a path to his computer monitor, which he switched on. "I've got several files going on the trials: a couple for my book and a couple just because the incident interests me. Most of what I have is on the trials that occurred in Salem itself, in particular the people who were executed, so I may not be able to answer all your questions. I can try, though."

"All right."

He turned to me. "First, is Mercy's diary legible? Were you able to transcribe the entire document word for word?"

"Yes, pretty much. Many pages were difficult to read, but I took my time and I think I was able to come up with a reasonably accurate transcription. Some of the ink has faded and portions of the parchment are damaged. But Abigail helped me, and most of the time we could see where Mercy was going even if a sentence or two was missing or faded beyond reading."

"Wow. That's really great."

I could see how anxious Professor Turrell was to read Mercy's diary. How envious he was that I had spent so much time with it.

"And you found it be historically accurate?" he continued.

"Well, I guess it is. Mercy wrote it as she saw everything happening around her. I have no reason to think her dates are wrong, but I suppose she could've written something on the tenth of August that actually happened on the eleventh. Nobody's perfect."

"No, certainly. And she lived in Salem Village, right? I've done a search for her name in my documents and it comes up a couple times. She was accused in late summer of 1692 and stood trial the first week in September. Does that sound right?"

"Yes. Yes, I think so. You really don't have much on her? Nothing about her diary or her story book or letters she wrote?"

Professor Turrell's fingers flew over his computer keyboard.

"She was arrested and taken to Salem Town. She was examined the same time as Mary Easty and that whole lot."

"Yes, that's correct."

"I have some of the transcript of her examination. I can e-mail that to you if you want. She was accused by a girl named Prudence Dawes. Does that sound right?"

"Yes, that's right." It was strange to hear Professor Turrell say names that had become as familiar to me as character names in a novel. But this had been real.

"I don't see much else," he said. "I'd have to do some digging to find more on her. Her name doesn't come up as often as some of the others. What exactly are you looking for?"

"In the diary, she mentions doing something the day before her execution, and I just wanted to know if maybe she had written a letter to—"

Professor Turrell interrupted me. "Did you say execution?"

"Yes."

"Mercy Hayworth wasn't executed."

"Yes, she was."

"She was convicted and sentenced to hang, but she died in prison. She wasn't executed."

A warm sensation like walking from an air-conditioned room into summer heat swept over me. What Professor Turrell was saying was impossible. His data was wrong. He had made a mistake.

"Yes, she was," I said.

"There were a lot of people accused of witchcraft back then, more than a hundred, but only nineteen were hanged. She's not one of the nineteen."

"She had to be," I whispered. Relief that Mercy had not been executed after all should have flooded my soul, but instead raw disappointment enveloped me. I had been tricked.

Professor Turrell looked pained, like he hated telling the naive sophomore she had her facts mixed up. "I can show you the list of nineteen names. She's not on it."

"Are you sure it's an accurate list?" I asked.

"This list is everywhere, Lauren. It's in books, it's on the Internet. Haven't you done any research on your own?"

I closed my eyes as the heat of embarrassment assailed me.

"I promised Abigail I wouldn't," I whispered. "She wanted me to wait until I had finished the diary."

"I see. And she's the one who told you Mercy was executed?"

"Yes."

"I wonder why she did that." Professor Turrell stared at his computer screen. Then he turned to me. "What else did she tell you?"

"I...I don't know. Nothing else, I guess. Everything I know about Mercy I read in the diary. And I know the diary is real. It's authentic. I know it is!"

"Oh, I don't doubt the diary is real. It probably really is Mercy Hayworth's diary, and it's still an amazing artifact. And of course Mercy couldn't possibly have written how she died. When she stopped writing, she was scheduled to hang. But she died before that happened."

"Does it say how she died?" The words shot out of my mouth. Embarrassment had given way to anger.

"I don't have that in my notes. I... We could do some research and find out. It might take a while, but we could probably do it. She must've been ill when she was arrested."

"She wasn't ill."

"She might've been. Conditions in the Salem jails weren't that great. Other people died in them, and the colonies were plagued with sickness all the time."

"Mercy wasn't ill. She would've written about it if she were. She didn't die because she was sick. She *did* something the night before she was to be hanged."

"What could she have done? Are you thinking she tried to escape?"

Mercy hadn't tried to escape. I was sure of that. But what if John Peter tried to break her out?

"What if someone helped her escape?" I asked, thinking out loud more than anything.

"The records say she died in prison."

"What if that's just what was said? What if she really did escape?" I sounded like a fool.

"There was a body," the professor said, still in that gentle voice of an educator revealing hard truth to the ignorant. "She was buried. She didn't escape, Lauren. Mercy Hayworth died in prison the day before her execution."

I felt sick to my stomach. I felt stupid. "Are you sure she's not on that list?"

Professor Turrell clicked a couple keys on his computer and sat back in his chair. He gestured with his hand, inviting me to see for myself. I leaned in, squinted, and read the names, whispering them.

Hanged on June 10

   Bridget Bishop, Salem

Hanged on July 19

   Sarah Goode, Salem Village

   Rebecca Nurse, Salem Village

   Susannah Martin, Amesbury

   Elizabeth Howe, Ipswich

   Sarah Wilds, Topsfield

Hanged on August 19

   George Burroughs, Wells, Maine

   John Proctor, Salem Village

   John Willard, Salem Village

   George Jacobs Sr., Salem Town

   Martha Carrier, Andover

September 19

   Giles Corey, Salem Farms, pressed to death

Hanged on September 22

   Martha Corey, Salem Farms

Mary Easty, Topsfield
Alice Parker, Salem Town
Ann Pudeater, Salem Town
Margaret Scott, Rowley
Wilmott Reed, Marblehead
Samuel Wardwell, Andover
Mary Parker, Andover

Mercy Hayworth's name wasn't there.
Abigail had lied to me.

Thirty-Two

I left Professor Turrell's office in a fog of disbelief. My thoughts were in a tumble. Why had Abigail lied? Why had she told me Mercy was executed when she really died in prison? Had she lied to me about other things?

And I couldn't accept the truth that Mercy hadn't been executed on Gallows Hill, even though she never deserved to be there. I'd envisioned the tragedy of her wrongful execution from the first moment I saw her handwriting. The others who'd been examined and convicted the same day as Mercy had met their sad end at the gallows. But not Mercy. I'd read the list of names three times. Professor Turrell even produced for me another list from another source. And another one from one of the books lying at his feet.

He wanted to see the diary more than ever. He asked me again if I would show it to him, and a war of wills broke out in my head.

I would show it to him.

I wouldn't show it to him.

I would.

I would not.

He asked if he could at least see a copy of the transcription. I told him I didn't have a copy and a wave of surprise washed over his face.

Professor Turrell had tipped his head in a thoughtful way and then leaned forward. "Do you have a thumb drive?"

"Yes."

"You should make a copy for yourself. You've done all the transcription work on your own, right?"

"Yes, I did."

"I can pretty much guarantee that if the diary is genuine…"

"It is genuine."

"My publisher will want it."

Professor Turrell had paused to let that notion sink in.

"It should be published," he continued. "That period of history is significant. What happened in Salem was tragic and astonishing."

"That doesn't sound like a book about economics," I said, a moment later.

"I'm not talking about my book. I'm talking about yours. The diary. It should be published."

I left a few minutes later, promising to return with the transcript on a thumb drive. He assured me that while I was gone, he would scour the Internet and the UC library system for the truth about Mercy Hayworth's death.

I went straight to my dorm room to get the thumb drive from my desk. It had taken me just seconds to rationalize what I was about to do. Making a copy of the transcription made perfect sense. It was an act of protection for me and the diary.

Clarissa was still asleep—in my bed, actually—and wearing her clothes from the night before. She stirred when she heard me rummaging through my desk drawer.

"You didn't come home last night, naughty girl," she mumbled.

"You're in my bed, do you know that?" I closed my hand around my silver-toned thumb drive.

"Yours is closer to the door."

I slipped the thumb drive into my purse. "Did you see if I was in my bed before you fell in it?"

"Don't shout." Clarissa screwed her eyes shut. "It was this morning already. I knew you hadn't slept here. Ugh. My brain feels like it's a thousand times too big for my head. God, I hate hangovers."

I grabbed an unopened water bottle off my desk and a bottle of Tylenol. I handed them to her. "You shouldn't drink so much, Clarissa."

She hesitated, then took the water and pills from me. "I know."

I turned to leave.

"If you're going to church, you can pray for my wretched soul," she said, popping two capsules in her mouth and taking a swig from the bottle.

I moved past her. "I missed church. I am going to Abigail's to take care of something."

A moment of silence passed, and I decided to tell her.

"I finished the diary last night, Clarissa."

"Hallelujah. No more witches."

"But Mercy wasn't a—"

"I know, I know. She wasn't a witch."

Clarissa pulled my blanket over her head and curled into a fetal position.

I closed the door quietly behind me.

I was disappointed to see Esperanza's car in the driveway when I arrived at Abigail's. What I needed to do would only take a few seconds. I had a key. Esperanza wouldn't have to let me in or out.

But I still wished she wasn't there.

I opened the front door and made for the library.

Everything was as I had left it an hour and a half before. I turned on the laptop and waited impatiently for it to boot up. I heard footsteps above me on the second floor. I fished for the thumb drive in my purse and inserted it into the USB port, all while tapping a nervous foot.

The footsteps were getting louder. Esperanza was coming down the stairs.

I quickly copied the transcription from the laptop's hard drive to the thumb drive. The footsteps sounded in the tiled entry. I removed the thumb drive, tossing it into my purse as Esperanza stepped into the library.

"Good morning, Esperanza," I said, feigning a casual manner.

She looked surprised to see me. "Are you here to work this morning?"

"No, actually, I'm not. I finished the diary last night. I, uh, just forgot something. I'm on my way out."

"Abigail is back. She'd like to see you."

It was only Sunday.

"When did she get back?" I asked.

"Not long ago. She got an earlier flight. The taxi just dropped her off. She called me at home."

Abigail was back. I was both scared and eager to confront her with her lies, but I thought I'd have another day to decide what I would say to her.

"She saw your car though the window. She'd like to see you," Esperanza said again.

"I'd like to see her too."

"She'll meet you on the patio." Esperanza stepped back from the doorway so I could walk past her.

"All right."

She watched me as I left.

I walked into the dining room, through the open french doors, and cautiously peered out onto the patio.

Abigail wasn't there yet.

I sighed and took a chair at the glass-topped table.

I breathed slowly, telling myself I would not raise my voice or let Abigail know how much she had hurt me. I would state the facts simply and ask for an explanation. Surely I was owed that much.

Several long minutes passed before I heard movement behind me. I turned. Abigail was framed in the doorway to the patio. She looked like she had aged a year or more in the three days she had been gone. If I hadn't been so mad at her, I would have asked if she was all right.

My surprise at her appearance must have been obvious. Her wan smile tugged at me.

"The early flight out of Boston is hard on a girl." She stepped onto the patio, walked over to the table, and took the chair across from mine.

"You're home early," I said.

"Yes."

Esperanza appeared with a coffee tray. She set it down and poured a cup for each of us.

"Thank you, Esperanza. You don't have to stay. I'm sure you'd rather be home with your family."

Esperanza looked from me to Abigail. "What about your lunch, señorita?" she said.

"I'll be fine. I ate on the plane. Please, Esperanza. It's Sunday. Go home to your family."

Esperanza hesitated. She caught my gaze and I knew she was trying to communicate something to me, but I didn't know what it was. She turned to Abigail.

"All right. But call me if you need me. Arturo and I have no plans today."

"I will."

Esperanza left, and we were alone. I didn't know how to begin. Or where.

Abigail began for me.

"You've finished the diary," she said simply.

"I did. Last night."

"And I suppose you have questions."

"I have a lot of questions."

Abigail picked up her coffee cup. "What would you like to know?" She was the picture of calm. Exhausted, but calm. Smug, even. She brought the coffee cup to her lips. My hastily hatched plan to stay unruffled began to fall apart.

"I'd like to know why you lied to me."

She raised her eyes over the rim of her cup and blinked at me, then brought the cup slowly down to its saucer.

"Why I *lied* to you?" she said.

"Yes. I'd like to know why you lied to me."

She hesitated for only a moment. "And what makes you think I lied to you?"

My foot resumed a nervous tap dance under the table and I fought to still it. "You told me Mercy was executed. She wasn't. She died in prison. That sounds like a lie to me."

Disappointment flooded Abigail's face. Disappointment and hurt. I knew that feeling. I had felt it just hours before, as I sat in Professor Turrell's office.

"Where did you come by such information?" she asked, exhaling heavily.

"What difference does that make? It's true, isn't it? You lied to me. I'd like to know why."

"Oh, it does matter. I said you would have questions when you finished the diary. I asked you to wait until I returned to find the answers. You told me you would. That sounds like you lied to *me*."

"But I…" I couldn't finish.

"You couldn't wait? You couldn't wait a day or two? You wouldn't have needed to wait even that. You finished last night and here I am!"

"But why did you let me believe she was executed when she wasn't?" I raised my voice, even though I had promised myself I wouldn't.

"I never asked you to believe anything. What you believed about Mercy was what you chose to believe."

"But you knew I was under the impression she had been executed. You knew that's what I thought! You made sure of it."

For a moment, she said nothing.

"Where did you go to find out what you couldn't wait to find out?" she finally asked.

I was silent.

"Where? Where did you learn this?"

"A professor at the college."

"A professor at the college? You've been talking to a professor at the college? Does he know about the diary?" Abigail looked stunned.

"Look, you never said the diary was a secret. And yes, he knows about the diary. So do my parents. So do my roommate and my cousins. You never said I couldn't tell anyone about it."

"Why this professor? Why him?"

I fidgeted in my chair and the metal made a whining sound. "He asked about it. He's writing a book about stigma and culture and economics and I don't know what else, but he's done research on the Salem witch trials. My roommate told him I was working on your diary. He wanted to talk to me."

"He's writing a book?" Abigail tossed the words out as if they tasted bad.

"He asked to see the diary, Abigail, and I told him it wasn't mine to show. I told him he'd have to talk to you and that you'd be gone until maybe Tuesday. I didn't do anything wrong."

She sat back in her chair. "You told me you would wait for me."

I sat back in mine. "You told me Mercy was hanged."

We stared at each other, both of us angry and disillusioned, for several long, silent moments.

"I just want to know why you lied to me," I finally said, removing any anger from voice but letting the hurt come through.

Abigail slowly stood. "I'd like to be alone now."

I stood too. "I think after all the work I've done, I deserve an answer. I think I deserve to know how Mercy died."

"You?" She stared at me. "You deserve an answer?" She turned and began to walk away.

"Yes!" I shouted. "I cared about her, Abigail. I even dreamed about her. I think I deserve to know!"

Abigail turned to face me. "I didn't lie to you. I swear to God, I didn't."

She stepped into the dining room and disappeared down the hall.

I stood there, unable to let myself out of the house, unable to accept the fact that Abigail must be crazy. She had to be.

Surely Abigail had seen the same list I had.

If Abigail truly believed she hadn't lied to me, then she must also believe Mercy Hayworth was the twentieth person hanged as a witch in Salem in 1692.

But there were only nineteen names on the list.

What Abigail believed was impossible.

I made my way back into the house. Abigail was nowhere to be seen. I went into the library, hovered over the diary for a moment, then carefully placed it back inside its protective covering. I eased it into its foam-padded box and closed the top. It was almost like putting Mercy in a casket, closing the lid, and saying good-bye.

I didn't know what to expect from Abigail. Were we finished? Did she want me to come back and proof the transcript? Print it out for her? But how could we even consider publishing it without including how Mercy died? And how could I convince Abigail that Mercy never saw the hangman's noose?

Hopefully Professor Turrell would be able to dig up the truth. In the meantime, I wanted to keep the lines of communication with Abigail open. I grabbed a piece of paper off the writing desk and wrote a quick note:

Abigail:

I'm very sorry I didn't wait for you. I hope you can forgive me. I want to finish this project for you and talk with you about what you can do with it now that the transcription is done. Call me when you're ready.

Lauren

I turned off the computer, closed it, and placed the note on top.

I drove back to campus, but Professor Turrell had left. Maybe just for lunch?

I decided to go to a church and pray for my dad's surgery since I had missed church that morning. Then I'd come back to North Hall and see if Professor Turrell had returned or if I had misjudged his interest in the diary. I reached into my purse to touch the thumb drive, the only part of the diary left to me.

I couldn't find it. I dug around inside my purse, dumped the contents onto the passenger seat, and prodded every inch of fabric. But it wasn't there.

The thumb drive was gone.

Thirty-Three

At first I didn't know what to do. After several frustrating moments in my car, I decided I should at least leave a message for Professor Turrell.

I wrote a quick note telling him I had been unable to get the copy of the transcription that day but I would try again and let him know as soon as I had it. I tacked it to his office door.

Then I pondered whether or not I should buy a new thumb drive, go back to Abigail's, tell her I wanted to fix a few things in the transcription, and copy it again. But if she had already seen my note, she knew I'd left the next move up to her. And if *she* took the thumb drive, there was no way I could go back there and pretend she hadn't.

But I didn't think Abigail had taken it. I was pretty sure it was Esperanza.

She came into the library as I tossed the thumb drive into my purse. Esperanza had seen me put it in there, had told me Abigail wanted to meet with me, and then stood at the door to the library instead of showing me out to the patio. As soon as I was in the dining room, she must have walked over to my purse and taken the thumb drive.

But why?

Esperanza had never read the diary. She didn't like it. Didn't like what it stood for.

And yet she had taken the thumb drive.

I couldn't go back to Abigail's, but I could try to find Esperanza.

It wasn't hard to locate Esperanza's address. I remembered her last name, and she had given me her husband's name on the patio: Arturo. There was only one Arturo De Salvo in the Santa Barbara phone book.

Her condo was easy to find too. Perched on a hill within a couple blocks of the ocean, Esperanza and Arturo lived in a rather stylish townhouse. Small, but nicely landscaped and well cared for.

I rang her doorbell and prayed silently for wisdom. I didn't want to say anything I would regret.

When the door opened and Esperanza saw me through the screen door, her eyes grew wide and she said something in Spanish.

"Hello, Esperanza."

"Why are you here? Something happen to Miss Abigail?"

"No. Nothing's happened to Abigail."

The look of panic fell away but her eyes were still wide. "Then why are you here?"

"I think you may have something that belongs to me," I said as nicely as I could.

Esperanza just looked at me through the screen.

"Please, Esperanza. I need it for school. It has assignments on it." That was partly true. I did need it for school, but I didn't have any current assignments saved on it.

"I don't have it," she said simply.

"I think you do."

"No, I don't. I gave it to Abigail. Before she came out to you on the patio."

"Why did you do that?" I didn't try to hide my frustration.

"Because the diary is hers. You can't take a copy for you. And I know that's what you did with that little silver thing. You can't do that."

"That little silver thing is mine!"

"But the diary is Miss Abigail's. You can't take it. Abigail has been very good to me and my family for many years. She bought for me and Arturo this lovely house. She helped send our children to college. She pays for Arturo's insulin. There is nothing I wouldn't do for her. I take care of her like she takes care of me. That is why I took it."

I sighed. "I wasn't going to do anything with it."

"Then you can ask her for it yourself. Ask her for copy. Don't just take it."

Esperanza was right. I should have asked. Abigail might have said yes. Not now of course, but before the argument on the patio, she might have.

"Is that why you were trying to get my attention this morning, when Abigail told you to go home?" I asked.

"No. I didn't think she should be left alone. I didn't know how long you'd be staying."

"What do you mean?"

Esperanza hesitated a moment and then swung open the screen door. "You want to come in?"

I stepped inside.

Esperanza's living room was decorated in bright oranges and greens, and tiled in soft beige. Lingering aromas of cumin and garlic wafted around the room. "Please, sit down," she said.

I took a seat on an ivory-hued sofa. Esperanza sat next to me.

"I'm worried about Abigail," she said. "She came home early from Maine, she looks very tired, and I think she had to give Graham more money. I think maybe he's in over his head. I don't know. But she's not herself these days."

"Do you know why she came home early?"

"No. She didn't tell me. But I think she left because they argued. They don't get along, those two. They never have."

Guilt crept across me. I had seen how sad Abigail looked when she walked out onto the patio. I'd been too mad to consider showing her any compassion, too sure she had purposely misled me. And then I had accused her of lying to me while she probably had my thumb drive in her pocket, a stolen copy of her diary tucked in its memory.

"Should I go back over there?" I asked Esperanza.

"I think maybe I should."

"I want to come with you. I…I owe Abigail an apology."

She shrugged. "I guess you can come with me. I'll tell Arturo where I'm going."

Esperanza was only gone a moment or two.

"Let me drive," I said. "I don't mind bringing you back here later."

Esperanza nodded, and we started for the front door.

"Why does Abigail feel like she has such an obligation to take care of Graham financially?" I asked. "Is he ill?"

Esperanza held the door open for me. "Graham is not ill. Graham is addicted. To money and gambling."

"And Abigail feels obligated to bail him out? Every time?"

"If he were my son, I would not do for him what she has done. She gives him too much. He takes advantage of her."

We walked across carefully laid paving stones to my car.

"Did Abigail promise Dorothea she'd take care of him or something?" I asked.

Esperanza stopped and looked at me. "Dorothea?"

Her surprised look startled me. "Isn't Graham her cousin Dorothea's son?"

Esperanza tossed her head back. "Ay yi yi. I thought you knew. Graham is hers. Graham is her son."

"Her son?" I gasped.

Esperanza looked off toward the ocean, probably wondering how much she should say. Then she turned to me. "She married a man long after the gardener's son moved away. His name was Edward Swift and he had a boy named Graham. Mama told me Abigail was quite a bit older than Edward. His wife had died in childbirth. Abigail adopted Graham and they lived in the Santa Barbara house with Mr. Boyles. Edward and her father argued about everything. My mother told me Abigail tried to make the marriage work but she didn't really love Edward. Edward loved the money, but I don't think he loved Abigail. He had some money of his own when they married, but he lost it. I don't know how. A bad investment of some kind. Graham was *un mocoso*—a brat. I remember him. He was older than me and I was afraid of him. And Edward had other women. Many, I hear. The marriage did not last. Mr. Boyles had made Edward sign an agreement—what is it called?"

"A prenuptial agreement?"

"Sí. So Edward, he got none of Abigail's money. But Abigail had adopted that little boy, and you don't divorce a child. Edward found a new rich lady to take him in, but Abigail, she's been paying for Graham ever since."

We resumed walking to my car. "That's such a sad story."

"This is why she tells me, she tells you, she wishes she had married the gardener's son. Even if it would have been hard, even if she had to move, even if she lost her rich friends. At least she would have love. And love you can't put price on, no? No price for it."

"Would she really have lost all her rich friends? Would she really have had to move?" I asked. Were people in her circle of friends that shallow?

"Maybe. I don't know. My mama said it would have been very hard. But my mama could see he loved her. And Abigail seemed fond of him. But I guess she didn't love him enough."

"Why would it have been so hard? Just because Abigail had money?"

Esperanza frowned at me and huffed. "I told you this wasn't about money!"

"Well, what was it about?" I felt like I had been sent to the corner.

"The gardener's son was Japanese. They fell in love during World War II, *comprende*? But after Pearl Harbor the gardener and his son were sent to an internment camp, even though they had had both been born in California, in San Francisco. No one trusted Japanese Americans then. My mama told me Miss Abigail decided she could not bear the stig... What is word? Stig..."

I closed my eyes. "Stigma."

"Stigma, sí. She let him go. She turned him down. And then she never found another man who loved her like he did. The gardener's son had done nothing wrong. Nothing. But he was Japanese. Now *that* is a sad story."

We stood at my car, but neither one of us got in.

"After the war, did she see him again?" I asked, though I think I knew already Abigail hadn't.

"I don't know. My mama didn't think so. Abigail was alone in that house with her father for twenty years before she met Edward. I think she had given up on marriage. Then Edward came along and, ay yi yi, nothing but trouble."

"So Abigail doesn't know what became of the gardener's son?"

"I don't think so."

Such a wasted life. No wonder reading the diary was too painful for Abigail. Mercy's life had been wasted too, but in a completely different way.

"What was his name?" I asked. "Do you know?"

"How come you want to know?"

I shrugged. "I don't know."

"Give me your cell phone."

I handed it to her across the car. Esperanza punched in a few numbers and a few seconds later began speaking in rapid Spanish. I understood only a few words. Mama, Abigail, *novio*. Boyfriend. She hung up and handed the phone back to me.

"Mama remembered his name. It was Tomoharu Kimura. Miss Abigail called him Tom."

≈≈≈

A few minutes later, we were at Abigail's front door, letting ourselves in.

"I'll go see if she is sleeping. You wait, okay?" Esperanza took the stairs.

I wandered into the library and saw that Abigail had removed the box that held the diary. She must have put it away.

The laptop was gone too.

That surprised me. The transcription hadn't been proofed yet. I had only just finished it. It was probably littered with typos and grammatical mistakes.

A tiny sliver of fear worked its way through my body as I stood there looking at the empty writing desk. No diary. No laptop.

And no thumb drive.

Abigail, what have you done?

I heard hurried footsteps on the stairs. A moment later, Esperanza appeared at the doorway to the library and confirmed what I suddenly knew was true.

Abigail had gone.

She had taken the laptop and the diary.

And left not so much as a sticky note telling us where she had gone.

Thirty-Four

There was nothing I could do but go to class the next day and see if Esperanza called to tell me Abigail had returned.

She didn't call.

I felt like I had been robbed. The diary wasn't mine, and technically I had finished the work I was hired to do. Abigail owed me a bit of money, but that was all. She didn't owe me anything else.

Except perhaps a new thumb drive.

It shouldn't have mattered that she'd disappeared with the laptop and the diary and left no way of reaching her. Esperanza said Abigail didn't carry a cell phone and she didn't drive. Wherever she had gone, she had called a taxi to take her there, and we had no reason to call the police. She was a grown woman in a right state of mind, and she could do what she wanted.

But it did matter. It mattered to me.

I saw Professor Turrell on campus late Monday afternoon, and I told him what had happened to the thumb drive. He found Abigail's sudden disappearance with the diary, its transcription, and my thumb drive troubling. He asked me to tell him what Mercy wrote in the last entry before she died. I had read that entry many times. Fragments of those sentences flitted about my memory and I repeated them back to him.

There is no escaping what awaits me. God knows I will hang.

But I fear the anguish. I am afraid for Prudence.

John Peter...

One thing remains that I can do, even in chains.
The ink is nearly gone. Is there enough?

Professor Turrell asked who John Peter was, and I told him how John Peter came under suspicion because he defended Mercy after her arrest. I described how she wrote the incriminating letter, how she fiddled with the mole on her arm during her examination, and how she had silently convinced the magistrates she had bewitched John Peter. She convinced them John Peter was innocent by persuading them of her own guilt.

"What do you suppose she wrote?" Professor Turrell asked.

"I don't know. Maybe a letter of forgiveness to her accusers? Prudence Dawes, especially."

Professor Turrell rubbed his hand absently across his stubbled chin. "I have a friend at Boston University who's looking into this for me. He should be getting back to me today or tomorrow. You going to be around?"

I told him I'd be at Good Samaritan Hospital in Los Angeles while my dad had bypass surgery. I told him to call me.

I drove to my parents' house Monday night, played a game of chess with my dad before bed—which I won fair and square—and woke up at 5:00 a.m. Tuesday to go with them to the hospital. The hospital wanted my dad there by 6:00 a.m.

Once there, my mother couldn't sit still, and I refused to pace the room with her. Uncle Loring and Aunt Denise arrived just before Dad was taken to surgery, and Denise joined my mother in her tireless pacing of my dad's room. Uncle Loring looked pale and uptight, and Denise told me my dad's heart condition was brought on by hereditary causes and Loring feared he'd be next.

Mom cried when the nurses arrived to take Dad to the operating room. Aunt Denise held her, and Dad told her he wanted lobster for dinner on Friday.

"Without the drawn butter," I said to him. He smiled at me. Then he grabbed for my hand, and I saw again the flicker of true fear in his eyes. He squeezed my hand and locked his eyes onto mine. He opened his mouth, and I could almost hear him start to say, *If anything should happen,* but I squeezed back and met his gaze.

"Without the drawn butter," he said.

And then he was whisked away.

The first two hours went by quickly, but then the novelty of courageous waiting began to wear off. Mom and Aunt Denise left to pace the entire third floor. Just as they rounded a corner and walked out of sight, I heard my uncle, who sat behind me, get to his feet and say, "You made it!"

I turned to see who he was talking to. Standing next to him was Cole.

And Raul.

"So it's going okay?" Cole asked.

I couldn't believe he was there. I knew Cole was close to my dad, and that of Loring's four sons, Cole was the one most like him. There were times growing up that I was a little jealous of Cole's fondness for my father and the return admiration my dad had for him.

But it was my dad in surgery, not his. And it was just after ten in the morning, which meant they had flown down in Raul's plane.

I stood up.

"Hello, Lauren," Raul said. His voice was polite, as always. Today he wore a simple T-shirt.

"Hi," I said back.

"So, where are we? How's it going?" Cole looked impatiently from his dad to me.

"We're probably past the halfway mark," my uncle said. "It's been three hours already. They told us it could take four to six."

"Okay. Good. So Raul and I have time to get some breakfast?"

"I would think so. Cafeteria's in the basement."

"Cool. Hey, Lars." Cole turned to leave. "Okay. Let's get a bite."

Raul turned too and then turned back. "Can we get you anything?" he asked me.

"I'm good," my uncle said, settling back into his chair.

Raul kept his eyes on me.

"No. Thanks anyway," I said.

He smiled and turned to follow Cole, who had already walked away and been caught in an embrace by his mother. My mom and aunt had returned from their first lap around the cardiac unit.

I watched as Cole and Raul disappeared down the hallway.

My mother and aunt continued to close the distance between us.

"He is such a nice young man," Denise said.

"Oh, I know. So polite," my mom replied.

"No kidding. He could give Cole a few lessons on how to behave around people. Isn't that true, Lauren?" Denise said to me. "Cole is so oblivious to other people."

"We're talking about Raul," my mother said.

"Yes," I replied.

"He's so sweet," Denise said, looking at me.

"Uh-huh."

"You know," Denise continued, in a softer voice. "Cole said Raul is simply brilliant. An IQ you wouldn't believe. And he's not even Asian."

I glanced about to see if anyone had heard her, though Denise practically whispered this.

Not even Asian.

Yep, Raul was the most polite, rich, brilliant Hispanic man I'd ever met.

My mom and my aunt continued their nervous stroll. I plopped down on the chair next to my uncle.

"Want some of the paper?" he asked, holding out the business section of the *L.A. Times*.

"No, thanks."

I reached into my purse and pulled out *My Ántonia*. Abigail had recommended it.

Half an hour later Raul and Cole came back. They took two chairs opposite my uncle and me, next to my mother and aunt. Mom and Denise were taking a break from pacing. I looked up when Cole sat down, and Raul nodded at me. He had a textbook in his hands.

"Test day after tomorrow," he said when he saw me looking at his book.

"Mmm."

He looked at the book I held. "For a class?"

"No. Abigail thought I'd like it."

"Did you finish that diary of hers?"

"Yes. I did."

"Congratulations. That must feel pretty good."

I had no idea what to say to that. "Um. Yeah. Thanks."

He opened his book. Next to him, Cole slouched in his chair, folded his arms across his chest, and closed his eyes. "Somebody wake me up when it's over," he said, yawning.

"I hope you're not missing anything important by skipping class today," my aunt said to Raul, leaning forward in her chair so she could see him.

"Oh, I'll be fine," he said. "I can get the notes from a buddy of mine."

"Like you need to study anything," Cole said, eyes closed.

"Well, it was very nice of you to come down," my mother chimed in. "I know it means a lot to Bryant to have us all here waiting and praying for him."

"It's my pleasure," Raul said.

"So you really came all this way to bring Cole down?" It was out of my mouth before I even considered why I said it.

Raul looked a bit surprised. "Yeah. But I don't mind. We're only missing one class today. One important one, anyway."

"And it's such nice weather for flying." I couldn't stop myself from saying that, either.

Raul stared at me. "Are you okay?" he mouthed.

Somehow he saw through me, saw that I was struggling to figure out why he was there. Thank God he couldn't see I was fighting an attraction to him—an attraction everyone in my father's world would applaud. Raul was rich, brilliant, and a true gentleman. He met every Durough expectation. I didn't want to do what everyone expected me to do. I think deep down I wanted to fall in love with a poor man so I could prove to everyone it wasn't about the money. Not for me.

I looked to see if anyone else noticed what Raul had asked me. But Cole was already falling asleep, my uncle had his nose buried in the newspaper, and my aunt was showing my mother an article in a *People* magazine.

Was I okay?

I shrugged. "Sometimes," I whispered.

His grin was soft, measured. Polite.

My cell phone began to vibrate. I took it out of my purse and looked at the screen. Professor Turrell was calling me. I excused myself and walked down the hallway to a set of windows by the elevator and away from the cardiac unit.

"Hello, Professor," I said.

"Steve."

"What?"

"You can just call me Steve."

"Oh. All right."

"I just got a call from that friend of mine at Boston University. He made some calls and had someone look into the jail records and other historical accounts. I finally have an answer for you."

"Tell me."

"Mercy Hayworth committed suicide."

Thirty-Five

I heard what Professor Turrell said. I heard every word. But I still made him repeat it.

"She committed suicide. She hanged herself in jail."

"I don't... I just... How?" I stammered.

"The record my friend found states she tore her apron and dress into shreds, tied the shreds together, and made a noose. She looped it over a rafter and stood on a wooden bench. When she was ready, she kicked the bench over."

"And no one heard her? No one tried to stop her?"

"She did it in the middle of the night. There's a letter in a Gloucester museum from a woman who was also arrested for witchcraft and in the Salem jail when Mercy died. She wrote to her sister after her release that one of her cellmates hanged herself. That cellmate was Mercy Hayworth. This woman wrote that she awoke when the bench hit the floor, and so did some of the other women, Mary Easty being one of them. But they couldn't reach the noose, and they couldn't get the bench back underneath Mercy's feet. Not in time to save her."

"But she had leg chains!" I said.

"Apparently they were long enough."

Images of Mercy swinging from a prison rafter from the remnants of her apron—the apron in which she hid her diary until she gave it away—invaded my mind. I wanted to sweep them away, wash them away, but they wouldn't leave. I leaned my head against the window.

"Why did she do that?" I whispered to no one.

But Professor Turrell heard me and assumed I was asking him. "Well, she could've decided to just get it over with by herself instead of being subjected to the spectacle of a public execution."

"I just don't... This isn't how I pictured it."

"She was probably distraught. Perhaps suicide seemed the easier way to go. Or maybe she wanted to deny her accusers the satisfaction of seeing her executed."

I sighed, letting my forehead rest against the cool glass. No. Mercy's last act had something to do with ink and everything to do with self-lessness. That was Mercy's way.

She wrote something to someone in her last hours. She had a plan. She hadn't been distraught.

I am ready.

Professor Turrell interrupted my thoughts. "Listen, my editor wants to see the diary. He wants your transcription, too. By this time next year you could have a book on the front table at Barnes & Noble. I can tell you right now mine won't be there. It will be in the back with all the other boring business books."

"I don't have it."

"I know you don't, but you should try to get it back. The diary should be published. It's a great story."

"It's a tragic story."

"Which is what makes it great. You're a lit major. You know exactly what I mean. I think it's kind of poetic what she did, and I'm only an econ prof."

"Poetic."

"Or something like that."

Two tears slipped from my eyes and slid down my cheeks. I had been moved by Mercy. I was baffled by her and awed by her. She had changed nothing and changed everything.

And Abigail had told the truth all along.

She told me Mercy died a needless death. That she had been unjustly tried, convicted, and sentenced. That the verdict had been execution by hanging.

And that Mercy died by hanging on September 22, 1692.

All true.

"Look, I've got class," Professor Turrell said when I said nothing. "If you want, call me when you get your thumb drive back. My editor said he'd come talk to Abigail in person if the diary is genuine."

"I already told you it's genuine."

"He needs to see it. He wants to see it."

"If I hear from her, I'll call you."

"Sounds good."

"Tell your Boston friend thanks."

"Will do."

We said good-bye. I shut my phone and turned my body so that the back of my head rested against the window. I wanted to reach across the ages. I wanted to fold time in two, slide myself into that jail cell, and bring Mercy back with me, alive. I wanted to know what it was like to see the world the way Mercy saw it. I closed my eyes for a moment, and when I opened them, I looked over at my family at the far end of the corridor. They were all absorbed in their own thoughts.

Except Raul. His book lay open on his lap, but he was staring at me.

I met his gaze for only a moment. Then I turned toward the elevators, the cafeteria, and momentary anonymity.

Raul followed me to the elevator doors. When I lifted my finger from the down button, he was at my side.

"You okay?" His polite tone was laced with concern.

"Yeah." Our eyes met for a second, and I looked away.

"I'm sure your dad's going to pull through this just fine. He's relatively young, in great physical shape, and this is a really good hospital."

I felt my face warm. I didn't know how to tell him I wasn't thinking about my dad at all. It was demoralizing enough just realizing it.

His hand reached out and I felt his fingers gently land on my shoulder. "You don't believe me?" He bent his head to catch my gaze.

"No. I mean, yes, I do believe you. I just…"

Raul waited. His thumb caressed the skin below the bones of my shoulder. I shivered.

"I just…"

I couldn't tell him my anxious thoughts were tumbling around in the seventeenth century instead of in the present, where my dad lay in an operating room, his chest splayed open.

Raul moved his hand away quickly, like he had read my thoughts and was ashamed of me. I looked up, startled to see that the elevator doors were open and had probably been open for several seconds. Raul held them for me. I forgot where I'd been headed.

I stared at the doors.

"Still want to go down?" he asked.

From somewhere deep inside me, my frustration burst through.

"I don't know what I want."

The minute I said it, I wished I hadn't. Those words had nothing to do with whether I still wanted to go to the cafeteria or not, and we both knew it.

For a second we were both silent.

"I really think everything's going to work out just fine. Most of the time it does." Raul's voice was gentle. He could have asked about the phone call, why it had moved me tears, why I was so torn between two warring concerns. But he didn't. It was one of the kindest things anyone had ever done for me.

He pulled his hand away and the doors swished closed, the car empty. "Want to pace?" He smiled.

I smiled back.

We walked the floor eight times.

Raul told me about growing up in Guadalajara. There was a lot to tell. I only had to listen.

Six and half hours after surgery began, we were told Dad was in recovery, heavily sedated and intubated, but doing well. We had been told at the five-hour mark that it was taking longer than expected and that we needed to just sit tight. My mother and Denise practically jogged the cardiac unit that last hour.

The surgeon suggested we wait to see him until the following day since he was sedated. My mom was allowed in for a few minutes, and I was told I could visit first thing in the morning.

Cole and Raul weren't allowed to see Dad because they weren't immediate family, and since they had to get back to Palo Alto, they got ready to leave.

"Want to take us back to the airport, Lars? I've borrowed a car from a friend of mine here, and he needs it to get to work. We'll need a ride from his place."

Cole didn't wait for me to answer. He just hugged his mom and mine and started for the elevators.

"Do you mind?" Raul asked.

"No," I said. I had nothing better to do. My aunt and uncle agreed to wait for my mom and take her home so I could use my parents' car.

Cole chattered the whole way to the municipal airport, expelling the nervous energy he had stored up in case something bad happened during the surgery. When we got to the airfield, Raul went inside the main building to okay his flight plan. I stood outside with Cole and waited. Behind the fence lay a sea of white and cream planes with splashes of color on their wings and sides.

"Which one is Raul's?" I asked.

"Huh?"

"Which plane is Raul's?"

"Oh." Cole pointed to a plane across the Tarmac with a bold blue stripe on the cockpit door. "That one. But it's not his."

"His is broken?"

"What?"

"Why aren't you in his plane?"

Cole made a face at me. "Raul doesn't have a plane. Did he tell you that plane was his?"

My face grew hot.

"Man, are you gullible, Lars. Good one, Raul." He laughed.

"Raul doesn't have a plane?"

Cole laughed harder. "I'm so sure! No, he doesn't have a plane. He has a pilot's license, though. At least he told me he does."

"Whose plane is that then?"

"A friend of my dad's at the West Valley Flying Club. He lets us borrow it for hardly anything, 'cause he hasn't been able to fly it in a while. He only charges us for the fuel. He likes Raul. Everybody likes Raul. And Raul takes good care of the plane."

"So Raul rented that plane."

"No, not rented. Borrowed."

The warmth continued to spread across my face and neck. I felt like I was melting.

Cole cocked his head at me. "Besides, Raul can't *rent* a plane. Do you know how much it would cost to rent a plane, Lars?"

I couldn't say anything.

"Okay, well, you and I don't have to worry about money but some people do. Raul can't afford to rent a plane whenever I want to come home. You think everybody's made of money?"

No, no, no.

"I just thought… I mean, he's at Stanford…"

"On a scholarship and student loans."

"He wore such nice shirts when you guys came home."

"What? Oh. Those were *my* shirts, Lauren. He borrowed them because he wanted to look nice while he was here. Man, are you red. People will think you spent the day at the beach instead of the hospital. I do believe you're embarrassed."

I wanted to rub the red and the heat away. I didn't want Raul to see me shamed out of my wits. I had done it again, done exactly what I loathed. Assumed I knew everything and was wrong all the way around.

"I can't believe I did that," I muttered.

"Me neither. You were always the nice one."

I looked at Cole. "Don't tell him, please?"

"Tell him what?" Cole's eyes danced with glee.

"Please, Cole, don't tell him!"

"Don't tell him you don't like him now that you know he's not rich?"

"That's not true, Cole. Don't you dare tell him that! I swear to God that's not true!"

"Yeah, right."

"Cole, please."

"I'll think about it."

I leaned against my car, wanting to dissolve into the warm metal. I wanted to leave. I didn't want to wait for Raul. And yet I did.

"Why did you guys even come?" I moaned.

Cole blinked. "Well, I came for my parents and for your dad."

"And you just used Raul as your personal taxi driver?"

He laughed, but it was a sour laugh. I didn't like it. "You really are dense, Lars. Wake up. Raul didn't come to be my chauffeur."

I met his eyes and waited for him to tell me.

"Raul said you e-mailed him and told him your dad was going to have surgery and that you were afraid." Cole folded his arms across his chest and leaned back against my mother's car. "He came for you."

Thirty-Six

I slept in the guest room by the little library. I don't know why. When my mom went up to bed a little after nine, I went into my bedroom, grabbed my overnight bag, and headed up to the third floor. I poked around in the library for a while, sat at my old writing desk awhile longer, and then climbed into a bed I had never slept in and begged sleep to take me to a place where I didn't have to think about who I really was.

For so long I had imagined I was different, that money wasn't important to me, that I was a new kind of Durough. I didn't evaluate people or tasks or ideas by their monetary worth. I was above all that.

I wasn't the person my dad was.

I was someone else.

I was someone worse.

I did evaluate people and ideas by their monetary worth, but I pretended I didn't. And that was worse.

I had judged Abigail that way. And Clarissa. And the gardener's son. And Raul.

Sleep didn't come for a long time.

I woke early, before the sun. My dreams were unremembered, but they left me unsettled and on edge. I didn't want to remember them.

I made my own breakfast, drank several cups of coffee, and waited for the day to break. As soon as the sky turned from pink to amber, I left a note for my mother apologizing for going to the hospital without her but I couldn't wait to see Dad. I knew she would at least be happy to hear that. I promised to come back and get her if she didn't want to drive down herself.

I wondered if I would collect frowns from the nursing staff for showing up so early, but no one seemed to mind that I had come before visitors typically showed up. Perhaps they thought I had camped out the night before in the waiting room like others had done.

My father had a restful night, the nurses said, which meant he did not burst his stitches or spike a fever or slip into cardiac arrest. He was barely awake when I stepped into his room. The breathing tube had been removed, and when he saw me, a quiver of a smile broke across his face.

"Lauren," he whispered.

"Shhh. I know it probably hurts to talk, Dad."

"It's not so bad," he croaked.

I took the seat next to his bed and ran my hand across his. He grabbed for my fingers.

"Does it hurt?" I asked.

He cracked another smile. "I've felt better."

"You've looked better," I whispered back and the smile increased before it fell away. He didn't have the strength to keep it.

"I was afraid," he whispered.

"What's that?"

"I was afraid I wouldn't wake up."

I didn't know what to say.

"I think maybe I was gone for a few minutes," he continued.

My heart stuttered. "What?"

"Just for few minutes. Don't tell your mother."

Another prancing beat. "But Dad, your doctor said you came through just fine."

"It wasn't during the surgery. It was afterward, in that hot, white room. I felt like I was slipping away, like I was leaving you. Leaving you all."

I stroked his hand and said nothing. My heart pounded.

"And do you know what I was thinking?" His hand stirred under mine.

"Tell me." My two-word answer was a whisper.

"That I hadn't done enough. I was afraid I'd see my father and he would know I hadn't done enough."

My grandfather, who I barely remembered because he died when I was six, came to the forefront of my mind as I sat with my father's hand under mine. I remembered my grandfather in snapshot images, moments of video when he waved the camera away while he puffed on a pipe. I remembered thinking he looked like Winston Churchill. I remembered him wearing gray suits and smelling of pine.

I remembered being afraid of him.

Charles Durough was a stranger to me. Not a mean or hostile stranger, but a stranger nonetheless. My father never talked much about Grandpa. I always thought he and my dad were just men who kept their feelings to themselves.

"What do you mean you hadn't done enough?" I asked.

"Duroughs have to make something of ourselves, don't we? We have to take the tobacco and the gold nugget and make something of ourselves. And we can't stop."

His voice fell away.

"Can't stop what?" I whispered. But I knew. In that moment I knew what my father feared more than anything, and it had nothing to do with money. He feared he wouldn't measure up.

I had underestimated everyone.

Everything I believed about my dad and me and the Durough legacy fell away, and the truth suddenly became crystal clear.

My father wasn't driven by a relentless desire to amass wealth. He was driven to please his father. And he worried that he couldn't do it.

Just like me.

Certain there could be no pleasing my father because I wasn't a son, I convinced myself to do the opposite of what he expected of me. I would be nothing like the sons the Duroughs before me had been. This is why I went to a state school and majored in English and told myself I had no desire to run the company—so that I would be nothing like my nonexistent brother, the heir who was never born.

I squeezed my father's hand as tears slipped down my cheeks. "You've done quite enough," I whispered. "Do you hear me, Dad? You've done more than enough."

He closed his eyes, but a tiny grin formed on his lips.

"I am so sorry, Daddy," I mumbled. The tears kept coming. I couldn't stop them.

My father slowly opened his eyes. "Why?"

"I'm sorry you never had the son you wanted. And I'm sorry I've made such a mess of things."

He could only stare at me as tears coursed down my cheeks. I had to look away to avoid his questioning eyes.

"What are you talking about?" he finally asked.

I caressed his hand and waited for my voice to return and my tears to lessen. He waited too.

"I don't know who I am," I said, shaking my head.

His fingers tightened around mine. He said my name and waited until I looked him full in the face. "You are my daughter. You are my flesh and blood. I have never wanted you to be anyone else. You will do wonders with your tobacco and nugget of gold. I know it."

We were silent for a few moments. I wiped away my tears with my free hand. He was so quiet I assumed he had fallen asleep, but he was looking at me still, waiting for me to acknowledge him.

"I've made so many mistakes," I said.

"Welcome to planet earth."

I smiled. "I just wish... I wish I didn't judge people by what they have or don't have. I wish I could see people for who they are on the inside before I come to any conclusions."

My dad blinked slowly and then said something so profound, I knew I would never forget it. The funny thing was, after that morning, he didn't remember saying it.

"Yes, that would be better than the other, but it still makes you their judge."

My father squeezed my hand and drifted back into his numbed slumber.

And I just sat there, mesmerized.

❧

Later that afternoon, as I stood in my father's study and prepared to head back to Santa Barbara, Esperanza called me. I hurried to answer my phone, anxious to talk to Abigail.

"Lauren, it's Esperanza."

"Yes, I know. Is she home?"

"No."

"Have you heard from her?"

"No. I have heard from someone else."

"Who?"

"Graham. He's coming."

Something about the way Esperanza said his name alarmed me. "What do you mean, he's coming?"

"I think he knows Abigail left without telling anyone where she is. And he saw how tired she looked when she was with him. And sad. He could tell too that she's not herself."

"So?"

"He told me he thinks she is, how do you say, losing it."

Losing it?

"Esperanza, what are you saying?"

"I think he's coming to take over her affairs. I think he wants to go to a judge and have him say Miss Abigail is not able to take care of herself."

"That's ridiculous."

"Sí, but that's what I think he wants to do."

"Well, he won't get away with it. Abigail is fine. She…she probably just needs some time alone."

"Perhaps."

Esperanza sounded so unsure.

"What?" I asked.

"I don't know. But I think you should be here when he comes."

"Me? Why me?"

"Because you are Miss Abigail's assistant. I am only the house-keeper. What if he brings a lawyer? A lawyer will not listen to a house-keeper."

"And you think he will listen to me?"

"You are her assistant. You are smart. You can talk to these people."

I couldn't believe Esperanza believed a twenty-year-old college student would be able to help Abigail.

"Surely she has other friends, business associates…," I began.

"Miss Abigail worked at the library twenty years ago. No one remembers her. And she only worked part-time. She didn't need the money. She just loved the books."

"What about her lawyer? She has to have a lawyer."

"I don't know his name, and I don't know how to find it. You should come and look for it. Look in her desk. In her files."

I was appalled. "I can't do that!"

"Then how can we prove Miss Abigail is not crazy? How can we keep Graham from taking everything? You should come. She likes you. She trusts you."

"No, she doesn't," I said, remembering my last conversation with Abigail.

"Yes, she does."

"I tried to take a copy of the diary."

"She was disappointed in me that I took that thing from your purse! More disappointed in me than in you."

"But she kept it."

"That doesn't mean she doesn't trust you."

I had no idea how to intervene on Abigail's behalf and was about to say so when my eyes fell upon an antiquated tin of tobacco on the mantle in my father's study. My father had had it for years. It was there to remind him, to remind all of the family, of the tin of tobacco that Abel Durough gave Wilbur Fellowes, the tin of tobacco that contained a gold nugget and changed a man's life.

My father's words came echoing back to me. *You will do wonders with your tobacco and nugget of gold.*

I had a choice.

My father had spent his life making not money but an image. An image of the successful man. He knew no other goal, and it haunted him.

I could spend my life making something else.

This is what Mercy taught me in her dark and dreadful classroom. The choice was mine, imperfect though I was. I could choose to make a difference in the life of someone else.

This one thing I could do, even in chains.

"I'll be there as soon as I can."

Thirty-Seven

Esperanza was alone at Abigail's house when I got back to Santa Barbara a few minutes after three in the afternoon. She let me in.

"When is he coming?" I asked as she closed the door behind me.

"Tomorrow. He said he would be on a flight first thing in the morning. You have classes tomorrow?"

"Yes. I can skip the last two, but not the first. I'll get here as soon as I can, a little before ten."

"Bueno. I think you should plan to sleep here until he goes back."

"Why?"

"Because you are a young single girl. It would not be right for him to stay here too. He will have to get a hotel room."

"But this is—"

"This is not his house. This is Miss Abigail's house. I will tell him you've been working on a project and staying here."

"But I haven't been staying here."

"You stayed here two nights."

"But the diary is finished. It's not even here!"

"Graham doesn't know that. I don't have any trouble lying to protect Miss Abigail. You say nothing about that. I will tell him you are staying here, and he will have to get a hotel room. Bring some clothes, pajamas. You are staying here."

"All right."

"Bueno. Now I show you Miss Abigail's files so you can find her lawyer."

"Okay."

Esperanza started to walk away, but then she stopped and turned to me. "Your father is okay, no?"

I fell in step with her. "He's okay. He's going to be fine."

It took an hour, but I found a file that included some legal documents and the name of Abigail's lawyer, Alexander Helming. The document related to some property Abigail owned in Long Beach and was dated two years earlier. I prayed he was still her lawyer and knew her personally.

I phoned his office and convinced the secretary who answered the phone that my call was urgent. As soon as she heard Abigail's name, she transferred the call. I took that as a good sign.

"This is Alex Helming."

"My name is Lauren Durough and I am Miss Boyles's literary assistant."

"Yes?"

"I think Miss Boyles might be in need of your assistance. Quick."

"Oh? What's the problem?"

"Do you know about Graham?" I figured that was as good a place as any to start.

"I'm afraid I do."

"Miss Boyles has…taken a vacation. She decided to keep her whereabouts private. Miss Boyles's housekeeper received a phone call from Graham. He's coming to Santa Barbara, and he knows Miss Boyles left without telling anyone where she was going. The housekeeper is afraid Graham wants to prove Abigail suffers from dementia and that's why she's disappeared. We think he wants to have her declared unfit to manage her affairs."

"That's preposterous. Miss Boyles is old, but she is not senile. That man just wants her estate."

"Yes, I know. But he's coming here. Tomorrow."

"So? Let him come. He won't be able to prove it. When Abigail returns, she can send him on his way."

"But Mr. Helming, Esperanza and I don't know where Abigail is. And when she left she was upset."

"Upset? How so?"

"She'd just returned from seeing Graham, and I don't think their visit went well."

"They never do."

"And she was angry at me."

"You? What did you do?"

I sighed. "We had a misunderstanding about a project I was working on. I thought she hadn't been up-front with me about something. It was my fault."

"You were working on a project?"

"Yes."

"The diary?"

So he knew about the diary, too. "Yes."

"And you really have no idea where she is? None at all?"

"No."

He hesitated for a moment. "What is it you'd like me to do?"

"If she contacts you, will you let her know what has happened? Tell her to come home."

"All right."

"And can you come over tomorrow in the afternoon sometime? I'd like you to be the one to talk with Graham."

"I'll see what I can do. If I can get away, I'll call before I come over."

"Okay. Thanks."

We hung up.

I turned to Esperanza. "He'll try to come."

"Bueno."

We stood there, unsure what to do next, until the phone rang. I assumed it was Mr. Helming with a last-minute change.

"Yes?" I said.

There was a momentary pause. And then a woman's voice.

"Who is this?"

Abigail.

"Abigail, it's me. Lauren."

"Lauren. Why are you answering my phone?"

"Listen. You need to come home. Graham is on his way out here. He told Esperanza you're losing your mind. He might be getting a lawyer. Esperanza thinks he wants you to be found unfit to manage your affairs."

She said nothing.

"Abigail, did you hear me?"

"I heard you."

"You need to come home."

Another long pause. "What for?"

A splinter of panic poked me. "Do you understand what I just said? Graham is coming here."

A second or two went by. "You know what? I don't care. Just let him have it. Let him have it all."

Esperanza had been right. I hadn't seen it. I hadn't seen anything but my own agenda. We should never have left her alone.

"You want Graham to have you declared mentally unfit?" I tried to keep my tone businesslike. "You want him to take over your house? Your library? Your *books*?"

I heard her sigh. "It just doesn't matter anymore."

"What doesn't matter?"

"Any of it."

"Please let me come get you."

"No."

"Then let me come, and we can just talk."

"I don't want to talk. I'm done talking."

I looked at Esperanza. Her eyes were wide with worry.

"Okay. What do you want to do, then?" I asked.

"I just want it to end."

The splinter of panic became a rod. I stiffened. "What do you mean? What do you want to end?" I asked.

She paused. "Everything. Everything I've ruined. I want it all to end."

"Abigail, please! Please tell me where you are!"

"Is Esperanza there?"

"Yes. Yes, she's right here. Do you want to talk to her?"

"No. Just tell her there's a stray cat in the backyard. I've been feeding him. And tell her I've left her well cared for in my will."

"Abigail!"

"Don't worry, Lauren. Graham won't get it all. My will is not to be contested. If he contests, he loses it all. I've left him a wealthy man."

"Abigail, please don't do this!"

"Don't do what? I'm just letting nature take its course. I'm an old woman. I've nothing to live for. I should have died long ago. I am not going to fight it anymore. I can't make anything right that I've made wrong. It's silly to hang on thinking I can."

"But what about the diary?"

"What about it?"

I thought quickly. "I can see now why you wanted me to transcribe it. I know how Mercy died. I know you didn't lie to me. And I think we could get her diary published. Then everyone could know what you and I know—that she gave her life for the man she loved."

Abigail was silent for a moment.

"The diary is yours, Lauren," she finally said. "You can do whatever you think is best."

"Abigail, please tell me where you are. Please?"

"Good-bye, Lauren. I enjoyed talking with you about books. You were the only enjoyable thing I've had in my life in a very long time. You and Esperanza and that cat."

"Abigail!"

"Good-bye."

She hung up.

Esperanza was crying. "What should we do? What should we do?"

I had no idea.

Thirty-Eight

I left Esperanza at the house. She promised to stay in case Abigail called again while I went to the dorm to gather a few things. We decided I would stay at Abigail's until she returned, starting that night. Neither of us wanted to consider her morbid comments about wanting her life to end.

Esperanza panicked when I told her what Abigail had said. I had a few panicked thoughts of my own. I wondered for a moment if Abigail had plans to hang herself, as Mercy had done, but quickly dismissed that thought. Abigail had tremendous admiration for Mercy's last act, misguided though it might have been. I didn't think she would want to mock Mercy's sacrifice by copying it and cheapening it. Mercy's death hadn't been about ending her own suffering; it had been about lessening someone else's. Any action on Abigail's part to end her life would be an insult to the woman she admired most in all the world. And she had said she was just letting nature take its course. I didn't think she was planning a suicide attempt that night.

I asked Esperanza if Abigail was taking any medication that was critical to keeping her alive. Esperanza said Abigail had a prescription for high blood pressure medicine and that was it. She took over-the-counter calcium tablets and pain reliever for her arthritis. Nothing else. It could take her months or years to die from high blood pressure.

"Maybe she will starve herself?" Esperanza asked, her eyes glassy with fear.

"Maybe."

"We have to find to her!"

"We have to find a reason for her to come home," I said. "Then we won't have to find her. She'll come."

"What reason? Where can you find this reason?" she asked.

I didn't know. I left to gather my things and hunt for an answer.

Clarissa was in our room when I arrived, typing on her laptop.

"Hey," she said when I walked in.

"Hi, Clarissa. I'm going to stay at Abigail's for a while. She...she needs me to housesit for her."

"Cool." Clarissa didn't look up. She popped her gum and kept typing.

I opened my drawers and closet and began laying clothes in a duffel bag.

Clarissa finally looked at me. At the amount of clothing I was packing. "Exactly how long are you going to be gone?"

"I really don't know."

She stared at me for a minute. "You finally had it with ordinary life in the dorm?"

I smiled at her. "No. That is so far from the reason I am doing this."

"What's the reason?"

I decided to tell Clarissa everything. I told her how Mercy had died. I told her about my argument on the patio with Abigail, the stolen thumb drive, the conversations I had with Professor Turrell and Esperanza. I even told her about Tomoharu Kimura and Edward Swift. And Graham.

And I told her Abigail had gone somewhere hoping to hasten her death.

When I was done, Clarissa blew a bubble with her gum, and for a moment I thought she found the whole thing trite and uninteresting.

"I know what you should do," she said.

"What?"

"I know what you should do to make her want to come home."

"What?"

Clarissa turned back to her keyboard. "Find the gardener's son. See if he's still alive. She wants to fix a mistake, right? She wants to make something right. Well, if you can find him, she can tell him she's sorry. That she's regretted her decision her whole life. Even if the guy had a great marriage and hardly thought about her at all in the last sixty years, he won't mind hearing the girl he proposed to first has always wished she'd said yes. His current wife may not like it, but hey, that's life."

It was an outlandish idea. Completely crazy.

"He's probably dead," I whispered.

"She's still alive and kicking. Lots of people live into their nineties. You won't know if he's dead until you start looking."

"But where would I start?"

"The Internet white pages, of course. What's his name?"

Clarissa opened an Internet browser on her computer. She typed in a Web address and then looked at me. "Name?"

There was no way it would be this easy.

"Um. Tomoharu Kimura."

Clarissa typed it in. "Hmm. No results found. You don't think he went back to Japan, do you?"

"He was never *in* Japan. He was born here."

"Well, there aren't any Tomoharu Kimuras listed in the U.S. Unless he has an unlisted number. Or he's dead."

I thought for a moment. "Try Tom Kimura."

Clarissa's fingers flew over the keys.

"Bingo," she said.

I leaned in to look at her screen. There were seven results. All of them included telephone numbers.

"I don't believe it," I whispered.

Clarissa turned to me, her eyes wild with excitement. "Let's call them!"

"I can't just call them!"

"Why not?"

"What in the world am I going to say?"

"Well, the truth works for most people."

I sank into my desk chair. "I can't just call some stranger and say, 'Hey, you don't know me, but I'm wondering if you're Tom Kimura, the son of a gardener who worked for the Boyles family in Santa Barbara in the 1940s.' "

Clarissa snapped her gum. "Sure you can."

"No, I can't."

She held out her hand. "Give me your phone."

"No, Clarissa!"

"Yes. You've got tons more minutes than me. Give me your phone." Clarissa wiggled her fingers.

"But—"

"Do you want this Abigail chick to come home?"

"What if he doesn't want to see her?"

"What if he does?"

"But what if he doesn't?"

Clarissa shrugged. "She'll never know, will she?"

I said nothing.

"Give me your phone."

I reached into my purse. "Maybe I should do it."

"No, no, no," Clarissa said, swiping the phone out my hands. "You're too emotionally involved. I'll do it." She pressed the first set of numbers.

She winked when someone answered. "Yes, my name is Demetria Howe and I'm researching landscaping in southern California in the 1940s. I'm looking for a Tom Kimura whose father was a gardener for a wealthy family in Santa Barbara in the 1940s. Would he happen to be at this number? No? Oh, sure, of course not. Well, thanks anyway."

Clarissa ended the call and immediately punched in the next set of numbers. "That Tom Kimura is thirty-six."

I listened as she gave the same story to the second Tom Kimura, who barely spoke English, and the third, who was two years old when Japan attacked Pearl Harbor. She tried the fourth. A Portland, Oregon, telephone number.

She tossed out the same lie she'd given the others, and then her eyes grew wide. "Really?" she said. Her eyes locked onto mine.

We've got him! she mouthed. I almost fell out of my chair.

"So Tom Kimura is your dad?" she continued. "Wow. How wonderful to have found you. I actually have someone with me who works for the Boyles family here in Santa Barbara. She sees those gardens every day. Yes. Oh, yes, they're still as lovely as ever." Clarissa crossed her eyes. *Small talk,* she mouthed. "Yes, that's so true. Say, would it be possible to speak with Mr. Kimura about his father's landscaping? No? Oh. Oh, I see. Um, perhaps you could speak with Miss Durough about that? I think she'd like to hear this from you. Okay. Here she is."

Clarissa's animated demeanor had vanished. She handed me the phone. Something was wrong. I took the phone, keeping my finger over the mouthpiece.

"What? What is it?" I whispered.

"Rotten luck, Lars. He's dying. Cancer. End stage. He's getting hospice care at home."

The man Abigail still loved was dying. I brought the phone slowly up to my ear.

"Hello. This is Lauren Durough. I work for Abigail Boyles."

"Hi. I'm Ken Kimura. Tom Kimura is my father."

"Mr. Kimura, I know the timing is terrible, but would it be possible to visit your father for a few minutes? I just need to ask him something. I promise it won't take long."

"About the gardens? You know, my father didn't work in landscaping after the war. My grandfather lost his business, and he never went back to it. My father taught English. He really can't tell you much about my grandfather's landscaping."

"Actually," I said, "it's not about the gardens. It's about someone he knew when he lived at the Boyleses' house."

"Oh, really? Who?"

I hesitated a second. "Mr. Boyles's daughter. Abigail."

"Oh."

"Is your father up to seeing visitors? It's...it's really important."

"What's this about?" Ken's voice had shifted from polite to protective.

"It's about something that happened a long time ago, when your father and Miss Boyles were young. Before the internment camp." *Before your father met your mother.* "May I see him?"

A long pause followed.

"Well, I guess that's up to him," Ken finally said. "Hold on a second."

Clarissa looked hopeful. "Well?"

"He's asking him."

Let him say yes, let him say yes.

A minute later, Ken Kimura returned.

"My father says he would like to see you. He wants to know when you can come."

My thoughts somersaulted. Tom Kimura wanted to see me. "I... I'll get there as soon as I can. Later this week, maybe?"

Clarissa began to dance in her seat.

"I don't think you'll want to wait that long, Miss Durough. Do you understand?"

I understood. I couldn't wait until after I'd spoken to Graham. I had to go now.

"I'll find a way to get there tomorrow."

"You need our address?"

"Yes, please." I scribbled the address on the back of a biology quiz.

"Perhaps you could call before you come over," Ken said.

"Sure."

We said good-bye and I closed my phone.

"See! What did I tell you?" Clarissa raised her hand to give me a high five. I met her hand with mine. "I can't believe you're really going to go there tomorrow. You really think you can get a flight on such short notice? Your dad own an airport or something?"

"Very funny."

"And you're playing hooky three days in a row. I must be a bad influence on you, girl."

I couldn't think about the classes I was missing. There was too much to do. I had calls to make.

I had to call Esperanza and tell her I wouldn't be staying at Abigail's that night and she'd have to find a way to keep Graham at bay until I got back. I hoped he didn't have a key or Esperanza's phone number. She would have to stay away from the house so he couldn't make her let him in.

I needed to call home and make sure Dad was still doing okay. And to tell my mom where I was going. Someone should know.

And I had to call Cole. I had to convince him to let me talk to Raul.

I needed a favor.

Thirty-Nine

It was after ten that night when I pulled into Palo Alto. Raul wanted to meet me at the parking lot of the Holiday Inn where I'd hastily booked a room to make sure I made it okay, but I convinced him I'd be fine. He asked me to call him when I got there, and I did.

He told me he'd file a flight plan for as early as he could, preferably so we could leave around seven in the morning, weather permitting. I got the impression that if it rained, he wouldn't be able to take me. He figured it would take us a little under four hours to get to Portland. Then we'd need to rent a car and drive to the Kimura house on the western side of the city. I hoped to be at the house by one o'clock in the afternoon.

I had difficulty falling asleep. The long drive from Santa Barbara, the stress of my dad's surgery, the curious pain of my self-discoveries, the anxiety I felt over Abigail's whereabouts, the safety of the diary, and the strange task that awaited me in the morning—the weight of these things hung on me. I lay awake for several hours before I fell asleep, my mind plagued by too many thoughts.

In the morning, the wake-up call I'd requested split the quiet of my predawn room. I jumped out of bed, afraid I'd overslept even though I'd allowed myself plenty of time to get ready for Raul to come for me. I wore the outfit my mom bought for me, the one he said looked good on me. I hoped he'd notice.

He came at 6:30 a.m., just like he said he would. A few minutes after he arrived, we were heading toward the municipal airport in the pearly gray dawn.

"I don't know how to thank you for doing this," I said, unsure of what to say to him.

"I don't mind." His voice was casual, relaxed.

"I really am very grateful. More than I can say."

He looked at me and smiled. "I really don't mind. I think it's nice, what you want to do. I hope it works."

"Works?"

"I hope it makes your friend Abigail want to come home."

I peered at him. Stared at him. I wanted so badly to apologize. But how do you apologize to someone who doesn't know what you've done? Unless Cole told him…

He peeked at me. "What is it?"

I looked away.

"What?" he asked, turning his attention back to the road.

"I…I…," I tried, but the words wouldn't come.

He stole another look at me. "You all right? You need me to stop?"

His utter kindnesses to me, in so many ways, that day and many other days, tore at me.

"Why are you doing this?" I asked without thinking, not much louder than a whisper.

Raul did a double take. "What was that?"

"Why are you doing this?"

"You don't want to go to Portland? I thought you wanted to go to Portland."

"Why are you nice to me?"

He gave me a funny look. "You like it better when guys are mean to you?"

I barely heard his question, lost in my own private world of self-loathing. "Why would you want to help me?"

Raul shifted in his seat and looked out his window. "You got a problem with people who want to help you?"

"I've got a problem with people like me."

He laughed. "People like you? There are more of you?"

"We're everywhere."

He laughed louder. "And what's the deal with people like you?"

I inhaled deeply. "We think we know everything. We think we can read people like they are books. We believe whatever we want about people, whatever others tell us to believe, and whatever we tell ourselves to believe."

I looked at Raul. He stole a glance at me.

"You've lost me," he said.

"I hope not," I whispered.

"What?"

"I'm as bad as the people I criticize all the time. Worse."

"Okay. Um. Who do you criticize all the time?"

The truth seemed inescapable. "Just about everybody."

"That bad, huh?" he said. He wasn't taking me seriously.

"Yes. It's that bad. We believe whatever we want! Do you know what I believed about you? I thought you were just another privileged guy, another rich kid flitting around in your own airplane, attending an exclusive school, rolling up the sleeves of expensive shirts like they were hand-me-downs, completely oblivious to real need."

Raul said nothing at first. "And that's what you *wanted* to believe about me?"

"No! It's what I assumed. But I didn't want it to be true."

His half smile surprised me. "You didn't want me to attend an exclusive school and fly my own plane and wear nice shirts?"

Why couldn't he take me seriously? "I didn't want you to be oblivious to real need. And the funny thing is, that's the one thing that is least true of you, Raul."

We were silent for a moment.

"Lauren, I don't want you to say another word until I say you can, okay? I want to show you something. Look, we're almost there."

"What do you mean?"

"Shhh."

We pulled into the little airport and Raul parked the car. We got out and Raul pointed to the same plane I had seen two days before in Los Angeles. "I'll meet you right over there."

"But I want to pay for the fuel," I countered.

"Hush. And you can't. Cole and I already took care of it. I'll be right back."

He returned from the clubhouse with a large bag. I watched him silently as he walked around the plane for the preflight check. When he was done, he placed a finger against his lips, letting me know I wasn't free to say anything yet. Then he helped me into the plane. I had never flown in anything so small. Nervous anticipation gripped my stomach.

Raul must have seen me pale.

"You okay?" He handed me a pair of earphones from inside the bag.

I nodded. I started to say something about being nervous, but he pressed a finger gently to my lips and said, "You're not supposed to talk."

Seconds later he was beside me in the cockpit, turning the ignition. The noise of the plane's engine filled the tiny space that surrounded us. Raul spoke into his mouthpiece and a conversation between him and the municipal airport's ground control began. They spoke English, but I understood little of what they said. I tuned them out and focused on settling my nerves while the plane shuddered to life.

Raul asked for permission to take off. Moments later we were taxiing down the small runway, and I could feel the air wanting to own us, wanting to lift us up from the ground and hurl us heavenward. The plane released its grip on the Tarmac and the propellers sent us to the sky. Inside, the cockpit rumbled with power, noise, and intensity. I leaned back in my seat and concentrated on breathing.

The flat world fell away and the rounded horizon took shape. A fat stretch of pinkish blue shimmered in the distance on my right, as the bay brightened in the morning light. Cars below us on the 101 inched along an asphalt necklace, and brown hills to the east looked caramel-topped in the breaking sun. We lifted higher, and I was never more aware of how tiny and insignificant I was, sitting in that tiny plane, a speck of metal in a shining sky.

It wasn't until we had passed Oakland that Raul finally turned to me.

"Beautiful, isn't it?" His voice sounded strange through the ear-phones.

I nodded, my mouth slightly open, my eyes taking it all in.

He must have felt I was sufficiently awed by our surroundings. "Now you can talk!"

Words failed me for a moment, not because I hadn't been in a plane before, but because I'd never bothered to truly consider what existed beyond me.

"I'm so small!" I gaped at the vastness that lay below us.

He laughed and shook his head like I had missed the point completely. "The world is so big!"

I blinked at him.

"It's not always about you, Lars," he said lightly, like he didn't want me to take offense.

I didn't.

"So what are you going to say?"

Raul sat next to me in the Honda Civic he'd rented since he was over twenty-one. I held the directions Ken Kimura had given me over the phone.

"I don't know exactly. I know what I'd like *him* to say."

"What's that?"

I'd rehearsed the scene several times as we flew over northern California. I pictured myself going to Tom Kimura's bedside and having him reach for me while he said over and over, "Does she remember me? Does she remember me?"

I pictured myself taking Tom Kimura's wrinkled hand and telling him Abigail did indeed remember him. Every day she remembered him. I even imagined telling him she was haunted by her memories of him. Of what she had turned away.

"I want him to tell me he's never forgotten her. That a day hasn't gone by in the last sixty years when he hasn't had at least one fleeting thought of her."

Raul was thoughtful for a moment. "Tom Kimura married someone else. Had a son."

"I know. I'm not saying I wish he'd never loved anyone else. I just want him to remember her. I want him to ask me if I can bring her to him before…before it's too late."

We were quiet for a few minutes as we drove down a wide tree-lined boulevard.

"What if you can't find her in time?" Raul looked at me.

I knew this was probably how things would turn out. I had no idea where Abigail had gone, and Ken Kimura made it sound like his dad wouldn't last through the week.

"I'll ask him to tell me what he would say to her if he could see her again. And then I'll tell her. When I find her."

"Okay. So what if he says he has nothing to say?"

Tom Kimura's street came into view. I was through with believing the worst about people I didn't even know. "He has something to say to her. He loved her. Besides, he asked me to come."

We pulled up to the curb in front of a cedar-paneled house flanked by a row of pines. Several cars were parked in front, silently attesting to an event taking place inside. For a moment I just sat in the car and looked at the house, preparing myself to meet the man who lay inside it, inches from another world.

God, do something nice for Abigail. For all of us.

Raul looked at me and the corners of his mouth rose slightly. "Ready?"

I started to get out of the car. Raul didn't move.

"Aren't you coming?" Alarm whispered through me.

"Do you want me to?"

"Of course!"

"Then I'll come."

We walked up the imbedded-stone path. Carefully manicured shrubs and rows of purple flowers lined the walk. A wind chime fluttered in the breeze, announcing our coming. A row of shoes let us know how many people were inside the house, waiting. When we stepped onto the porch we could see that a man stood at the screen door, watching us. Ken Kimura. We had called from the car rental agency.

"Miss Durough?" he said, opening the door.

"Please call me Lauren."

"Ken Kimura."

"This is my friend, Raul," I said.

"Pleased to meet you," Ken said, almost mechanically. "Won't you come in?"

We slipped off our shoes and stepped inside. The entry was cool and fragrant. The décor, decidedly Asian, exuded peace and simplicity. I drank it in.

Tom Kimura's son was probably in his early sixties. His salt-and-pepper hair was trimmed short, and he wore a pair of rimless glasses. He looked tired. He showed us to a living room where six people waited. Six sets of sad eyes looked up at us. No one said a word.

"I'm really sorry to be coming at such…such a hard time," I finally said. "If it wasn't important, I wouldn't have bothered you. Honestly, I wouldn't have."

Ken shrugged his shoulders and closed his eyes, like it hurt to have me say anything at all about my mission. Like he didn't want to know why I came. He was just honoring his father, who'd asked that I be allowed to come.

"It's no bother," he said. "Why don't you come on back? I told my father you were on your way. He's expecting you."

Ken turned toward a hallway and walked away from us. The six silent witnesses kept their eyes on me. I started to follow Ken, and when Raul didn't come with us, I turned and begged him with my eyes to stay with me. He took a step toward me, and I resumed following Ken down the hall.

Tom Kimura lay in a rented hospital bed. His weathered, wrinkled face was ashen, his body thin and wasted away under the blankets that embraced him. The room was furnished with a mix of medical machinery and serene Japanese artwork. A row of bonsai trees stood on a mahogany cabinet by the window. Inky black Japanese characters painted on creamy rice paper hung on the walls. A small desktop fountain bubbled over stones, its motor the only sound in the room besides the shallow breathing of the dying man.

The gardener's son.

Ken stood over his father. "The woman from Santa Barbara is here," he said.

I cringed. Perhaps I had made a terrible mistake. I looked at Raul and his eyes spoke confidence. I stepped forward. Tom turned his head and his narrow eyes met mine.

"You can leave us," Tom said softly to his son. Gently. But it was a command nonetheless.

Ken looked at me, flashed me a wordless plea to be brief, and left the room.

"Come," Tom Kimura said. I stepped closer to his bed.

"My name is Lauren Durough," I said. "This is my friend Raul. He brought me here. I'm Abigail Boyles's assistant."

"Abigail," Tom said.

"Yes."

"Did she send you?"

"She…" I didn't know how to answer. The weight of not wanting to screw things up for Abigail tugged at me. "Actually, I don't know where she is."

Tom blinked slowly. "Is she all right?"

"Not really."

"I don't understand."

"She left the house without telling anyone where she was going. She has only called once and it was to give instructions about… I think she has gone somewhere to…to die."

Again the slow blink. "To die."

I couldn't help the choice of words. Abigail had gone somewhere to die.

"She is sick?"

I chose my next words and actions carefully, praying they'd be the right ones. I had no idea what Tom Kimura expected or wanted to hear.

"Not physically." I touched the left side of my chest. "This is where she hurts."

His eyes widened.

"She still loves you, Mr. Kimura. She has always loved you. Regret is what is killing her." Two tears slipped out of my eyes as two tears slipped out of his.

"How did you find me?"

"I looked for you. And I found you."

Tom said nothing for a moment. "Why didn't she look for me?"

"She was afraid," I said. It was as accurate an answer as any.

"Afraid of what?"

"Afraid you had moved on. Forgotten about her."

Tom turned his head to look at the row of bonsai trees. "I had to move on. I had no choice. But I did not forget her." Two more tears slipped away from me and I rubbed them away. Tom slowly turned his head to look at me again. "Is that what you came to hear?"

I nodded. "And it's what I came to tell you. She has always regretted what she did. You should know that. She would want you to know that."

He turned his head again to look at the bonsai trees. "Will you tell her something for me?"

"Of course."

Tom drew in a long breath and continued to stare at the trees. "Tell her the evening primroses will always come back. Every year. The winter chill will try to kill them, but they always come back. She liked those."

I told him I would tell her.

"Open that cabinet for me," he whispered. His eyes never left the bonsai trees, and I realized he was staring at the cabinet on which they sat, not the trees themselves.

I went to the cabinet and opened one of its polished doors. Inside was a collection of books and papers and a cedar box about the size of a turkey roaster.

"Take out the box."

I obeyed.

"The key is in the drawer above it, taped to the top."

I opened the drawer, which was full of pens, paper clips, and packages of mints, and felt inside for the key. I peeled away the tape and the key fell into my hand.

"Open," Tom breathed. His voice was weakening.

I set the box down on the floor, inserted the key, and turned it. Inside the box were more papers and several bound journals. "The red one," Tom whispered.

I moved the contents around until I found a burgundy-hued, leather-bound journal. I lifted it out and showed it to him. "This one?"

"Yes. Hand it to me. And a pen."

I stood, reached for one of the pens in the drawer, and handed it to him along with the journal.

His weak arms reached for them but fell back against the blanket. He sighed.

"What do you want me to do?" I asked, anxiety coursing through me.

"Open the book. Hold it steady. Hand me the pen."

I did as he asked. Tom held the pen over the open front page and rested it there for a moment. Then he slowly began to write.

Abby,
   All is remembered, all is forgiven.
   Live.
   Tom

The pen fell away from his fingers and I took it. Raul moved toward me and I handed it to him.

"These are poems I wrote. They're not very good, but she might like the one on page twenty-six. Take the book to her. Don't let Ken see you have it. When you are gone, if he asks, I will tell him I gave it to you. He will think I did not love his mother. I did. I loved them both. In different ways."

I hesitated.

With a shaking hand, he thrust the book toward me. "Take it. Give it to her when you find her."

I closed my hands around the book.

"She liked the primroses," Tom whispered.

"Yes," I said, aware of Raul closing the box behind me, returning it to the shelf in the cabinet, and replacing the key under the tape.

"Thank you for coming." Tom's voice was but a breath surrounded by transparent words.

I leaned over and kissed him on the forehead, letting my lips linger. I wanted him to think, just for a moment, that it was Abigail's lips that caressed his ancient skin, thanking him for the book and for releasing her from her pain.

Tom fell into an exhausted sleep. I slipped the book into my purse, and we left him.

Ken waited for us in the living room, concern covering his face. He asked us politely if we wanted any tea. Raul declined for us, thanking Ken for allowing us to come, and we slipped our shoes back on. I had no words to say good-bye.

Ken stared at us as we left, wondering I'm sure why my face was wet with tears.

"I'll drive," Raul said as he walked to the car. I wordlessly handed him the keys.

We got into the car and I took the journal out of my purse.

I turned to page twenty-six and read what the gardener's son had written there.

Abigail Rose

You, in your nightgown among the lilies
Eyes on the glittering night sky
Pacing the flat stones beneath your feet
Milky white in the moonlight

You, mourning the simple
Shaking your head
Raising your fist against heaven
Against earth

You will not choose me
In anger you will not choose me
Fear holds you close and I am jealous of it
But I will learn to let you go

You, alone in the garden
In the middle of the night, after hard words
Before the sun, before I learned I would survive
And so would you

You think you were alone in that stillness
But you were not
I saw—and still see—
You.

Forty

I had six phone messages waiting for me when I finally turned on my cell phone after Raul and I returned to Palo Alto. It was after six in the evening, and though I had managed to sleep some in the Cessna, I was bone tired. Two of the messages were from my mother, two from Esperanza, one from Alex Helming. I didn't feel like listening to any of them.

"You should stay another night," Raul said, as he took me back to my car.

"I can't. I have to get back."

"But you're exhausted."

"We can get some coffee. I'll load up on caffeine. I'll be fine."

Raul wasn't convinced, but he didn't argue with me. I wouldn't have minded if he had. I was starting to enjoy his concern for me.

We stopped by a Starbucks and I ordered a venti latte with three shots of espresso. When we got to the hotel parking lot, Raul walked with me to my car. I unlocked the driver's side door and then we just stood there. I didn't know how to say good-bye and apparently neither did he.

"Thanks for doing this for me," I finally said, though I had already said it half a dozen times that day.

"I'm really glad you asked me. I think some good may come out of all of this. It's kind of cool, actually."

He stood so close to me, and I still felt such shame for the things I had believed about him. "This isn't the first time you've stepped in for me," I whispered.

Raul tipped his head, unsure what I meant.

I looked down at my feet, unable to look him in the eye. "Cole said you came to the hospital the other day for me." I lifted my head, summoned some inner strength, and met his gaze. "You came for me."

"Yes." His eyes never left mine.

A sliver of silence passed between us as we just looked at each other.

"I'm sorry, Raul. I'm sorry for every—"

But I could say nothing else. He leaned in and kissed me, silencing my unwanted apology with his lips. For a moment I was back in the clouds, far away from the cursed ground and the messy world. I never wanted to come back down.

When he slowly broke away, Raul lifted his hand to my cheek. I had started to cry again and he brushed away the tears.

"You're not the person you think you are, Lauren," he said.

Speechless, I stood, unable to move, as what he'd said echoed in my mind. I wanted to hear it over and over and over.

"Can I call you later to make sure you made it home okay?" he asked.

"Yes."

He opened my door for me, but I turned to him and wrapped my arms around him. Some of my coffee spurted out of the cup I held and dropped to the asphalt. His arms were at once tight around my waist.

I wanted to thank him again, but I couldn't, and I knew he didn't need to hear it.

He kissed me again and stepped away. "You need to go so you can get home."

I was amazed how much I didn't want to get into my car and leave.

Raul walked toward his car. "Call me when you get home. Call me if you get sleepy!"

"I will."

He got into his car and I got into mine, and for a few minutes we shared the same road, our cars just yards apart. Then he honked a farewell and I headed toward the highway and home.

Once on the open road, I relived those last moments with Raul, replaying them in my mind again and again. I felt what Mercy tried to describe in her diary when John Peter kissed her. I knew now exactly what she meant. I couldn't keep myself from smiling as I drove.

How had Abigail ever turned her back on this? This feeling that swept you breathless into the sky?

I was nearly an hour into my commute before I pulled myself away from what happened in the parking lot to listen to my phone messages.

My mother first called with a progress report on my dad—he was doing well, the chest tubes had been removed—and then called to see how I was. Esperanza called twice to ask the same question—when was I getting back? And Alex Helming called to say Graham had arrived in Santa Barbara and wanted to speak with him. Alex had told Graham it might have to wait until next week. "But I can't put him off much longer than that, Miss Durough. It would be much easier if Abigail were here. I trust she will contact you before then."

But I really didn't think Abigail had any plans to do that. Why would she? She had plenty of money. She could stay wherever she was as long as she wanted.

I eyed Tom Kimura's book peeking out of my purse on the passenger seat. I had to get that book to Abigail before she did something stupid. I had to give her Tom's message.

I pressed the speed dial for Esperanza.

"It's me—Lauren."

"Did you see him?" she asked, meaning Tom Kimura.

"I did. He gave me a book of poems to give her. And he forgave her a long time ago. But he's dying, Esperanza. He's not expected to live much longer."

Esperanza said something softly in Spanish. It sounded like a prayer.

"Graham is in town," she said a moment later. "He left messages on Miss Abigail's phone. I saw him drive by the house twice."

"Did he see you?"

"No. Arturo dropped me off around the corner, and I went in the back gate. Graham can't get to the door. He doesn't know the code for the front gate."

"Esperanza, we've got to figure out where Abigail went." An idea came to me. "Listen. She might have wanted to be near where Mercy died. Are you at home? Do you and Arturo have Internet access?"

"Sí, sí,"

"Go onto the Web and find as many five-star hotels in the Danvers—that's what Salem Village is called now—and Boston area as you can, call them up and ask to speak Abigail Boyles. Tell them she's a guest."

"But we don't know if she's at any of those places."

"If she's not, they'll tell you she's not registered there. Then you try the next one."

"Okay. And you will stay at Miss Abigail's tonight?"

"I'll be there in a few hours."

"Graham may drive by and see the lights on in the house."

"We'll just let him think Abigail has timers on her lights."

"He may buzz the gate."

"I won't answer it."

"Don't let him in, Lauren."

"I promise I won't. Call me if you find Abigail at one of those hotels."

"Bueno."

I got back to Santa Barbara after eleven o'clock.

I spent the last hour on my cell phone with Raul, talking about everything and nothing. I was prepared to put him on hold if Esperanza called, but she didn't. He told me more about his dad, his childhood in

Guadalajara, what it was like to move to America when he was eight, what it was like the first time he flew a plane. He told me when he knew he wanted to be a heart surgeon—the day his father died of a massive heart attack—and when he knew he was falling for me—the day I found him in the little library looking at all the old books.

I told him what my favorite foods were, what kind of music I liked, what I liked to do when I had nothing to do. I also told him something I hadn't told anyone before—what it was like to grow up wondering what happened to the son your parents were supposed to have.

"You don't still wonder that, do you?" he'd asked.

It felt good to tell him I was finally learning not to.

We hung up when I arrived at Abigail's. The street was dark and quiet. There were no cars parked curbside, and Graham was nowhere to be seen. I opened the gate, drove through, and watched in my rearview mirror as it closed behind me.

Inside, the house was deathly still. When I had stayed at Abigail's before, the diary had been there. It made me feel like I wasn't alone. Without it, the house felt like a crypt. I didn't want to climb the stairs to the guest room. Not with Raul's kisses still lingering on my lips, reminding me of what Abigail had turned her back on. I grabbed an afghan from the library sofa and went into the sitting room. I knew the morning light would flood the room with warmth, even if the room itself did not look warm.

I curled up on the sofa with one of Abigail's perfectly plumped pillows and pulled the afghan around me.

On the long table across from me, Abigail's framed photos stood like sentinels guarding the past. Moonlight danced on the image of Abigail and Dorothea sitting on a sun-drenched porch railing with their matching parasols.

Abigail looked truly happy.

I fell asleep thinking of her that way. Laughing. Smiling. Holding Dorothea's hand. Spinning her parasol.

Life before loss.

Hours later, when dawn spread a blanket of golden light around me, I awoke with the same image in my head. Abigail and her parasol.

I sat up and looked at the photo across from me.

I knew where Abigail was.

Forty~One

Esperanza didn't know where Dorothea's parents' property on Pismo Beach had been. Alex Helming knew Abigail had bought property in Pismo Beach a few years prior, but he hadn't been involved in the transaction. After several calls to the San Luis Obispo County Historical Society, I was finally given the number of a retired staff member who remembered that the Sand Dollar Bed and Breakfast off Ocean Boulevard had once been the summer beach house for Theodore Boyles and his family.

Theodore Boyles. Dorothea's father.

"But that B and B's not open anymore," the woman told me. "Someone bought it a while back. I don't know what they're doing with it, but it's not a hotel anymore."

I thanked her and hung up. I knew who bought it.

It was less than a hundred miles to Pismo Beach. I wanted to call Raul and tell him where I was headed, but he was in class—where I should have been. I sent him a text message and called Esperanza instead. I told her where I was going and asked her to look up an address for me on the Internet, wishing the whole time I had a top-of-the-line phone like my dad's and could look it up myself.

A moment later, Esperanza rattled off the address for the former Sand Dollar Bed and Breakfast.

"Bring Miss Abigail home," she said.

"I plan to."

I took the coastal road, letting the beauty of the Pacific Coast Highway calm and invigorate me. I prayed Abigail wouldn't be angry that I found and saw Tom Kimura. I prayed she'd be able to accept that he was dying—I didn't see how I'd be able to avoid telling her. I prayed that the book of poems, especially the one on page twenty-six, would soothe her tortured mind, not wound it.

It wasn't hard to find the former hotel. The Boyleses' old beach house sat on a quiet street that ended in a cul-de-sac. I saw the gabled windows and steeply pitched roof first when I turned onto the street, then the commanding view of the sea, then the wooden porch. I parked my car on the street and walked slowly up the front path. I could see the invisible frame the photographer had chosen on that long ago day when two girls sat on the porch railing and held matching parasols. The railing was still there, painted a glistening white. Above the railing on the second floor, a lacy curtain fluttered at an open window. I walked up to the door and hesitated, then rang the doorbell.

I rehearsed in my mind what I would say when Abigail opened the door.

But the door didn't open.

I rang the bell again and waited.

No answer.

As I stood there, wondering what to do, wondering if Abigail was even here, my eyes fell on a flower bed below the porch railing. Rows of primroses in magenta, saffron, and coral peeked at me.

She was here.

I rang the bell. Again, no answer.

Did she know it was me? Was she hiding from me?

I tried the doorknob, but it was locked. She had to be here. I stepped off the porch and made my way to the back of the house. Perhaps a back door was open. I had to find a way to get in.

I rounded a corner and saw her.

Abigail sat at the far end of the yard at a patio table that overlooked the sea. In front of her lay the diary, open to the sea air. She sat very still.

I walked toward her, doing nothing to mask my footsteps. When she didn't turn, I said her name. When she still didn't turn, I quickened my pace until I stood at her side.

She seemed not to see me, and I reached out to touch her on the shoulder.

"Abigail," I said gently.

She flinched and snapped her head around. Fear and dread shone in her watery eyes, like she was looking at a ghost. She seemed not to recognize me.

"Abigail, it's Lauren."

She stared at me for a moment, and the dread fell away. It was replaced by utter disappointment.

I had found her. And she hadn't wanted to be found.

Abigail turned her head back to the sea. "What took you so long?" she murmured in a voice I almost recognized.

I slid into a chair next to her. "You picked a great hiding place."

Abigail looked at me and then away again. "I'm not hiding," she said.

"You left without telling anyone where you were going."

"What I do is my own business."

She was her same cynical self, but the bitter edge to her voice alarmed me.

I reached for the book in my purse.

"You shouldn't have come, Lauren."

"I have something for you." I ignored her remark and placed Tom's book on the table.

She kept her eyes on the ocean. "I don't want it."

"It's a book of poems."

"I don't want it."

"It's a special book of poems. The author signed the book to you. He even wrote one of the poems to you."

She glanced at the book and then raised her head, narrowing her eyes at me. "You're lying."

I matched her tone. "You and I are done with lies, Abigail. Take the book. The poem is on page twenty-six." I picked up Tom's book and held it out to her.

She hesitated and then took it.

Abigail opened the cover, and I watched as her eyes traveled across the words Tom Kimura had written. Her chest rose and fell rapidly and I reached out to steady her heaving body.

"Where did you get this?" she rasped.

"He gave it to me."

Abigail slowly turned to face me. In her eyes I saw the ache and agony of countless days of regret. "You saw him?"

"Yes."

The next question hovered on her lips, unspoken. Maybe she couldn't decide which to ask first.

"Esperanza's mother remembered his name, and Clarissa and I found him using the Internet," I continued. "I wanted to give you a reason to come home. I think I have."

"Where did you find him?" Abigail whispered, her gaze returning to the open book. Her fingers trailed over the words *All is remembered.*

"He's in Portland, Oregon."

"Is… Does he have a family?" Her fingers traced *All is forgiven.*

"He has at least one son. I think his wife has passed away."

Tears formed in Abigail's steel blue eyes. "Why did he give you this?"

"Because he wanted you to have it. He wanted you to know he never forgot you."

Abigail ran her index finger over Tom's name. "Why did he give you this?" she asked again, this time to no one.

I laid my hand over hers and moved it so her finger rested on the word *Live*.

"Because he is dying and you are not."

Abigail raised her other hand to her eyes and covered them as she wept.

I stayed with her until her sobs subsided. When she had taken a tissue from her sleeve and dried her tears, I stood. "His poem for you is on page twenty-six."

I reached across the table to Mercy's diary and gently folded its pages shut. I lifted it into my arms and walked toward the house, leaving her alone with her memories of Tomoharu Kimura.

The back door opened to a kitchen. I put the diary on the table and busied myself with finding what I needed to make tea. I kept an eye on Abigail from the window. Half an hour later, when she closed the journal and cast her gaze over the ocean, I went out to her with a tea tray.

She said nothing when I set the tray down. I handed her a cup and she took it silently. I sat next to her with my own cup.

"Do you want me to take you to him?" I asked.

Abigail didn't answer right away. The words caught in her throat. She laid a hand across the journal. "You've already done that for me."

"He's dying, Abigail. Do you want to see him?"

"I see him as I saw him then. And that's how he sees me. Who wants to mess with that?" She inclined her head, and I smiled.

I wanted to ask her so many questions, but I didn't know if any of them were appropriate. Abigail must have seen my unspoken thoughts.

"I didn't know I loved him until it was too late. When I finally realized it, I'd already sent him away and he was already in that awful camp."

"You didn't try to find him or write to him?"

Abigail looked away, her eyes glistening with moisture. "I was afraid to love him. He was Japanese. I was afraid of what people would say about us. And I was embarrassed that he was in that camp. And that I had let him kiss me."

She paused and I waited.

"The night before he was taken away, we met in the garden. He and his father lived in the gardener's cottage out past the pool. We often met in the garden at night. We would talk and laugh, and I could tell Tom anything. He wasn't like any of the men my father found suitable for me. He was genuine. I knew I could trust him. He was my best friend."

Abigail looked at her lap. "But that night he told me he loved me. I was so angry with him. It changed everything. It changed me. I sent him away."

She raised her head and exhaled heavily. "I was a fool, Lauren. Worse than a fool. A fool doesn't know what he's doing is foolish. I knew and did it anyway."

"But he forgave you," I whispered. "He went on with his life. He wants you to live, Abigail."

She said nothing.

"Abigail?"

When she finally spoke, her voice was different than it had been a moment earlier. Softer, less sure, like that of a young girl.

"My resolve is crumbling," she said. "I've always been able to pretend I'm indestructible, that I'm strong enough to bear the consequences of my blunders, the weight of my misfortunes. But it's all crashing in around me and I'm starting to wobble."

She turned to face me and her voice became her own again. "I never factored in how bringing you into my life to give you the diary would shatter the glass. I should've guessed."

A queer shiver ran through me. "What glass? What do you mean 'give me the diary'?"

"The glass around the diary. I was protected from the diary's indictment against me as long as it was hidden away. But the glass is shattered now because I've given the diary to you. That was my sole objective. I never considered having it published. I never cared about it being rewritten in today's language for a host of strangers to read. I wanted you to transcribe it for *you*. I chose you to transcribe it so you would fall in love with it. I wanted it to become important to you so I could pass it on to you."

"Why me?"

"I couldn't leave it with just anyone, Lauren. Surely you can see that."

"But why me?"

A tepid smile spread across her lips. Someone standing ten feet away would not have seen it.

"You are the girl in between. You are young like Mercy, a writer like Mercy, and the sole daughter like Mercy. And you've lived a life of privilege like me. You've seen its every side, just like I have, and you are the heir to an accomplished man's legacy, as I was. You, like me, will always have choices to make because of it. Who better to give the diary to than you, Lauren?"

I couldn't wrap my brain around the notion that the diary was mine, nor that Abigail had hired me for reasons that went far beyond her job posting. But her wanting me to possess the diary didn't explain why she had taken off with it.

"Then why are you here? Why not just give me the diary?"

She sighed. Abigail from eight weeks ago might have said, "What I do and why I do it is not your concern." This Abigail turned to me but did not raise her eyes to meet mine.

"I'm afraid."

"Because I want to have the diary published?"

"Because the glass is broken," she said, shrugging. "And I don't know how to live without it."

Forty-Two

The breeze off the ocean below lifted a lock of Abigail's hair and twirled it about her ancient face. She didn't seem to notice.

"I never told you how my family got the diary," she said, swiveling her head to face the breeze, forcing the wild strand of hair back where it belonged.

I waited.

"John Peter Collier did indeed get the diary from the girl Benevolence several weeks after Mercy died. I don't know how she got it to him, but she did. John Peter kept it for many years. At some point, he must have felt Mercy's family should have it. He went to Wells and gave the diary to Samuel, Mercy's cousin, who never went back to Salem after Mercy died and her land was seized. He stayed in Maine with his new bride. Samuel apparently never told anyone he had Mercy's diary."

"Why?" I asked.

Abigail absently smoothed an eyebrow. "The family believed in Mercy's innocence, but she had committed suicide, and that was against Puritan law. I don't think Samuel was proud of what his cousin had done."

"But surely Samuel read the diary after John Peter gave it to him. He knew why Mercy did what she did."

Abigail shook her head. "Apparently it wasn't reason enough for Samuel. It is amazing to me he didn't destroy the diary."

She took a sip of her tea, set her cup down, and continued. "Samuel's daughter Elizabeth found the diary after her father died. She wrote to John Peter Collier in Salem after she read it, she was so taken by what the cousin she wasn't supposed to talk about had written. But John Peter had died several years earlier, having never married. Elizabeth's letter was delivered to one of his sisters, Anna. Anna and Elizabeth decided to meet, and when they did, Anna gave Elizabeth something she had found among John Peter's things after her brother died. A letter."

Abigail paused and I filled the space. "Mercy wrote a letter to John Peter the night she died, not Prudence Dawes."

Abigail lifted her head and gazed out over the vast blue water. "She wrote a letter to each of them. Her letter to Prudence was very short. She simply told her she forgave her. Anna knew of the letter to Prudence. John Peter had shown it to her and asked her to deliver it, as he could not. Elizabeth never saw that letter, of course. But family legend has it that there was one. Mercy's letter to John Peter was the longer of the two, and she ran out of ink writing it. It was not even signed."

"Do you have it?" I whispered. I wanted so badly for Abigail to say she did.

But she shook her head.

"No. I don't know what happened to it. No one in the family does. It was apparently tucked into the diary for many decades, but something happened to it in the early 1800s. No one could account for it after that. But what was written in that letter has been passed down through the generations. My mother told me what the letter said, but of course I cannot prove it, nor can I prove there even was a letter."

"Tell me." I leaned in.

"Mercy told John Peter she loved him and she wanted him to be happy, to live a full life and to spend it at peace. She wanted him to remember her as they last touched, fingertips to fingertips. She didn't want him to be burdened with the image of her execution, nor did she want his life to be endangered should he attend the hanging and shout an opposition. She told him she was to be hanged; it was the providence of God and the will of man, and he could not stop it. No one could. So she would hasten the inevitable and allow him only sweet memories of her. She asked him to pray for her immortal soul, as she hoped God would look favorably on this last act of mercy and gladly receive her spirit a few hours early."

Abigail touched the corners of her eyes. Her fingertips came away wet, and she rubbed them gently into her palms, absorbing the tears into the skin of her hands.

We were silent for several moments, lost in the extravagance of Mercy's love for the man she would have married had she lived.

"Do you not want the diary published, Abigail?" I asked when I was able.

"I know I told you in the beginning that I wanted her to be remembered, but now I'm afraid."

"Afraid of what?"

"I just wish I had the letter." Abigail's eyes closed slowly, as if she were in pain. "I don't want anyone to think Mercy was a coward because she killed herself. Mercy was no coward."

I reached for Abigail and clasped my hand over hers. "No one will think that. Even without the letter, no one will. We can re-create the letter, you and me. We can put it at the end as an epilogue."

"But we've no proof there was a letter. Will anyone believe it?" Abigail opened her eyes and looked at me.

"Everyone will believe it. They'll want to believe this is what Mercy would have done."

Abigail stared at me for several long minutes.

"I am so tired of pretending," she said.

"Then stop."

Abigail folded a palm under her jaw and rested her elbow on the table. "What am I going to do, Lauren?"

"Come home. Publish the diary. Entertain people in your sitting room. Adopt the stray cat. Find more shelves for your books. Get your driver's license. Set up Internet service. Have a garden party."

The corners of her mouth rose. "And what about Graham? He's mine, you know. In a strange way, he's mine. What am I going to do with him?"

I shrugged. "All I know about him is he gambles. He has a problem with money."

"Yes."

"That's all I know and that's not enough. I know Esperanza thinks he's after your estate. But I've never met him. What if he's coming because he's concerned for you? What if he's coming because he's desperate and needs help?"

"I've tried helping him."

"You pay his debts. That just allows him to keep gambling."

Abigail's brow crumpled and she lowered her hands to her lap. "What else can I do? I don't know what else to do."

"I don't either. But you can live and find out."

Abigail's gaze drifted to the house. "You really think we should publish the diary?"

I liked that she said "we."

"I do," I replied.

"She was an amazing person. I've never met anyone who loved like Mercy did, without any thought for herself. That is love of another kind."

We were quiet for a moment.

"Is that why you stopped reading the diary, Abigail?" I asked.

She answered me slowly. "It killed me to read it, so I stopped. A long time ago. But then when I wanted to die, I wanted it to kill me. I've read it dozens of times the last few days. I've barely eaten or slept. I wanted it to kill me. Then you came, and for a moment I thought you were her, coming to take it from me."

Abigail inhaled deeply.

"I've made such a mess of my life, Lauren. I pushed Tom away. I couldn't save Dorothea from her depression, and I didn't fight her parents to raise her child. I tried to make amends with myself by marrying Edward and adopting Graham. I thought I could make up for my bad choices by being a good wife, but Edward didn't love me and Graham knew I didn't really want to be his mother. I could have made the effort, but I didn't. It's no wonder he grew up the way he did."

Abigail looked down at her hands. "After Edward and Graham left me, my father developed dementia and by the time he died five years later, he had no idea who I was. He didn't like the person he had to live with—me. Every day I had to tell him my name, and every day he told me he didn't like me."

"Abigail," I began, but she stopped me.

"Terrible things happened to Mercy, too, but somehow she didn't end up like me. I found that so remarkable. That's one of the many reasons I hired you to transcribe the diary, because I thought Mercy had so much to teach us. But then I was afraid you, too, would see her suicide as weakness. That she did what she did for herself. She was young and naive, and reason tells me she ought not to have taken her own life, but Lauren, the strength it must have taken for her to make that kind of sacrifice! I want people to understand! I don't want Mercy to be remembered as the young woman who committed suicide in the Salem jail. She was a brave girl who willingly traded her life to save another. She was everything I was not. Everything."

I laid my hand over hers. "Not everything. If you didn't care deeply, none of this would matter to you."

Her hands trembled under mine.

"Tom had a message for you, Abigail. Something besides the poem."

She looked up, trepidation and expectancy splashed across her face.

"He remembered you liked primroses," I continued. "He told me to remind you the primroses always come back. Even after a hard winter, they find a way to survive. They come back every spring."

Abigail swallowed and her gaze dropped to the red journal on the table as if it, rather than I, had spoken those words to her.

"Let's go home," I whispered.

Abigail was silent for several moments. Then she looked out over the ocean. "I'd like to keep this place."

"Okay."

"I was happy here."

"I know."

She turned to me. "Do you really think I should adopt the cat?"

I smiled at her. "Definitely."

I stood and helped her to her feet. She picked up the book of poems and tucked it under her arm. "So Graham is in Santa Barbara?"

"Yes."

"Perhaps I can borrow your phone on the drive down. I need to talk to him."

"Sure."

We took two steps, and she stopped.

"Thank you. For this." She patted the book.

I smiled and said nothing.

As we walked back to the house—and to what awaited us both in Santa Barbara—I wondered if I would still dream of Mercy now that the transcription was finished. Would she still invade my sleep if we published the diary and Mercy no longer belonged to just me and Abigail?

Even then, as we made our way to the back porch, I knew there was no "if." The diary would be published, and Mercy would be embraced for what she had been all along. She was an echo from the past, a link to our origins, and an observer of those things about us that never seem to change.

I used to think mercy meant showing kindness to someone who didn't deserve it, as if only the recipient defined the act. The girl in between has learned that mercy is defined by its giver. Our flaws are obvious, yet we are loved and able to love, if we choose, because there is that bit of the divine still smoldering in us.

Mercy showed us our true selves—the beautiful and the awful, the deep and the shallow, the marvelous and the mortal.

She revealed it all and begged us to take heed.

I thought of Raul as this revelation took hold of me. As Abigail reached for the door, I must have smiled.

Abigail hesitated. Her hand froze over the doorknob and she cocked her head.

"Something's happened to you. You're different somehow," she said. She tightened her other hand on my arm.

Then her brows suddenly knitted together in a weave of surprise and elation.

"You've met someone," she breathed.

Yes.

Behind us, the sea crashed onto waiting rocks below, as it had done for ten thousand years.

READERS GUIDE

1. *The Shape of Mercy* is about three distinct women from vastly different generations: Mercy, Abigail, and Lauren. What do you feel they have in common? What separates them?

2. The diary's pages reveal a time and place of tragic historical significance. What emotions did the diary evoke in you? If you were faced with Mercy's choices, which would you have chosen? Discuss why.

3. Mercy writes about a bird seeking shelter in her barn during the first few weeks of January 1692. What do you think the bird represents for Mercy? Lauren? Abigail?

4. Lauren describes Abigail's library as suffocating, overly decorated, and bursting with books—a room in sharp contrast to the rest of the house. Why do you think this room was like that? Does Lauren's opinion of the library remain consistent throughout the story?

5. When Lauren first meets Raul, she assumes he is a member of the catering staff. Later she assumes he is a rich, upwardly mobile, premed student who cavalierly rolls up the sleeves of two-hundred-dollar Armani shirts. Discuss how you believe we fall into the trap of such assumptions. Think of a personal experience when, based on first impressions, you assumed someone to be different than they actually were.

6. Esperanza is convinced Graham wants to have Abigail declared unfit to manage her affairs. Why does she think that? Do you agree?

7. Were you satisfied with Tom Kimura's response to Lauren's visit and revelations about Abigail? How might Abigail's life have been different if she had married Tom Kimura? What might have happened to the diary then?

8. When Raul takes Lauren up in the plane, she makes the comment, "I'm so small!" He tells her, "It's not always about you." What do you think he means in that moment?

9. What do you think Lauren does after she graduates from college? What kind of career do you imagine her in?

10. John Peter tells Mercy shortly before her arrest that it "is easier to believe ill of someone than good." Discuss whether you think he is right, and why.

11. What do you think of Mercy's final act of compassion? Did she do the right thing?

12. *The Shape of Mercy* is a story about choices, stigma, and preconceived notions. In light of these themes, what did you discover about yourself?

ACKNOWLEDGMENTS

I am deeply grateful to…
- my writing colleagues, Susie Larson and Sharon Hinck, for coming alongside to applaud me as Mercy's story and persona took on flesh, and Brandilyn Collins and James Scott Bell, for advice, direction, and perspective.
- an amazingly gifted editorial team at WaterBrook Multnomah, especially Shannon Hill, Jessica Barnes, Laura Wright, and Mick Silva. Your insights sharpened this story's every page.
- my family, particularly my husband, Bob, and my parents, Bill and Judy Horning, for unflagging encouragement.
- Chip MacGregor at MacGregor Literary, for affirmation at every turn.
- kindred spirits Kathy Sanders Zufelt, Linda Emmert, and Tanya Siebert, for life support during the hectic cross-country move when this tale took form.
- God, the very essence and shape of everything wonderful and good.

Author's Note

The Salem witch trials comprise a sad collection of events in American history, events that illustrate what can happen when judgment is cast without knowledge. Though they are a fitting backdrop for *The Shape of Mercy*, this book is foremost a story, not a commentary; a story about three women—all fictional—who wrestle with the concept that we tend to judge people based on notions rather than on truth, and without stopping to consider if we even have the right to judge them at all.

Only a few liberties were taken with the historicity of the witch trials, and these purely for the sake of crafting Mercy Hayworth's story.

I love hearing from readers and would treasure your thoughts on this book. You are the reason I write.

Susan Meissner
www.susanmeissner.com

RESOURCES

Carlson, Laurie Winn. *A Fever in Salem—A New Interpretation of the New England Witch Trials.* Chicago: Ivan R. Dee, 1999.

Francis, Richard. *Judge Sewall's Apology—The Salem Witch Trials and the Forming of an American Conscience.* New York: Harper Collins, 2005.

Fraustino, Lisa Rowe. *I Walk in Dread: The Diary of Deliverance Trembley, Witness to the Salem Witch Trials.* New York: Scholastic, 2004.

Gaskill, Malcolm. *Witchfinders.* Cambridge, MA: Harvard University Press, 2005.

Hill, Frances. *A Delusion of Satan—The Full Story of the Salem Witch Trials.* New York: Da Capo, 1997.

Hill, Frances. *The Salem Witch Trials Reader.* New York: Da Capo, 2000.

Karlsen, Carol F. *The Devil in the Shape of a Woman.* New York: W. W. Norton, 1998.

Warner, John F. *Colonial American Homelife.* New York: Franklin Watts, 1993.

About the Author

From early school-day projects to becoming editor of a local newspaper in Minnesota, Susan Meissner's love for writing has been apparent her entire life. *The Shape of Mercy* is her latest novel in a string of books that delve into the deeper issues of life. She is the author of nine novels and lives with her family in San Diego. Find out more about her at www.susanmeissner.com.

Visit Susan's blog at http://theshapeofmercy.blogspot.com

An exclusive sneak peak of
SUSAN MEISSNER'S
newest book.

THE
GIRL
IN THE
A NOVEL
GLASS

Available everywhere September 18, 2012.

Prologue

The sun is setting on my last day in Florence. Tomorrow I will marry the man my uncle has chosen for me and Florence will be at my back, perhaps forever. My soon-to-be husband will have no reason to come here after we marry, and my uncle will not expect to see me again. His responsibilities for me, such as they are, will be done.

My cousin Maria does not understand my melancholy at the prospect of leaving forever the place where my life began. "What has Florence ever brought you but heartache?" she has said more than once.

And if I've any kindred souls in this world besides her, perhaps they would say she is right.

But within my heart so cruelly handled, there are unseen places that have been shaped by Florence's beauty. Florence is a coin with two sides, a room with two doors, a river with two banks. Everything that wounded me happened here. And everything that brought me solace happened here too.

Maria brought me to Rome with her to see me out of Florence, out of the maelstrom of Medici woe that she believes Florence is to me. Maria does not know that Florence alone speaks condolence to me; I couldn't wait to return. Only Florence, in all her vast majesty, assures me that as much as people can create ugliness, they can create splendor. It is all around me in Florence: the ache of loveliness, in every work forged by human hands that can kill as soundly as they heal.

And now it seems I must bid farewell to my very soul.

Maria is calling for me. The carriage is ready. My uncle would have us leave for the Villa dell'Ambrogiana before darkness falls.

As I depart, Florence safeguards my childhood treasures, buried beneath the marble and within the frescoes and in the threads of the canvases. All my longings, whispered on dark nights and gray days, I press them now into the folds of my city, so that as my shadow falls away from Florence forevermore, I shall not be forgotten by her.

Nora Orsini

October 1592

1

When I close my eyes and think of home, I always envision Florence—a place I've never been.

The red and cream hues, remembered from the paintings on my Italian grandmother's walls, speak "home" to me as much as any address where I've ever lived. My grandmother is gone now, and her pictures and paintings have been scattered among my father's family members. But with my eyes shut, I can picture the rosy cap of the cathedral dome, the toast-colored stucco, the lizard-green Arno River as it lazes down its course. I can hear the odd cadence of European emergency sirens, the zipping of Vespas down asymmetrical streets, and the acoustic darts of a language I don't understand beyond simple endearments spoken by my *nonna*. I can smell the cappuccino—because she told me hers smelled just like it—the perfumed doorways of the fashion houses, the dense exhaust of too many cars. And I can feel the cool, silken flesh of *David*'s marbled feet if I were allowed to stretch out my hand and touch them.

Even now, so many years later, I can see the canvases on my grandmother's living room walls—the litho of Botticelli's *Primavera*, the oil Nonna had done of a woman walking in the rain in a puddled piazza, the watercolor of rows of Italian cypress, and a young man on a bicycle.

But the one of a young girl reaching toward a beckoning statue is the only one I still dream about. My great-great-grandfather painted it when Nonna was young, before she and her parents immigrated to America. My grandmother was the girl in the painting, and the statue stood in the Florentine background. A palette of russets and burgundy and ocher filled the rest of the painting with depth and elegance, with a hint of blossoms to come.

Nonna used to tell me I was the girl in the painting, just as she had been when she was a little girl, an impossibly wondrous thought that I clung to until well after my eleventh birthday. Nonna, as the young girl, whose back was to my great-great-grandfather as he painted, wears a rosy-pink gown that glistens in the sunlight playing behind her. I used to imagine the statue was speaking to the girl and that's why her hand was extended—as if she were inviting my grandmother to dance, to join her world of joy where anything unexpected was possible. I loved that painting and thought of it often, long after my parents divorced, long after my mother and I moved to San Diego and the visits to Nonna's dwindled. Nonna was going to take me to Florence when I graduated from high school to find the statue, but she died when I was twelve. I never saw that painting again after she died.

My father promised his mother, as she lay dying, that he would take me to Florence in her stead. I wasn't there when he promised her this. My mother and I were in San Diego when we got the call two days after she died that Nonna had had a massive heart attack. But Dad told me of the promise when my passionate grief over Nonna's death left him grappling for words to make me stop crying. Six years later, however, in the summer months following my high-school graduation, Dad had knee surgery. From then until now, the promised trip to Florence has been in a perpetual state of postponement. From time to time he'll remark that we need to take that trip. He hasn't forgotten, but it's almost as if he's waiting for something to happen—or change—before he can make good on that promise.

Eighteen years after Nonna's death, I marvel that the mention of her birthplace still sounds like the name of a matronly soul, kind and sweet. Florence—a woman with ample arms, a soft voice, and silver wisps in her hair. I've been to London and Paris and to Aruba twice for publishing conferences. But the closest I've come to visiting Florence are the phone calls I make to one of my authors who happens to live there.

A phone call to Lorenzo always makes me feel decidedly homesick.

⁜

I awoke to early-April coastal fog, frothy white like a bridal veil, and my first thought after remembering I'd be Skyping with Lorenzo before nine, was that my ex-fiancé would marry that evening.

A blanket of mist coddled Bird Rock and the rest of the San Diego coast with a ghostlike embrace as I lay scrunched under the covers, wondering if Miles was feeling nervous or afraid. Was he thinking of me, even just a little? Would the unintended wound I gave him two years ago needle him as he got ready for the day? I hoped not. I didn't want to ruin his wedding day twice.

Coffee drunk, cheese omelet eaten, I gave scant thought as to what to wear to work. I wouldn't be rushing to Balboa Park for twilight nuptials. I chose a denim skirt, red-and-white-striped knit top, black flats. Chrome jewelry. Ponytail.

I was pouring a second cup of coffee into a travel mug when my cell phone rang. My mother's ringtone. I fished the phone out of my purse and answered with a cheerful "Hello, Mom."

"Meg. You don't have to pretend. It's me."

"Good morning to you too."

"You doing okay? Really?" In the background I could hear her pushing buttons on her microwave.

"Really."

"But today is not just any old Friday."

I replaced the carafe on the coffee maker and pressed the Off button. "I'm fine. I'm the one who broke up with Miles, remember?"

"Of course I remember. That's doesn't mean you enjoyed having to do it. Or that you are enjoying this. You and Miles dated for two years. He's marrying someone else today."

"But I'm happy for him." I screwed the top on my travel mug.

"Yes, well, I didn't call him to see how he's doing today. I called you."

"And I'm fine."

"Well, if you're sure."

"I am. But thanks."

I heard the sound of the microwave whirring to life.

"So, I was thinking if you're free tonight, we could meet up at the Melting Pot for dinner."

My mother loves fondue restaurants. No one touches your food while it's cooking but you. No one touches it when it's done cooking but you.

"Why? Something up?" I grabbed my car keys and then knelt to unlatch the kitty door for Alex, my borrowed cat. He brushed past me, meowing his thanks, and disappeared through it into the tiny backyard of the cottage that I am caretaker for.

"I just want to have dinner with you. I… There's…" But she didn't continue.

I stood up. "There's what?"

"Nothing. Can you come? Are you busy?"

Since breaking off my engagement with Miles, I'd given myself a year to heal—wounding someone could be just as painful as being wounded by someone—and then had spent the next twelve months slowly reentering the dating life. I'd gone out on a few dates, but I hadn't met anyone I'd wanted to rush into a relationship with. My mother had applauded my caution. Elaine Pomeroy always applauds caution. "Better safe than sorry" would be tattooed on my mother's forearm if she wasn't convinced tattoo artists don't properly clean their needles. She was all for me taking it slow. Gabe, the graphic designer at the same publishing house where I work, is the closest I have come to dating anyone exclusively. We've gone out a few times. The thing is, a dating relationship is always going somewhere. Even nowhere is a place. I didn't want to mess up Gabe's and my workplace friendship with a potential dating destination like nowhere. So I recently backed off—a sublimely cautionary move my mother applauded—and Gabe gallantly retreated. And I am not dating anyone else at the moment.

I had no plans for the evening of Miles's wedding.

"What time?" I asked.

"How about seven thirty? Unless you want to do it earlier. I was thinking we'd miss the worst of the evening traffic."

"Seven thirty is fine." I turned off the kitchen light and reached for my purse. "See you then."

"Oh. And your father is probably going to call you today."

My arm reaching for my purse paused midstretch. It wasn't odd that my father might call. Our amicable relationship includes occasional phone calls and the even more occasional visit. But it seemed odd to me that he'd call today, out of the blue. Dad surely didn't know Miles was getting married that night. He couldn't have known. Unless my mother had called and told him. Seventeen years postdivorce my mother still calls my father to remind him of things she thinks he will forget, as if it still matters what he does and doesn't do.

"I'm telling you I'm fine, Mom."

"It's not about Miles getting married. I'm sure your father couldn't care less about that. I didn't call him. He called me."

"What for?"

"He lost your new cell phone number. All he has is your work number. So I gave it to him. I wasn't going to without asking you first, but he said he needed it to talk to you about something. And he didn't want to call you on your work phone."

As my mother talked, I began to conjure possibilities as to what my father would think important for me to know that he couldn't tell me at work. Maybe at long last he was setting a date for our trip to Florence?

"If he is coming down today and wants to see you, do what you must," my mother continued. "But don't bring him to the Melting Pot."

The tone in my mother's voice was a mix of apprehension and distaste.

"I won't bring him. And I doubt he's coming down. He could tell me that at work."

"There've always been a great many things he could have done and didn't."

Sunlight was peeking through the marine layer outside my kitchen window, reminding me that a full day at work awaited. I was due to talk with Lorenzo in less than fifteen minutes. It could take that long just to get from the cottage in Bird Rock to the office in downtown La Jolla, especially if all the good street parking was taken.

"Hey, Mom. I've got to run. I'm Skyping with one of my authors, and I don't want to keep him waiting."

"Call me if you're going to be late tonight. And tell your father to give you a bit more notice next time."

"I doubt he's coming down. I'll see you tonight." I headed for the front door, travel mug in hand. "Okay?"

"All right. Oh. And it's quite foggy this morning on the coast. Saw it on the morning news. Don't rush out into it. If it's too bad, just go in later."

I hung up and stepped out into the lacy vapor.

Nora

I was the first child born to my mother who lived.

When I was little, Nurse liked to tell me that when I was born, I had lips as pink as a Florence sunrise and a howl to set the castle dogs to barking. Such a fine, healthy baby, she said. I didn't know until I was older about my mother's other babies or that rose-hued lips and a throaty cry were the difference between us.

Had I been a boy, my father might have decided to come from Rome to greet the first of his children to survive childbirth. But again, perhaps not. When my brother, Virginio, was born a year after me, it was many days before my father came to Florence to met his infant heir.

I'm a Medici *principessa,* and my christened name is Francesca Eleonora Orsini, but no one calls me that. All those letters are reduced to *Nora,* which sounds like a breath expelled without hurry or pretense or significance. I like it. It suits me.

Paolo Orsini, my father, was betrothed to my mother, Isabella de' Medici, when she was eleven and he was twelve. They married when my mother was sixteen, and I was born, alive and wailing, thirteen long years later. I was a miracle, Nurse told me time and again. And I believed her; long after my mother was taken from me, certainly after I learned of the other unborn babies, and even for many years after the last time I saw my father. As childhood fancies began to thin and stretch, I was tempted to see the miracle of my being born as something else entirely. But I blew the temptation away, and it floated off like thistledown.

2

The crinkly paint tubes in the garage corner where my grandmother painted had beckoned me in a way that seemed almost familial. A visit to her house always meant touching those metal tubes and fingering the horsehair brushes. The artistic gene showed up often on my father's side. He even dabbles in watercolors when he allows himself the luxury of time spent in front of a canvas, which isn't often. When I was little, I used to tell people that I was going to be an artist too.

But while I favored my dad's side in looks—my one-quarter Italian appears three-quarters when I wear knockoff Gucci and stilettos—I wasn't gifted with the family flair for art. After a less-than-stellar first year in college as an art major, my mother reminded me that my SAT English scores were a better indicator of what I was good at. I changed schools, changed majors, and graduated three years later with a degree in English. An internship at Crowne & Castillo Press led to a job as an editorial assistant after graduation. Four years later, I was named an assistant editor. Four years after that, I was promoted to editor. Crowne & Castillo publishes travel books: how-tos, planning guides, travel essays, and pictorial coffee-table books. It's my personal goal to one day soon produce travel memoirs, but the once-married publishers, Geoffrey Crowne and Beatriz Castillo, have yet to be convinced that a travel memoir has enough commercial appeal for the typical Crowne & Castillo buyer.

"Who really wants to read about one person's cerebral contemplations of a place?" Geoffrey said only a few days ago. I replied that I would want to. Lots of people would. And that not all memoirs are cerebral contemplations. He said that memoirs don't have photographs to engage the senses and that's what sells a Crowne & Castillo book—the photos. I said that's why ours would be different. Ours would have full-color photos. He said he'd think about it some more.

As I came in to the office out of the fog, this recent conversation with Geoffrey was on my mind, along with my father's imminent phone call, and Miles, too, and the fact that I was a few minutes late for my Skype appointment with Lorenzo. I mumbled hello to the front-office staff, rushed into my office to open my Skype account, and found Lorenzo waiting for me.

Lorenzo DiSantis and his sister, Renata, an Italian brother-and-sister writing and photography team, have authored five books for Crowne & Castillo: two on Italy, two on the South of France, and one on the Catalonia region of Spain. Their sixth project, still in the production stage, is a guide to planning intimate Italian destination weddings. Lorenzo and Renata live in a flat in the heart of Florence; no small wonder they are my favorite Crowne & Castillo authors.

I like talking with Lorenzo, and not just because he and Renata live in the one place I've always wanted to visit. Lorenzo is the only person who calls me by my full name—Marguerite. I like the way it sounds falling off his tongue. When Americans say it, like the woman at the DMV last week, my full name sounds like a bunch of concrete bricks rolling around in a wheelbarrow. But Lorenzo says my name the way my grandmother said it, light and sweet. Everything Lorenzo says sounds a little like my grandmother. Nonna's melodic Italian accent produced an unnecessary yet enchanting *a* sound at the end of every word and so does Lorenzo's. Lorenzo just turned forty, and Renata's a year older. They are apparently perfectly happy being single and sharing a flat.

When my Skype account finally connected with his, I could see that he was sitting back in his desk chair, a Florentine evening just beginning to fall on the world outside the window behind him. He was unshaven, a look that went well with his nearly hairless head. Lorenzo told me that when he started to go bald in his twenties, he promptly took matters into his own hands. He bought an electric razor and clipped his hair down to the scalp. Some men can expertly pull off the sophisticated five-o'clock-shadow-on-top look. Lorenzo is one of them.

I apologized for being late.

"Nothing to worry about, Marguerite," he soothed. "Ten minutes is nothing. Fifteen? Nothing."

I checked my watch. "It's only five minutes."

He leaned in and smiled. "Less than nothing!"

The little *a* sound on that end of "nothing" made me laugh.

"Do not worry so much. It puts wrinkles on the face." He stroked his stubbled chin.

"I get that from my mom, I'm afraid."

"Ah. Give it back to her, eh?"

Again, I laughed. "So how was Florence today?"

"Enchanting as always. When are you coming?"

For the last four years I've been telling Lorenzo and Renata that my dad has promised me a trip to Florence, but Lorenzo doesn't fully get why I don't want to come alone. He doesn't understand that when my father and I finally go, it will be more than just a trip to Italy. It will be something special and long awaited, like a lost thing found. I like to imagine that it will happen that way.

"Soon, I hope."

"So. You do not like the photo Renata and I suggested for the cover?"

"I never said that."

"I have your e-mail right here. You say 'Beatriz had pictured Venice or Rome.'"

"Yes. Beatriz was thinking either Venice or Rome."

"And you do not disagree with her?"

I riffled through the photos on my desk and uncovered Lorenzo's shot of a man in a black suit holding a woman's hand as they walked barefoot on the beach on the Amalfi coast. A grove of nodding lemon trees bloomed on the hillside above them. The woman was dressed in a gauzy white strapless gown. The skirt was caught in a breeze that wanted the ocean; its hem reached for the foam. I could almost hear the rush of surf and smell the tangy twin scents of citrus and salt water.

"It's a great shot, Lorenzo. But Beatriz wants the cover photo to be of a city people will instantly recognize."

"And you think we should give them Venice because everyone will be expecting Venice?"

"Is there something wrong with giving people what they expect?"

He laughed. "You know I like the unexpected, Marguerite. Besides, the Amalfi coast is a lover's bliss. Tell Beatriz that. Venice is for tourists with cameras. The Amalfi coast woos and flatters; it celebrates romance, eh? That is what the bride and the groom will remember when they go back home to wherever their real lives are.

The romance of the place. If the romance does not matter, they can marry in a courthouse in Detroit and save a lot of money. It is all about the romance."

A tiny comma of pain poked me. I had loved Miles as a friend. But I had not been *in* love. There is a difference.

"You do not believe me?"

I must have grimaced, and he had seen it. "I believe you."

"So you will sell Beatriz on the Amalfi coast? If she doesn't like that photo, I have others. At Positano, Ravello. Many others."

I nodded. "I will try."

"Good. Now I have something else to ask of you, *cara*. My neighbor, she is writing a book and needs some advice. She asked if I would ask you to look at a chapter or two. I said I would."

I replaced the photo of the Amalfi coast in its file. It is usually a bit awkward when a friend says he knows somebody who has written a book—worse when it's the friend who has written the book. I once had an acquaintance at a cocktail party insist on showing me three hundred pages of her poetry, all of it about birds. "What kind of book?" I asked. "If it's not travel related, there's really no point in my giving her advice."

"It is not exactly a travel book. But I think you may want to look at it anyway."

"Why would I want to do that?"

"Because Sofia's book is more like a memoir, cara. Memoir. Like what you told me you wanted to publish."

I reached for my travel mug, interested. "Really? What kind of memoir? Is it related to a place? Beatriz and Geoffrey won't consider anything that doesn't revolve around a travel destination."

"It is set in Florence. Your favorite place." He grinned. "And it's in English. Sofia is fluent. She was married to a British man once. Long time ago."

"But you and Renata have already written a book about Florence. It's only been out a couple years. How can I convince Beatriz and Geoffrey we need another one?"

"Ah, you will find Sofia's book to be very different, I think."

"How? Have you read any of it?"

"Some. Sofia has talent but needs direction, perhaps. But that is what a good editor is for, eh?" He laughed. I didn't.

"So what makes hers different from other travel books about Florence? You know how many are out there. There would have to be something amazingly unique about it. Especially if it's a memoir."

"Oh, that's easy. Sofia says she's one of the last known Medici."

I heard what Lorenzo said, but it didn't quite register in my head. "What did you say?"

"She says she's one of the last of the Medici."

I hadn't tanked every art class in my first year in college. I aced art history. I knew the Medici family ruled Florence for three hundred years and then evaporated in the eighteenth century because the last one died childless. The Medicis were extinct and had been for more than two hundred years.

"So you're telling me your neighbor's delusional?" I asked, half-laughing.

Lorenzo smiled easily. "Sofia is a very interesting person. Easily the kindest person I know. You would like her, cara. And her story is very out of the ordinary. She is sweet. If she is delusional, we should all sign up for it, no?"

"I didn't mean to sound insulting. But it just sounds a little odd."

Lorenzo shrugged. "I don't think it's so odd that a Medici still lives. Big family. Lots of little Medicis. It's possible."

"Does anyone else believe she's one of the last of the Medici?"

His smile was conciliatory. "But that is what makes her interesting, Marguerite. So you want me to send the first two chapters to you? I have them on my computer. She e-mailed them to me when she knew I would be talking to you today."

I had nothing to lose by agreeing to look at those two chapters. I could tell it would mean a lot to Lorenzo. And my interest was certainly piqued.

"But you won't promise her anything, right? She can't think that just because I am looking at her chapters, that we will publish her. She can't even think that I will be able to help her get it to the point where some other house will publish it, okay? I don't want her to have false hope."

"Of course. Here they come." Lorenzo tapped on his computer keyboard, then leaned back. "So you will speak to Beatriz about the photo, yes?"

"I will. I promise. And I will try to take a look at uh, Miss Medici-Whatever's chapters this weekend."

"Borelli. Sofia's last name is Borelli."

"She's a Medici with the last name Borelli."

Lorenzo shrugged. "The ladies don't get to keep the family name, do they, Miss Pomeroy?" He winked.

"All right. I will try to take a look at Ms. *Borelli's* chapters this weekend."

"*Buono.* No rush. And now help me choose a tie. Renata is in

Greece this week." Lorenzo produced two ties and held them to the webcam. One was solid blue with frenetic silver swirls; the other was a rosy pink with thick, black diagonal stripes.

"Where are you going? Date with Alessandra or business meeting?"

"Alessandra? No. When was the last time we talked? Date with Rosabel."

A tiny Cheshire cat–like grin tugged at the corners of my mouth. It was none of my concern who Lorenzo dated. Yet for no apparent reason other than she'd distracted Lorenzo from meeting a few deadlines, I was glad that fair-haired Alessandra must be out of the picture. I had no idea who Rosabel was, though, and that wasn't any of my business either. I tamped the grin down to a thin line, as though I could barely decide between the ties. "The pink one, then. Rosabel?"

Lorenzo dropped the blue tie and held the rosy one up to his neck and looked down at it. "*Grazie.* She's here from Milan for eight weeks. Met her at a party. And where will you be going tonight?"

"Dinner with my mother."

He lifted his head to stare into the webcam. "Your mother."

"Don't say a word, Lorenzo."

He ignored my command. "Is it her birthday?"

"No."

He clucked his tongue. "If you were in Florence tonight, *cara mia,* you would not be having dinner with your mother."

True.

I'd be having it with my father.

Nora

My mother's sisters died of illness as young maidens, seventeen and sixteen. I believe it was for this reason that my grandfather doted on my mother the way he did and let her live whatever kind of life made her happy. My grandfather, Cosimo de' Medici, loved his daughters. He was fond of his sons as well; for what titled man does not want sons? But oh, the affection toward his daughters! The deaths of my mother's sisters—one before my mother married and one after—devastated him. It is said he turned all his affection toward my mother, lavishly so. What she wanted, my grandfather gave her. What she didn't want, he took.

All this was whispered about my grandfather when people didn't think I was paying attention to them.

I barely remember him. He died when I was three, and all I can remember of him is the feel of his tunic against my skin. It was smooth and warm and smelled of mint and limes.

There is a painting of him in the Uffizi by Master Bronzino. He is young, like me, and he wears armor, and his gaze is off to the right, as though he might have to don the helmet he is holding and rush off to direct a battle. But that is not how I imagine him. I imagine him silver-haired and smiling and ready to chase away the mere shadows of imps and goblins that would conspire to threaten a little girl's dreams.

3

I pushed the photo of the Amalfi coast across Geoffrey's desk.

"Lorenzo really wants this photo on the front. People who've the money and motivation for an Italian destination wedding already know about Venice and Rome. He's thinking they've probably even been to those places already. They want a place that is romantic and special. And not crawling with a million tourists."

Geoffrey glanced at the photo. "Yes, but this book isn't just for people who've already decided they want an Italian destination wedding. It's to entice those who've never even considered it to consider it. Those people have never been to Venice and Rome, Meg. And that group of buyers is the bigger group. Exponentially bigger."

He pushed the photo back.

"So it's a no? You want me to tell him it's a no?"

Geoffrey sat back in his chair and rubbed an eyebrow. "Let me talk to Beatriz. I doubt she'll change her mind, but I'll talk to her. In the meantime you need to inspire confidence in that Venice photo. It's a good photo. Or the Florence one. That's the one you like, isn't it? The cover has to sell the book, Meg, not plan the wedding. Big difference."

"I think Lorenzo appreciates that, Geoffrey. He thinks this one *will* sell the book."

"He's a photographer."

"He's a romantic."

Geoffrey laughed lightly. "My point exactly. Photographers and lovers don't sell books." He turned to his computer. "Assure Lorenzo we will make the best decision for the book. We always do. And tell Gabe to start on the cover using the Venice photo for now."

I stepped out of Geoffrey's office. My cell phone in my skirt pocket began to vibrate, and I pulled it out.

My father.

I let the call go to voice mail. Whatever it was my dad wanted to tell me, I didn't want to talk about it in the hallway. When I arrived at Gabe's office, I found him standing over his desk, comparing two cover mock-ups of our latest guide to urban getaways. He smiled at me when I stepped inside.

Gabe is only a few inches taller than I am with short, curly brown hair that would probably grow in ringlets if he let it. He is missing two fingers on his right hand from a motorcycle accident when he was sixteen, but that hasn't hindered his skill. Sometimes I find myself a little jealous of his obvious artistic talent. The walls of his office are covered with his designs; some of them he drew freehand.

"Can't go wrong with Boston," I said, nodding toward the design at Gabe's left.

He pointed to another mock-up featuring a toned-down urban landscape. "Savannah's not on your bucket list?"

I cocked my head to look at the Savannah skyline. "I'd go. I guess I'd go to either."

"Savannah's pretty cool. Great art school there. Almost went to it. Guess we'll just have to see where Beatriz lands on it."

"Speaking of Beatriz, it looks like she wants you to go with the Venice shot for Lorenzo and Renata's book."

He regarded me for a moment. "Not one of Florence, eh?" His smile was subtle and knowing.

My face grew warm. "Everyone knows my secret loves. Not fair."

Gabe gathered the two mock-ups and sat down at his desk. "Everyone thinks you should just go, Meg. What are you waiting for? Just go."

His candor stung a little. And I knew he didn't mean for it to.

"I want my dad to take me. You know that. He said he would. I'm not ready to give up on him. I don't like giving up on people. Hey, want to join me and my mom at the Melting Pot tonight?" The invitation flew out of my mouth before I had a chance to consider it fully. But it was a safe enough request. Not a date. Not with my mom there.

Gabe looked down at the folio in his hands. I had taken him by surprise. "I, uh, can't do it tonight." He looked up. "I've got plans, I'm afraid."

"Oh. Too bad."

"I've a date, actually."

Gabe had a date.

"Oh. Well. That's…that's cool. Anyone I know?" My voice sounded distant in my ears, as if the question came from someone standing behind me.

Gable shook his head and smiled. "I don't think so. I met her at my sister's party last weekend."

A party Gabe had casually invited me to and which I had casually declined.

"Sounds like fun."

Gabe's smile widened. "Does it? I didn't even say where we're going."

Increased embarrassment warmed my face further. "Legoland, right?" Time to go. I turned to leave. "Have fun."

I heard him laughing behind me. "Another time, Meg?"

"Sure. The Melting Pot with my mother and me. Round two. Check."

More gentle laughter.

I chanced a look back at him, supposing he had returned his attention to the mock-ups on his desk. But he was watching me leave.

My phone vibrated in my pocket, reminding me I had a voice mail waiting. The distraction was a welcome one. I pulled it out as I walked away. "Voice mail," I said.

Gabe nodded thoughtfully.

Back in my office, I slid into my chair, annoyed that Gabe's date bothered me. He had every right to go on a date. So did I, had there been someone I wanted to go on a date with. I pressed the button on my phone for voice mail, ready to hear my dad's message and then get on with the business of the day. I began to read an e-mail message as I listened but stopped when I heard his voice. He sounded tired. Old.

"Meg, it's Dad. Sorry to bother you at work, but I need to talk to you about something. When you have a minute, can you call me back on my cell? Don't wait until tonight. And don't call me at the house. I mean, I'd appreciate it if you could call me back before I go home tonight. Okay. I guess that's it. Talk to you later."

I replayed the message, listening to the tone of my father's voice, the strange ache behind the words. I couldn't remember my father ever sounding so...defeated.

He was definitely not happy about something, and it was something he felt I needed to know about, something that would have some indirect effect on me.

I'd been up to see him and his wife, Allison, only a few months earlier at New Year's. Everything seemed fine. The last phone conversation my father and I had was three weeks ago. Nothing seemed amiss then either. Whatever it was, it was recent, and something he'd been able to mask in his earlier phone call to my mother. She would have said something if she'd detected something was wrong.

I punched the button to call him back. When he answered, he seemed to exhale gently before saying my name.

"Dad, what is it? What's up?" I asked.

He hesitated only a second. "Hey, I'm coming down to San Diego tomorrow. I know it's really short notice, but I'd really like to talk to you. Will you be around? I won't need more than an hour."

My father's voice was calm but thin, as if he was saving the air in his lungs for nobler purposes than a quick phone conversation.

"So you're not going to tell me what this is about?" I laughed nervously.

"How about I bring breakfast over to your place? Around ten?"

He had ignored my first question and now my second. Something was very wrong. Maybe Allison had kicked him out. Maybe he was the one who'd had the affair. It wouldn't be the first time.

"Dad, I think I deserve to know what the urgency is, don't I?" I asked tentatively. "If this is about you and Allison, it's not like it's any of my—"

"I'd rather tell you in person, Meg."

He paused a moment, waiting for me to agree to his terms.

"All right."

"So is ten okay? I'll bring poppy-seed bagels. That's the kind you like, right? The poppy-seed ones?"

"Uh, sure."

"Good. Okay. Then it's all set."

"All right, I'll see you at ten. And Dad, honestly, you could've called me on my work phone to ask me this. Beatriz and Geoffrey wouldn't have cared."

"I...I wanted your new cell phone number. I know you gave it to me already, but I lost it."

I was about to tell him he could've called me at work to get my new cell phone number and I would have been happy to give it to him, but I stopped before the words came out of my mouth. He had wanted to talk to my mother. It's why he called her before calling me. I've always been amazed that my father will still call my mother for advice and that she will still dispense it. But apparently he'd decided not to ask her opinion on whatever it was that was on his mind. Instead, he'd just asked for my cell phone number. The brief conversation with my mother had affected him somehow. Made him change his mind about what he wanted to say.

Poppy-seed bagels were not my favorite. They were my mother's.

A white picket fence
is no guarantee that all is well.

Amanda's family may look picture-perfect, but it is splintered by
discontent, heartache, and secrets. It isn't until her son, Chase,
and niece, Tally, interview a pair of Holocaust survivors that they
are challenged to face their pain.

Read an excerpt from this book and more at
WaterBrookMultnomah.com!

An ancient *ring,* *two women* separated
by nearly five hundred years,
and the *freedom* to *choose* one's life.

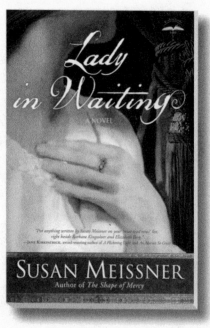

Manhattan antique shop owner Jane Lindsay is jolted into a new reality
when she suddenly has to face the fact that her marriage is crumbling.
While she grapples with her husband's abandonment, she comes across
an ancient ring that may have belonged to Lady Jane Grey. As she traces
the origins of the ring and Lady Grey's story, Jane has to decide whether
she will default to habits of powerlessness or whether she will take the first
steps towards real truth and happiness.

A HOUSE SHROUDED *in* TIME.
A LINE *of* WOMEN WITH
a HERITAGE *of* LOSS.

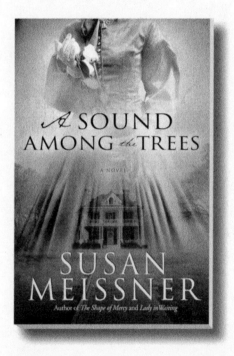

Marielle Bishop marries into an instant family and an antebellum home rumored to be haunted. How can she find the truth without losing herself in the painful past surrounding her?

Read an excerpt from this book and more at
WaterBrookMultnomah.com!